BOY I HARDLY KNOW

LISA HEATHFIELD

ANDERSEN PRESS

First published in Great Britain in 2026 by
Andersen Press Limited
6 Coptic Street, London, WC1A 1NH, UK
Vijverlaan 48, 3062 HL Rotterdam, Nederland
www.andersenpress.co.uk

2 4 6 8 10 9 7 5 3 1

British Library Cataloguing in Publication Data available.

ISBN 978 1 83913 783 9

Printed and bound in Great Britain by Clays Ltd, Elcograf S.p.A.

Praise for *This Boy I Hardly Know*

'This is one of those rare books that shines a light on a world we don't often see – the lives of children in care. Dusty's story is raw, real, and full of heart, showing just how powerful love and loyalty can be when the odds are stacked against you'

Ciara Smyth

'What Dusty and Cooper want is love. They'll do anything to find it, and once found, they'll cross the country and break their hearts to hang on to it'

Melvin Burgess

'Packed with colour and burning with life's force . . . Lisa Heathfield's brilliant protagonist is full of urgent love, complex betrayals, and ferocious secrets'

Luke Palmer

'Dusty and Cooper have my heart entirely. How do we live in a world where such precious lives are trampled so brutally?'

Louisa Reid

Other books by Lisa Heathfield

Seed

Paper Butterflies

Flight of a Starling

I am Not a Number

Such Pretty Things

Lisa Heathfield's YA novels have all won or been shortlisted for awards, including the Waterstones Children's Book Prize (twice), the YA Book Prize, the Virginia Reader's Choice Award, the North East Teen Award, the Fabulous Book Award, the Leeds Book Award, the Concorde Book Award, the Southern Schools Book Award and the GDST Award.

Having worked in a school for students with mental health challenges and also a residential children's home, Lisa now teaches teens who are unable to be in school for a variety of reasons. She lives in Brighton, UK, with her husband and three sons.

THIS BOY I HARDLY KNOW

For every child in the care
system – this book is for you.

Chapter One

There's a boy I don't know in my bedroom. I thought that sneaking him in would make me feel like I'm in charge of my life, but this Joe person doesn't look as fit as when I met him at the bus stop earlier. Plus, he's definitely been drinking.

'We've got to be quiet,' I tell him, because my sister is sleeping next door.

He stumbles into the cupboard, reaching into his hoodie pocket to bring out a bottle of vodka.

'Want some?' he asks.

I don't feel threatened by him or anything, I kind of just wish that he wasn't here. But I take the bottle and have a gulp that I swear rips the skin off my tonsils. We're both laughing as I cough and when he smiles, he's not as bad as I thought.

'What's all this?' he asks, going to my desk.

'My paints,' I say. I want to tell him that art is the one

subject I'm good at, that I'm going to be studying it for A level next term, but I get the feeling Joe wouldn't be that interested.

He picks up one of the tubes and squeezes loads on to the waiting piece of paper. He flattens his hand into it and then holds it up to me.

'Face paints,' he laughs.

I dodge his hand and press my own into the paint. It feels like when Poppy and I walked barefoot in the mud last winter. It was the best feeling, until our foster carer gave us hell for walking our footprints across her floor, when it wasn't even carpet and the wood washed clean as if we'd never been there.

Joe falls, his hand flat to the pristine wall.

'Shit,' I say. He's left a handprint of red paint.

'It looks cool,' he says.

'They're going to kill me.'

'For making a pretty picture?' Joe puts his hand on the wall again, the print fainter this time. 'I'm making a flower.'

I pull him away, laughing, but the door opens and my foster carer is standing there. I wish Poppy could see her face, because it's almost worth the trouble I'm going to be in.

'What the hell is going on?' she asks.

Joe stands straight, hiding the bottle of vodka behind his back.

'Sorry, Dusty's mum,' he says.

'She's not my mum,' I correct him. And feel the tiniest

bit bad, because Sue looks like she's swallowed a whole lemon.

'But this is my home,' she tells Joe. 'And you need to leave.' She steps back, her arm pointing in the direction of the front door.

'Fair enough,' Joe says, turning to me. 'See you around.' And he does a ridiculous salute with his hand that's smeared with the red paint.

I watch him disappear from my room and more than anything I feel relieved, even though the anger simmering from Sue is almost at boiling point. She stares at me and I keep my expression blank.

'None of this is OK, Dusty,' she says.

I don't reply.

'You thought you could just bring someone into our home without asking us? At this time of night?'

'I'm going to bed now,' I say.

'You should've been in bed ages ago,' she says.

'Well, I wasn't,' I reply and turn my back on her and pray that she doesn't notice the paint on the wall before she goes.

Chapter Two

Sue hasn't said anything about Joe all morning and I'm just waiting for the bomb to go off. I can tell she's stressed by the way her shoulders are too high, her knuckles white as she chops veg for later. I wish I could tell her to just leave Poppy and me to eat our lunch in peace, without her listening in on our conversation.

I nudge my sister. 'Prim?' It's not her name, but she once bought me Katniss socks, just because she wanted to buy them for me, and that hurts my heart in a whole new way. 'Want to go to the beach after?'

'To swim?' she asks.

'If you want,' I tell her.

She has a bit of ketchup on the side of her mouth and I should tell her to wipe it away. She'd have ketchup with everything if she could, but Sue decides what few meals she's allowed it. Poppy slides her finger through the last smear of sauce on her empty plate, squints at it on her skin, before licking her finger clean. That's heaven right there for her. If I had it my way, she'd be allowed ketchup every day, which is why I wish I could force Sue's whole head into the toilet and pull the flush.

Poppy and I get up and clear away our plates, stacking them in the dishwasher. I swear Sue steps away from me as if I'm contagious.

Not all houses have been this bad. But it's almost better when you hate it, because when they let you down, the pain is easier to patch up. When we had to leave Guy and Chris, it hurt so much I thought I'd never be able to breathe normally again.

Poppy and I sit with our feet in the sand, pushing our toes deeper until we hit the cold bit. Her arms have got freckles that I'm sure weren't there before and I wonder if I should've brought sun cream. They did predict a heatwave, but I didn't think it'd be warm enough to burn.

'Would you rather,' Poppy says, 'have a giraffe's tongue forever, or a baboon's butt?'

I look at her, with that glint in her eye that no one else has, yet her face so serious that she might as well have just asked me if I know how deep the ocean is.

'Baboon's bum,' I say.

'You serious?' Poppy raises one eyebrow in a way that I can't do. 'Like all red and raw?'

'How many people are going to want to kiss me if I have

a tongue as long as a giraffe's?' I ask her, straightening my dyed-pink fringe.

'How many people want to kiss you in any case?' she laughs.

I slap her arm, guilt springing that it's harder than I meant.

'Would you rather wipe Snarky Sue's arse,' I say.

'I'm never going anywhere near Salty Sue's butt-cheeks.' Poppy pulls a face that makes me laugh so hard that I can hardly carry on.

'Or pick straws to do a dare?' I say.

'We haven't got any straws.'

'Metaphorically,' I say.

'Big word,' Poppy says.

'From a big sister who's got big exams soon.' It's too weird that after them I'll be leaving school, going to college to study art, and I don't even know what else. I scoop up a handful of sand and hold it behind my back, transferring the sand from one palm to the next. 'If you get the sand, you do the dare.'

I hold out my hands in front of me, edging the empty one further forward in a double-bluff. Poppy's fingers hover above it and touch down on my knuckles.

'Sure?' I ask her.

'Yes.' She doesn't hesitate.

'What's the dare going to be?' I ask her.

'Show me first.'

'So you'll make it worse if it's me?'

'Of course,' she says and I uncurl my left hand and there's not a grain in my palm. 'That's what I'm talking about.' She slaps the sand either side of her.

'You're some kind of gangster now?' I laugh.

She's looking around the beach. 'That guy. The one with the blue shorts.' She points to a group of boys kicking a ball. 'Go up and ask him if he's Jude Bellingham. But you've got to do it really seriously.'

'I really don't want to do that,' I say.

'You really don't have a choice.'

'I'll buy you an ice cream instead,' I tell her.

There's a moment's pause.

'Nope,' Poppy says.

'You're brutal,' I tell her.

'I learned it from the best.'

I shake my head but know the rules. The day that one of us refuses, it's game over. Literally. We made a pact that if we ever back out, the bad luck will fall. And we've had enough bad luck in our life to fill a small country.

I stand up and wipe the sand from my denim shorts, ruffle my fringe and tighten the inch-long ponytails that stick straight up on my head, my insect antennae.

'You're seriously set on humiliating me?' I ask, pulling my bra strap straight, but it just slips off my shoulder again.

'Do it properly,' Poppy says, her face serious again. 'He's got to totally believe that you think he's Bellingham. And then you've got to kick the ball away.'

'You're cruel,' I tell her.

'But brilliant.' She smiles and her whole face lights up. She's like a little angel sitting there.

'A brilliant demon,' I say, walking away from her.

The boys must see me approaching, because they start doing that thing when they know girls are watching, they get plugged into the showing-off socket. One of them does a long hog of the ball, bluffing a kick, before messing up completely and the rest of them start shouting at him.

I'm getting closer and I wish I wasn't doing this. I look back to where Poppy sits alone on the sand. She's smiling at me and I think that if this is going to make her happy, then so be it.

I barge into the middle of the group, way more aggressively than I mean to.

'Are you Jude Bellingham?' I ask the boy in the blue shorts. He stops the football dead with his foot.

'What?' He looks genuinely confused and I feel a bit bad because he's definitely starting to blush.

'You look like him,' I say. 'That's all.'

And I know it's now or never for the second part of the dare, so I kick at the football and the boy topples, because he was leaning on it, and then I'm booting the ball and running to catch up with it.

I can't turn to look at Poppy at the same time, but I know she'll be loving this bit of improvisation, so I carry on, even when the Bellingham boy starts to tackle me.

We're both laughing and when he kicks the football high in an arc into the sea, I don't hesitate to charge after it, as though it's the most normal thing in the world. He splashes me and I'm knee-deep and it's freezing and I'm trying to run to the ball, but it's like wading through slushed ice. He's got more chance of getting it than me, so I whip up a ton of water and cover him.

'You win,' he says, his palms towards me.

His T-shirt is clinging to his chest now and it shows how toned his arms are. He actually isn't that bad-looking either. I realise my own T-shirt is soaking too, so I pull at the hem to bag it out a bit, but think that perhaps I quite like the way it makes my boobs look.

'What's your name?' he asks me, the sea swirling round his legs.

'Dusty,' I tell him.

'I'm Jude,' he says. 'Bellingham.' And he laughs and dives towards the football, managing to grab it, standing up again, flicking his hair in a way that makes me think I wouldn't mind kissing him, right here in the sea.

'You local?' he asks.

'Yeah.' I won't tell him that it's not my home, though. 'You?'

'Carnaby Avenue,' he says. 'Number thirty-four.'

I'm thinking he wants me to remember it and I smile at him and wonder if I'll have the courage to go and knock on his door.

'You don't go to Bridlington School?' he asks.

'No. Headlands,' I tell him.

'Year Twelve?' he asks.

I could pretend I'm older, but I don't. 'Year Eleven.'

I look back to see Poppy's reaction to this outcome of the dare, but she's gone. I shield the sun from my eyes and I'm sure I'm looking at the spot where I left her, but she's not there.

'You OK?' the boy asks me.

'I can't see my sister,' I say, moving away from him.

'Can I have your number?' he asks, but suddenly I don't care about anything, other than the fact that the place on the sand where Poppy should be is empty.

I'm out of the sea and walking up the beach and I want to call her name, but she'll be embarrassed if everyone looks. My sliders are here where I left them. And there's a dip in the sand where Poppy was sitting. I'm spinning round, thinking she's playing with me, but I can't see her. She's not anywhere.

I grab my sliders and I'm running now, heading towards the toilets, because that's got to be where she's gone. They're in a grey block set back from the beach and I run in and bang on every closed metal door.

'Poppy?' I shout.

A woman at the sink stares at me in the mirror.

'Did you see a girl come in here?' I ask her. 'She's wearing a white T-shirt and denim cut-offs. She's got brown hair.' I'm trying to keep my voice steady.

'How old is she?' the woman asks.

But there's no point explaining, because if I tell her that Poppy is twelve, she'll think she's old enough to be safe, when she's not.

The men's toilets stink and I can't go in, but I shout my sister's name as close as I can get. There's no one here, no one around. Only graffiti on a wall that's too smudged to read.

A much older man comes out.

'Is there a girl in there?' I ask him.

'Not that I saw,' he says. 'Have you tried phoning her?' And he just walks away. And I haven't got my phone because I never bring it to the beach, where the only person I ever want to speak to is Poppy.

I run back down to the sand, looking at every person, every gap between them. I go all the way to the shore and scan the people in the sea, but none of them are her.

All I can hear is my heart. It's cracking in two. Because I see it in my mind and I try to stop it, but I think of the police coming here and Poppy being gone, really gone and it's all my fault.

Someone taps me on the shoulder and the relief is like being flooded in light, because it'll be Poppy, laughing. So I turn, but it's not her. It's the boy with the football.

'Did you find your sister?' he asks me.

'Does it look like I have?' I shout and he looks at me as if I'm mad and I don't care that I'm running away from him and I don't care that I'm still carrying my sliders, so I'm barefoot on the pavement.

Poppy will be back at the house, in her room, I know she will, thinking it's funny, that this was all part of her plan. But I can't get there fast enough and it's like I'm in one of those dreams where fog is pushing me back.

I'm in our street and the house is there. I slow down and look behind me, because perhaps Poppy has been following and she's going to jump-scare me. But the road is empty.

Poppy?

Her name echoes inside me, finding its way to the dark places where I usually hide my fear.

I open the front door into the silent hallway and try not to run along the corridor. Poppy's door is closed and I open it into an empty room. I look in her cupboard and I'm kneeling to see beneath her bed and there's a sound behind me.

'Where's Poppy?' Sue asks me.

I stand up and walk past her, into my room, but she follows me and won't let me close the door.

'Dusty?' she says.

I can't take on her worry when there's not enough air for me. I pick up my phone from the desk.

'Where is she?' she asks.

'I'm finding out.' I want to hurl the phone at her, but all my focus has to be on pressing in Poppy's number.

It rings. I stare at the curtains. At the repeat patterns

there, the squares overlapping, and the phone keeps on ringing.

'Hello?' she answers.

'Poppy?'

A million dying moths lift from my brain.

'Where did you go?' she asks me.

'Where did *I* go?' I want to kill her and hug her all in the same moment. 'You disappeared.' My voice is weird and quiet.

'I went to get you an ice cream,' she says. 'But it's melted now.'

I think of my sister standing there in the sun, ice cream dripping down a cone, down her thumb. Waiting for me.

'I couldn't love you more,' I tell her and I don't care that Sue hears it all.

They've taken my paints. All of them. Simon and Sue were angrier than I've ever seen them, with Simon shouting about how irresponsible I am and Sue's mouth clamped shut into a thin line. And then they took my paints, leaving a big gap on my desk where they should be.

I sit on my bed, with my duvet over my legs and look at the handprints Joe left on the wall. In the shadows, the pattern looks like the head of one of those creatures in *Stranger Things*. The ones that open up like some insane Venus flytrap.

Not having my paints with me does something weird

to my stomach. It hollows it, then fills it with drying clay. I clench my hands and dig my nails into my palms. *Breathe, Dusty*. I can feel rage starting, pinpricks beneath my skin, hundreds of them that melt and swim into my bloodstream. I just want my paints. I need to see their colours, create something from nothing. It's the only thing that really calms me, that takes me to a different place where I can escape. But Simon and Sue have taken them from me, so I can't.

I remember when Poppy and I had been here only a few weeks and things were going OK and I was desperate to stay, because I was with my sister in a house with sofas and a TV and I had my own duvet that Sue cleaned. And she made food that was fine and I was allowed to lie in the bath as long as I wanted. So I painted these foster carers a picture of their house and I knew it was good. I used a technique we'd been learning in school, so it looked a mixture between realistic, but modernist too. Simon didn't say much when I gave it to them, but Sue seemed to love it and I thought she might frame it, or at least put it on the fridge, as Jo used to do in house number four, when I was ten. But I found it in the recycling. And there's not a word in the dictionary to describe the feeling I had in me when I saw it there.

There are plenty of words for how I feel now, though, and none of them are pretty. I get up and it takes all my willpower not to smash the room to pieces. I breathe from the pit of my stomach in the way that Jen, my social worker, told me I have to, and I creep out of the bedroom to the only place that'll calm me down.

In the utility room, next to the washing machine, Rex is curled in his basket, taking up all the space. He looks at me, his tail thumping. It's cold lying on the floor, but I rest my head on him and feel his heartbeat beneath his fur. It helps slow my own heart. It's the one place where I feel safe to cry.

Chapter Three

There's no getting around the fact that school is an endurance test. Poppy and I have been shifted from place to place so often that I don't bother trying to make friends any more and I put on a pretty convincing exterior that I don't care. I always tell myself on day one to keep looking forward, never at the ground. Don't freak out at sudden noises. Ignore the deliberate shoves and keep my expression blank as I get the inevitable *sweep you into the trash, Dusty.*

It's no surprise when I'm yanked by the elbow into the toilets. And no surprise that it's Tessa B doing the yanking. A bit more of a surprise to see so many people crammed in here, including boys, surrounding a girl called Janey. She looks at me as if begging to get her away, but there's no chance in hell I'll manage that.

'What do you want this time?' I ask Tessa. I sound confident, but my stomach has evaporated and I'm not sure my legs are going to keep me standing.

'You two are going to kiss,' Tessa says and there's sniggering in the crowd.

I reply to Tessa with a stare that I'm hoping will summon every damn snake from the underworld to writhe up and drag her down.

People are holding their phones ready, obscuring their faces, waiting to record the moment that two Year 11 outcasts were forced together.

I shrug. 'I'd prefer to kiss her than any of you freaks.'

Tessa grabs the front of my shirt, pulling me towards her. 'Who are you calling a freak?'

I stare into her eyes. 'Your breath stinks,' I tell her. It causes chaos among the boys.

Tessa's cheeks blush pink beneath her foundation. She shoves me towards Janey.

'Do it,' she says. 'Now.'

Janey looks like she's going to cry. Something tells me that she's never kissed anyone before, as she usually scuttles around in the shadows. I know exactly why they've picked us two.

'You want to keep your glasses on, or off?' I ask her.

'On,' she whispers.

'You'll be fine,' I tell her. 'At least I'm not halitosis Tessa.' I smile and before Tessa has time to grab me again, I step closer to Janey and kiss her. I've never kissed a girl and her lips feel a bit different, softer. It'd be nice if I couldn't feel her shaking so much. I keep my eyes closed, but know that cameras are immortalising the moment.

I run my hand down Janey's arm until we're linking fingers and I stop kissing her.

'That was good,' I say and I mean it. I pull her with me through the crowd, not rushing, pretending that I'm cool with all of this.

Outside the door, with a few phones still on us, I squeeze Janey's hand and lean towards her ear.

'You're more beautiful than any one of them,' I tell her.

If I had longer hair, I'd fling it over my shoulder, but still I walk away giving the same attitude. That I'm invincible, that they can't touch me. I don't let on that I can feel the claws of every single one of them scraping away at my fragile soul.

There's a knock on the maths room door. Sir stops talking, hand mid-motion and we all look to where Miss Mason comes in, her shoes clacking on the floor. I'm surprised she doesn't feel self-conscious with that sound following her around all day. She says something to sir and he nods and it's definitely my direction he's looking in.

Miss Mason is coming towards me, her noisy shoes mimicking my heart. She must've seen the videos of me and Janey. But I don't think there are rules about kissing in break time?

She stops by my table and has a weird smile on. Great, so all the staff are laughing at me too.

'Can you gather your things and come with me?' she asks.

As if I have a choice. I'm seeing my hands pick up my

pen and chuck it into my bag, along with my maths book. I'm trying to pretend that I'm not shaking as I do up the zip and swing the bag over my shoulder and follow Miss Mason between the tables.

'So long, suckers,' I say. I think I'll turn and flip them all the finger, but sir is about the only teacher I like and I don't want him to see me do it.

It's always weird being out of lessons when the corridors are empty. It feels a bit like being underwater, that none of the air sits quite right. I wonder how I could catch the feeling in a painting. I calm myself by thinking about how I could make it look like mist. Or perhaps it wouldn't need that, perhaps just emptiness would do it.

We walk past Poppy's tutor room and although she wouldn't be in there now, it suddenly hits me.

'Is something wrong with Poppy?' I stop as I ask it. I won't be moving until I know she's OK.

'No,' Miss Mason says. 'Poppy is absolutely fine.'

I start walking again. Poppy will definitely see the footage of me and Janey. She won't mind me kissing her, but she'll hate that I was forced to do it. Katniss would've whipped out a crossbow and decimated them all.

We go up some stairs and Miss Mason opens the door to the small pastoral room.

'After you,' she says. I go inside, when everything is telling me to run the other way. Jen, my social worker, is sitting on one of the chairs. It takes me a moment to figure out it's really her, because she never comes here. And I feel a familiar rush of shame. Of course Miss Mason knows I'm in care, but having my social worker in front of us completely confirms it.

'Dusty.' Jen's smile isn't the same as usual, but she gets up to hug me and it's familiar and for a spilt second I feel safe. But she lets go and I'm here, adrift in the middle of some ocean I don't think I want to be in. 'You can sit here.' She points to the comfiest-looking chair in the room, but instead I sit on the plastic one nearest me.

'Tessa B forced me to do it,' I say. But all this feels wrong for a kiss. Maybe Janey's mum has complained. But an even worse thought flares up. 'Is Janey OK? Has she done something?'

Jen glances up at Miss Mason. 'Janey?'

'Shall I leave you two for a bit?' Miss Mason asks.

'Thanks,' Jen says. 'We won't be long.'

We both watch Miss Mason leave. I should tell her that the hem of her skirt is coming down at the back, but she's shut the door and is gone.

'What's going on?' I ask.

Jen inhales deeper than I've ever seen her do before, letting the air out through puffed lips.

'Your foster carers phoned me. About the boy you had in your room.'

'Joe,' I say and have to swallow down a laugh. This isn't

about Poppy and it's not about Janey and I'm so flooded with relief that anything else I can cope with.

'Dusty, you had someone they didn't know in their home. You were drinking. And on top of it all, you smeared red paint all over their wall.'

'I didn't smear it,' I tell her.

'I've seen it,' Jen says. 'It's not OK.'

'You went to the house?'

'Your carers insist it showed malicious intent. That it's even something ritualistic.'

'What's that supposed to mean?' I ask. 'It was handprints.'

'Made from what looked like blood.'

'Blood?' And now I do laugh. 'It was red paint.'

'We know that, but they felt that it symbolised something.'

'Are you joking me?'

I'm so close to telling her that Simon and Sue were probably too drunk to see it straight. That they've been drinking more and more since Poppy and I moved in, but we've never said, because we don't want to be moved on again and at least in this house we're never hungry.

'No, Dusty, I'm not joking you,' Jen says. 'They say you're behaving too irresponsibly. You left Poppy on the beach.'

'I didn't leave her there,' I say.

'You know you were on your final warning.'

'But no one really meant that, though.'

'They did mean that. They've meant it for a long time. They've had enough.'

'Enough?' And there they are, the words that follow me everywhere. 'Of me?' I'm not good enough. I'm never good enough.

'You've pushed them to this conclusion, Dusty.'

I've a sharp pain in my throat, but I scratch the back of my palm to make it go away.

'They're not nice to us,' I tell her. 'If they were nice, then I would be too.'

'They're entitled to be angry with you for sneaking someone into their home.'

'There's other stuff,' I say.

'Is this about you not being allowed the dog in your room at night?' Jen asks. 'That's a perfectly normal request.'

I look at Jen and think about all the things I never told her, the little cruelties that add up. Simon sprinkling pepper all over Poppy's comfort blanket, saying it was a joke. Tearing the last page out of the book she was reading. He gave it back to her, but by then the damage had already been done.

I look down at my lap, my leg shaking. I don't need to keep my eyes forward for Jen, she knows the real me.

'Dusty,' she says, but I won't look at her. If I can block her out, then I won't hear the words that are coming next. 'This placement has broken down.'

I nod and it's not just my leg shaking now. My whole body is shivering, even though the room is hot.

'They're getting rid of us,' I say. Like rubbish. Easily disposable.

'They felt they had no choice.'

I can't tell whether I feel bad for Poppy or not. Because of me she's being uprooted again, but perhaps we'll go to a better place.

Jen passes me the box of tissues, the top one pulled up like the wing of a dove. I shake my head. I don't need them. I won't cry.

'I've packed up as much of your stuff as I could,' she says. 'If I've forgotten anything, I'll easily get it to you.'

'Why didn't I pack myself?' I ask, looking at her now.

'They don't want you back there.'

'At all?'

'At all,' Jen repeats.

'Not even to say goodbye?'

It feels like a drill is twisting deep into my heart.

'I'm sorry, Dusty.'

'But what about Rex? I can't just never see him again.' The drill slips and finds its way into my lungs.

Jen leans over and puts her hands on my knees.

'It'll be OK,' she says.

OK? I want to scream it in her face, but the word is lost and I can't find it. I can't find anything, apart from tiny gasps of air.

'I've managed to find a place for you,' Jen says. 'It wasn't easy, but we've been really lucky.'

Lucky?

My brain is smoke.

'It's difficult to find somewhere for sixteen-year-olds, as you know.'

'Especially when there are two of us.' I know how this works. It's written behind my eyelids to step into my dreams every night.

Jen looks like I've slapped her. She literally winces.

'Poppy is going to stay where she is for a while,' she says. 'It'll only be you who's moving.'

'Well, that's not happening,' I say. That's a definite. Jen knows that Poppy and I don't get separated, ever.

'Your foster carers don't have a problem with Poppy,' Jen tells me. 'They say that you're the disruptive one.'

I stare at her. She's narrowed me down to that one word. Disruptive. Forget that I can be funny, that I help clean, that I walk Rex and that I'm practically a mum for Poppy. Forget that I endure all their nasty shit. I'm *disruptive*. Kick her out. Move on.

'Poppy isn't staying there without me,' I say.

'That is what's going to happen for the moment,' Jen tells me.

'No,' I say. 'It's not.'

Jen takes her hands from my knees. 'There's no choice in this, Dusty.'

'They're not good people.' I'm the one leaning forward now. 'Poppy isn't safe there without me.'

'We've never been concerned about either of your safety in that home.'

'Because I never tell you what they do.'

Jen's face doesn't give away any of her thoughts. 'You've told me plenty of times. But not getting to watch what you want is not enough to get them struck off the register.'

I think again of what I didn't tell her. Like when Simon thought it was funny to force Poppy to watch the worst horror movie when she was only ten. And once, when they were annoyed with me, they locked me in the kitchen for ages and I smashed every piece of their china. And I never said, because I was always so scared that they'd separate us.

'You can't do this,' I say.

'I'm afraid we can,' Jen says. 'Believe me, it's the last thing I want to do, but there are no other options.'

'Why can't Poppy come with me to this new place?'

'There's no space for her. We were lucky to find anything at such short notice. It's taken a lot of phone calls and wrangling.'

As if she's doing me a favour.

'Well, I'm sorry for the inconvenience,' I say.

'You're never an inconvenience, Dusty,' Jen says. 'You've just got to try harder to control yourself when things don't go your way.'

I can't look at her any more. Instead, I stare out of the window. It was sunny this morning, but now the sky is the colour of ash.

‘I’m going to come with you, to settle you in,’ Jen says.

‘Now?’

‘Yes. I’ve got your clothes and everything in the car.’

‘I need to tell Poppy what’s going on,’ I say.

‘I discussed that with my supervisor,’ Jen says. ‘We both made the decision that wouldn’t be in Poppy’s best interest.’

‘I’m the only one who knows what my sister’s best interests are.’ The ash clouds from outside have seeped into the room and into my mouth.

‘She’d find it too much to process,’ Jen says. ‘It’d be unfair for her in a school setting.’

‘Then take us out of the school setting,’ I say. ‘We can go to the park. I can explain to her what’s going on there.’

‘Leave us to explain it,’ Jen says. ‘And hopefully tonight you can speak to her.’

I think of Poppy in Sue and Simon’s house without me, curled on the sofa, the phone to her ear.

When I woke up this morning, I had no idea that the end of the world was coming.

‘I need to see her,’ I say.

‘It would be too difficult for her,’ Jen says. ‘She can either be told later in the safety of her home, or we can pull her out of lessons now, with the potential of a traumatic scene that other students will see. We both know that’s not the best option.’

I feel like I’m in quicksand and it’s swallowing me whole.

Jen stands, but I can’t move. She reaches for my hand,

but I won't take it and her fingers circle my wrist so she can pull me up. She hugs me again, but it's so different this time. I'm caught in the jaws of a shark.

We go out and there's no sign of Miss Mason.

We go down the stairs and I know that somewhere in this building there's my sister. She'll be sitting there, her shirt tucked in, leaning over her work, trying her best. I always tell her to just try her best.

I think I'm going to be sick. I swallow back bile, but my stomach cramps. I hold on to the banister and there's the sudden, deafening, end-of-lesson bell. There'll be students everywhere and so I let Jen lead me by the arm, out the double doors to Reception. She nods to Miss Clark, who sits behind the front desk and doesn't stop us to ask where we're going, to tell us we've got to sign out.

We're in the car park and Jen gets a key from her pocket and points it towards her small green car. She opens the passenger door and I see myself step inside. I don't run, I don't scream, I don't smash every window in the school. I sit here, my school rucksack by my feet, and Jen pulls the seat belt across me and clicks it into place.

Her car smells like a taxi and it makes me want to vomit.

She passes me a bag of sweets, but I don't touch them. They sit on my lap as Jen starts her car, reverses us out and drives me away.

Chapter Four

We've been driving for over an hour and we're still driving and all I can think of is that I'm going to be miles away from Poppy tonight and this is the furthest apart we've ever been. There's just so much road and so many cars and every time we slow down, I want to open the door and hurl myself out and run back to her.

The sweets sit unopened and Jen turns on the radio, but the music is so shit that I want to scream. If I could have a normal phone like everyone else, I could be listening to whatever I want to listen to. But all I'm allowed is a brick-phone and I look at it and it's silent. Poppy doesn't ring. It means she won't know yet and that's good, because when I think of her face when she's told that I'm gone and I'm not there to comfort her, I want to grab the steering wheel from Jen and ram us into the biggest truck to take me to oblivion.

*

Another half an hour. I turn off the radio.

'This is going to be a long way to drive to school every day,' I say. 'Can I go by train?'

Jen stares straight ahead. 'You won't be commuting to Headlands,' she says.

'So this is just for one night? Then you'll find me somewhere closer?'

'No,' Jen says. 'At the moment, this is our only option.'

'I don't get what you mean,' I say. But I do. I get it completely, but I can pretend for a moment that this isn't happening.

'Dusty,' Jen says. 'I promise I tried every place I could. I called on every contact, phoned every agency. This is the closest I could get.'

'I'm in Year Eleven,' I remind her. 'My exams are literally in a couple of weeks. I can't just not go to school.'

'I'm not suggesting that you don't go to school. The home you're going to has a school attached to it, so you can carry on your education.'

'How can a family have a school attached to their house?'

Jen rubs her thumb on the steering wheel, as though there's something there that she's trying to erase. I want to tell her that she needs to redo her nails, that the paint has lifted away from her cuticles and it looks a mess.

'You're not going to a family, Dusty.'

'A single parent, then?'

But I can tell it in the tension in Jen's shoulders, even the way she's blinking. I'm not going to help her out, though. I want her to have to say it.

'It's a residential home.'

There it is.

'A children's home?' The words leave a bitter trail in my mouth.

'A residential home for children, yes,' Jen says.

The end of the line, then.

'You couldn't find one family, one person in the whole of the fucking country who wanted me?' I ask.

'It's not that people don't want you, Dusty,' Jen says. The road beneath us goes on and on, the lanes divided by a split line of white paint. 'It's that they can't have you. There's a big difference.'

I feel such a surge of hatred for her right now.

'It's got a really good reputation,' Jen continues. 'The company has a few homes dotted around the country.'

I look out of the window, at a red car we're overtaking. A woman is driving and in the passenger seat a girl sits with her legs up on the dashboard, a phone in her hand. I've enough time to see a much younger boy in the back and he looks up just at the moment that I'm looking at him. I want to open my window and open theirs and step into their life. Buckle a seat belt across me in their car, go where they're going.

'I can put a mattress on my floor for Poppy,' I tell Jen. 'Until there's a place for her there.'

'I'm afraid you won't be able to do that,' Jen says. 'We have to do what's best for Poppy too. We can't just uproot her whole life for no reason.'

'I'm her reason,' I say.

Pain flares bright and brutal in my chest.

'Honey,' Jen says and she reaches to me, but I slap away her hand.

'Don't fucking *honey* me,' I say, each word a spike in my throat. 'Don't you fucking dare pretend you care.'

'You know I care,' she says.

I don't even bother to wipe my tears any more. They drip from my chin, down my neck into the collar of my school shirt. The school I don't go to any more.

'All I know is that you're leaving my sister alone with those psychopaths and you're not listening shit to what I say. And I swear to God, if anything happens to her . . . '

'Nothing is going to happen to her, Dusty.'

I close my eyes and try to find somewhere in my head I can hide, somewhere away from this hell I've stumbled upon. But all I can see is Poppy, standing alone, calling for me.

We pull up next to the pavement in front of a house, three hours and seventeen minutes' drive away from Poppy. The house is huge, three floors, with big windows either side of the front door. There are blinds pulled down, so I can't see in.

'Here we are, then,' Jen says. 'That was a smooth journey.'

Her smile doesn't look like her own. I don't think she wants me here either.

She's shocked when I grab her arm. Not scared, but surprised.

'Please don't leave me here,' I beg her.

'It might not be for long,' she tells me. I can feel the subtle shift in her arm, moving away from me.

'One night is too long,' I say.

'I promise I'll keep looking for something closer to Poppy.'

Poppy. I fold over and put my head on to my knees. They would've told her by now. She'll be without me in that house, sitting alone at that kitchen table.

Fury is a switch and I sit up straight and I'm shouting. 'Don't you care that she'll be frightened? I'm the only person in the world who makes her feel safe.'

'She's perfectly safe where she is,' Jen says.

And she must sense that I'm on the edge of doing something I know I'll regret, because she turns away from me, opens the door and gets out.

'I'll go and let them know we're here.'

I watch her walk up a stone path between mowed grass. The terror that's been building in me turns into a swarm of beetles burrowing with quick legs beneath my skin, battling for space in my bloodstream. I see Jen knock on the door of the house and it opens and there's a man there and I should run, run now, get out of the car and escape down the street.

I could hide and then someone would help me. But I don't move. I watch the man and Jen walk towards the car and I swear my heart has slipped free from its place and is sliding, loose, beating into every inch of me.

The man opens Jen's door and leans down to speak to me.

'Hey, Dusty. Good to meet you. I'm John.' All I can see is his beard that Poppy would hate.

Jen opens the door on my side. They've got me trapped. I should've run when I could, but I didn't.

John stands up. 'Shall I grab the luggage?' he asks over the roof above my head.

'Can you manage it?' Jen asks him.

'No problem.' He goes to open the boot and takes out a suitcase and a bin bag, putting them on to the pavement.

'You got rocks in these?' he laughs.

Jen holds out her hand for me. 'Come on, Dusty. I'll help you get settled.'

'I don't want to be settled here,' I tell her. Surely she can see how wrong this is.

She doesn't answer, just looks at me with that useless expression of pity, balled up with sadness.

That man, John, walks towards the house, carrying all my things. He's a stranger and he's got his hands on everything I own. I shake my head and try to dislodge this fucked up dream I'm having, but it's all still there. I hit my palm on my head, needing to get rid of it.

'Dusty,' Jen says, but I hit and hit the sides of my head, because it's the only thing I can think of to get this madness to go away. Jen grabs my wrists and pulls them down. 'You don't want this to be the first thing the other kids see of you.'

'Please,' I whisper, because if I speak louder, I know I'm going to cry again. 'Please take me back.'

'This won't be as bad as you think,' she says. 'Come on.'

I feel her pulling me gently from the car and I'm letting her. I don't know what else I'm meant to do. She reaches to where my feet had been and gets my school rucksack.

'Here,' she says, passing it to me, and I hold it as a shield to my chest as we walk around the front of the car and up the path. With each step, I put my mask back on, covering the real Dusty, pushing her down.

Chapter Five

We're standing in a hallway and I'm trying to hold my rucksack casually, but knowing that if I move it, my heart will break out of my skin.

'The office area is through there.' John puts down the bin bag and my suitcase and points to the closed door on our right. 'And in here,' he pushes the door on our left further open, 'is the lounge.'

Jen peers in. 'It's lovely.' She waves into the room. There's someone in there.

John smiles at me. 'Alfie loves films,' he says. 'He won't stop watching them for anyone.'

We carry on walking and I can feel Alfie try to look at me. We go past carpeted stairs to a kitchen at the end. In another life I'd love this room, the colour of the turquoise paint on the walls and the long table in the middle. But it's not another life, this is my life and I don't want to be here. A woman is by the sink, with black hair in a plait all the way down her back, and standing near her is a girl, younger than me, maybe even younger than Poppy.

'Kelly, Casey,' John says, scratching his disgusting beard. 'This is Dusty.'

Kelly, the woman, walks towards me as if to shake my hand, but I ignore it. I'm not being rude, but I can't lift my arm. If I do, the whole of me will collapse.

'Smells good in here,' Jen says. 'What are you cooking?'

'Meatballs,' Kelly says. She has a string of purple beads twisted over and over on her wrist that rattle when she lifts her arm. 'Don't worry if you're a veggie, Dusty. We've got that covered.'

'Every day at least one of the kids helps the adults to cook,' John says. 'And then we all eat together.'

'I don't have to wash up, as I'm cooking,' Casey says, not looking up, slicing through a carrot.

'Casey offers to cook most nights, to escape the washing-up,' John laughs.

'Luckily for us.' Kelly smiles. 'As she's a brilliant chef.'

I turn to Jen. 'I need to phone Poppy,' I tell her.

The atmosphere shifts.

'Let's see your room, first,' Jen says.

She ignores the way I look at her and I have to follow them from the kitchen, with its smell of frying onions, back along the corridor, and I'm going up stairs I don't want to go up, with people I don't want to be with, in a place I should never have come to.

At the top, on the right, another closed door.

'There's another office in there and also the adults' sleeping area,' John says. 'So, out of bounds. This one is Liv's room. She's with Rina at the shops at the moment. They'll be back for dinner.' The door in front of us has heavy boot marks near the bottom. We go along the landing. 'Casey's in the end one, looking over the garden.' There's a handmade sign on her door, decorated with unicorns. John points to the next closed door. 'This is Alfie's room. Cooper and Jemal are up there.' He gestures to some more stairs. 'And you're in here.'

John nudges open a door and stands back to let me in first. It feels like I'm pushing through a thick fog that no one else seems to be able to see. Everything is muffled and too far away.

'It's really nice,' Jen says.

There's a bed in front of us in the corner and next to it a desk, with a window above. Poppy would call the curtains cat-puke pink. On the floor there's a blue beanbag and along the wall, a row of built-in cupboards.

'Plenty of space for everything,' John says.

I turn to Jen. 'Can I phone my sister now?'

'I'll get your bags,' John says and he's gone and I can hear him walking back along the landing and down the stairs.

'I'm settled in,' I tell Jen. 'You said I could call her then.'

'You don't want to unpack first? Meet a few more people?'

'You said I could speak to her.'

Jen nods. She looks tired. 'I'll phone Sue and see if she can put her on.'

'I can phone her from my phone,' I say.

'No. It's better this way.'

She takes her handbag from her shoulder, the same one that I used to rummage through for sweets when I first met her. Our social worker before Jen would never have let us do that.

John puts everything I own in the bedroom doorway. 'I'll leave you to it,' he says. 'You're welcome to stay for dinner, Jen.'

'Thanks,' she says, her phone in her hand. 'But I have to be off soon. It's quite a drive.'

I look at her, with all the millions of words I want to say crashing into each other in my throat. *You're really going to drive off and leave me here? With these strangers? On my own?* But my voice box is a mangled wreck and nothing comes out.

'If you do get to speak to Poppy,' Jen says, 'then you must try not to upset her.'

Anger lights me. I have to swallow it down, or she could change her mind in a moment.

'She's my sister.' I don't need to say any more.

I watch Jen scroll through her contacts, find the right one. I see her listen into the phone and it's only a moment before she's speaking. Sue must have answered, but I zone her out. She's there with Poppy, and I'm not.

Jen nods and she's passing me the phone. I keep my rucksack clutched to my stomach with one hand and hold the phone to my ear with the other.

'Poppy?' I say.

And there's no answer, because she's crying. My little sister is crying and I made this happen.

'Prim?' I say and the word begins to break in two. I cough and dig my hand into my rucksack, hold it so tight to me that it pushes into my ribs. 'We're going to be OK.'

I never lie to my sister, but now I have.

'Where are you?' she whispers and sniffs and I imagine her wiping her nose with her sleeve and I'm not with her to tell her not to do that.

'I'm in a house.'

'Can I come there?'

Needles dig deep into my bones.

'It's not a family,' I say. 'It's a residential home.'

'That's fine,' she says. 'I don't mind.'

I should tell her that she's better off staying with Sue and Simon, but I can't lie to her again.

'Jen is looking for something else. There'll be a new family for the two of us.'

'When?' She's crying again and it makes me feel like I'm tied to a rack and am being stretched and my body will tear down the middle.

'As soon as she can,' I tell her. 'It won't be long.'

I can't do this. I want more than anything to stay listening to her voice, but I can't.

'I'll phone you tomorrow, OK?'

Poppy doesn't answer.

'Be good at school,' I say. 'I love you.'

I don't turn off the phone. I drop it on the bed, curl on to my knees. Jen's hand rubs my back and I hate that it's there, because it can't make the pain go away. It's too deep and red and it burrows into me, dragging me towards a black hole that I won't be able to get out of.

'Do you want me to help you unpack before I go?' Jen stands in the middle of the room, me on the bed, my rucksack on the floor.

'I'm not going to unpack,' I tell her.

'OK,' she replies. She's run out of steam for me. She just wants to get back to her life now, the flat she lives in with her husband and their two cats, Salt and Spice. 'Do you want to come down and be with the others, or stay in your bedroom for a while?'

'It's not my bedroom,' I say.

'It won't feel like it yet,' Jen says. 'But once you've got all your things around it.'

I won't look at her, so she crouches in front of me and puts her hands on her knees. 'You need this place to keep you. You won't like the alternatives.'

I move away from her.

'I'll phone you tomorrow,' she says. 'Check how you're doing. OK?'

I look through the window, into the grey sky.

'You can do this, Dusty,' Jen says and she stands up.

I only look at her when she's walking out of the door. She doesn't even look back.

I haven't moved. I keep staring at the tops of the trees outside. This house I'm in is on a hill, roofs slanting away from us. And I'm here without Poppy, without my sister, without the only person who gives my life meaning. It creates a terrifying windmill of spikes in my brain. The only way to stop them is to try to keep Poppy out of reach of my thoughts, before I hurtle into an abyss with nothing to stop me.

Below, car doors bang and there's the sound of people rushing up the path, the loud voice of a girl. Louder still, as they come in the front door, slamming it behind them.

'Food!' I hear her shout. It sounds like there are loads of them down there, but it can't be that many. 'What's for dinner?'

Someone thumps their way up the stairs. I know they're coming this way. I haven't enough time to work out what expression I need on my face.

A girl appears in the doorway, wearing grey trackies and a pink hoodie. She lifts her hands up to her high ponytail, splits it in two and tightens it. 'You the new girl?' she asks me.

'Yeah,' I say.

'Dusty's a funny name,' she says.

'I guess,' I say, ready to get defensive, but the predictable comments about me don't come.

'I'm Liv. You a veggie?' she asks.

'No.'

'Good,' she says. 'Dinner's almost ready.' She steps out of my room and shouts up the stairs to the next floor. 'Dinner.'

And she's gone.

I can hear them all in the kitchen, but I don't go down.

'Cooper!' someone shouts from below and there's someone walking on the floor above me, a door opening and closing, feet on the stairs. My door is right opposite where he appears, so he can't not see me.

'You coming to eat?' he asks.

'I'm not hungry,' I lie.

God, I wish Poppy was here. She'd love him instantly. His black hair looks like he's either hacked at it himself, or paid tons of money to have it done, dots of black eyeliner under one eye, a beautiful face.

'You'll be hungry if you don't eat,' he says. There's the smallest scar on his forehead. 'I'll go in with you if you'd like. Jemal and Liv will be down there. It won't be too scary.'

'I'm not scared,' I tell him.

He shrugs. 'Do what you want.' He's walking away. 'But it'll become a much bigger deal if you don't come down.'

There are only a very few things in life that I genuinely have a choice in and this is one of them. I can stay up here and make a scene, or I can go down, blend in and hopefully never have to eat here again after tomorrow.

I stand up and realise that I'm still in my school clothes, but I'm not going to go through my stuff now to find something to change into. What would Katniss do? She'd walk into that kitchen and turn her uniform into fire. I keep the knowledge of that with me as I get up and go along the landing, hand on the banister rail, down the stairs, to a room where I don't know anyone.

'Dusty,' John says. 'Grab a seat.'

There are a couple of empty chairs, one beside Cooper.

'You can sit here,' Liv says and I go round the table to sit next to her. Opposite me there's another boy, the one I'd seen briefly in the lounge. He looks about nine, but he's possibly older. I think John said he was called Alfie. 'She's not a veggie,' Liv shouts to where Kelly stands, serving the food at the cooker.

Casey brings us the plates, one by one. It's slow and I've time to look around at everyone here. Next to Cooper is a boy with cropped short hair and deep black skin. He barely looks at me and keeps digging the prongs of his fork into the plastic tablecloth. John leans over and taps the back of his hand.

'It'll come out of your pocket money if you make a hole,' he says.

The boy pushes the fork into the tablecloth again.

'I mean it, Jemal,' John says.

Cooper leans over and takes the fork from him. 'I reckon he does this time.' He whispers something to Jemal and they both laugh.

'Let's make this a nice meal, as it's Dusty's first one,' Kelly says, ladling food on to the last plate.

There are too many eyes on me and I hate it. Kelly comes and sits on the other side of me. She moves the end of her plait from her shoulder, the beads on her wrist doing that really irritating clinking that makes me want to rip them from her and throw them across the table.

'Before we start,' John says. 'Tradition dictates that when someone is new, they're the ones to say grace.' He points to me. 'All yours, Dusty.'

Grace? Like praying to God before a meal? I feel myself blushing in a way that I haven't since Marcus Lendrid kicked away my chair in Year 7.

Suddenly they're laughing, and Alfie, the boy across the table from me, laughs so much that he pretends to fall off his chair. Kelly pats me on the arm.

'Not really,' she says, glaring at John and I can tell she's pissed off. 'It's just John's idea of a joke.'

Fucking funny one, I want to say, my cheeks still blazing.

'Wanker,' I hear someone mumble and I'm sure it's either Cooper or Jemal.

I don't want to be here, I don't want their food, but I

eat it. Every meatball and every bit of garlic bread. I imagine Poppy sitting beside me and Skanky Sue telling her not to pick at the crumbs with her fingers. I have to concentrate on the sounds of the cutlery on the plates to stop myself crying.

It's easier when we're clearing up. There are less people in here and Kelly seems to get that I don't want to talk and is somehow reassuring in her silence. Alfie is like a spinning top on constant spin. He keeps asking me questions and I give him one-word answers, or none at all. He doesn't need to know about Sue and Simon, about why I'm still in school uniform, about where my real mum is, my real dad.

'I've got a sister,' I tell him. 'She's called Poppy.' That's all he needs to know.

Casey and Alfie have gone to bed and Liv has made space for me on the sofa in the living room. She's being friendly enough, but it's like I'm in an alternative universe that I should no way be in. Cooper and Jemal are in an armchair each and Kelly stands in front of a massive TV, pointing the controls towards it.

'Not that one,' she says. 'Not until you're fifteen, Jemal.'

'He is next week,' Cooper tells her.

'Come on, Kel,' Liv says. 'No one will know.'

'I'll know.'

'Erase it from your head,' Liv says. 'Pretend it never happened.'

'We won't tell anyone.' It's the only words that Jemal adds to the conversation. He's got what Poppy would call a silent soul.

'It's not that I'm just following rules,' Kelly says. 'I do actually care that you don't watch something grim.'

I don't bother to tell her that my stepdad forced me to watch adult stuff on repeat when I was barely out of nappies.

We watch her flick through the choices.

'I'm putting this one on,' Kelly says, starting a film. 'It's got The Rock in it.'

'Can't complain at that,' Liv says.

'I just want it noted that I am complaining,' Cooper says.

'You'll get your choice next time, Cooper,' Kelly tells him, leaving the room.

'Kelly!' Liv shouts after her, even though she's easily within earshot. 'We need popcorn.'

Kelly reappears in the doorway. 'You seem to be missing something.'

'Yes, popcorn,' Liv says. Kelly raises an eyebrow at her and smiles. 'Please,' Liv adds.

'Salted or sugar?' Kelly asks. 'Jemal, you decide, as it's your birthday soon.'

'Caramel,' he says. Poppy's favourite.

'I'm not doing that at this time. It takes ages.'

'Can we have melted butter with salt?' he asks.

'Coming up.' Kelly begins to walk back towards the kitchen.

'Turn the light off,' Liv shouts again.

'Only allowed when I'm in there,' she calls back.

On the screen, we're flying over mountains and it looks so free that I feel even more trapped.

'You should've asked for sugar, Jemal,' Liv says, her volume still switched to loud.

'Can you actually be quiet now,' he says.

'Can you actually shut your mouth,' Liv retorts.

Jemal stares at her, but doesn't say anything more.

I curl my feet beneath me. There's no point keeping them on the ground without Rex to keep them warm. If he was here, I could reach down and have him nuzzle into my hand. I feel a cramp in my heart, a pain so overwhelming, with no way to make it go. I shift my position, but it's like a balloon getting bigger inside me, taking up all the space.

Cooper taps my arm and I jump. 'You OK?' he asks.

I nod. *Don't cry, Dusty.* I stare at the enormous TV and tell myself that tomorrow I'll be out of here.

I don't think that I'm going to be able to concentrate on the film, but I do. I sink into it. It's a blanket, blocking out all the cold. I even laugh, properly laugh. But when it's finished and the credits are rolling, I'm spat out into reality.

I don't wait for any of them to speak to me. I get up from the sofa, smooth down my school skirt, go out the room and up the stairs. I hadn't noticed the pictures on the wall before, three of them, all of roses, the petals in each slightly different. I want to stop and see how the artist has managed to get the folds of the flowers to look like velvet, whether they've used acrylic, or crayon, but I keep walking, turning left at the top and left again, to the room where I'm going to have to try to sleep.

I lift the suitcase on to the bed and open it, push the clothes aside, but can't find my paintbrushes, or my sketchbooks. I get the bin bag and throw the clothes from it and my art things aren't in there either. They were on my desk in my bedroom, I know they were. Simon locked away my paints, but he couldn't make a fuss about my dry brushes, sketchbooks and pencils. Jen told me that she'd packed everything.

Panic begins, the taut grey of bat wings inside my lungs. I find my phone and get Jen's number. It rings and rings. I know I'm not meant to phone her out of working hours, but surely tonight is different. She knows where I am and she knows I need her. I hang up and ring her again. She doesn't answer.

I'm about to hurl the phone against the wall when I remember that it's my lifeline to Poppy. I stare at the keypad. I could call her now, check on her again. Remind her to brush her teeth. But she might already be asleep and then I'd wake her and that'd definitely upset her. And I remember that Sue takes her phone at night in any case, so it'd be useless to try.

With the door closed, I can see where it's been kicked near its hinges and a deep line cut across it. It looks like the road that brought me here, the endless blur taking me miles and miles from anything familiar.

Someone knocks and John puts his head round the door, itching that wiry beard.

'We encourage lights off soon,' he says, 'as it's school tomorrow.'

Not my school, though.

'Have you got everything you need?' he asks. 'Anything else I can get you?'

'Paints,' I answer, without hesitating.

'Paints?' he laughs.

'Jen didn't pack my paintbrushes. Or my sketchbooks.'

'Oh right, OK, no problem.'

'Proper ones, though,' I say. 'Not kids' ones.'

'They've got some in the school. I'm sure they can spare some.'

'Can I have them now?' I ask.

It's the only way to get rid of this creeping terror. I need to free it, make colours of it to make sense of it.

'It's too late now,' John tells me. 'But we'll definitely make sure you get some tomorrow.' And he goes out, before I can argue.

Among my pile of clothes, there's the only other thing that might calm me. I kneel down and untangle them from each other and pull them on to my feet. My Katniss socks.

Poppy was so excited when she gave them to me, tearing them from the bag before I even got a chance.

I bring my knees to my chest, but I feel too small and so stretch out my legs, kicking them into the clothes.

You can do this, Dusty, I tell myself. And I know I can. Six foster carers in eight years. I know how to say goodbye and lose it all and start again. And be thrown away again. I get a plain piece of paper in my mind and I paint Katniss on it, the bit where she's standing on the cornucopia, waiting for that sound of the klaxon. And when it comes, she runs.

Chapter Six

'Dusty.'

I burrow my head deeper into the duvet. It smells strange, not like mine.

'Breakfast in half an hour.'

I open my eyes and remember.

'Did you hear OK?' It sounds like Kelly in the bedroom doorway. 'I know it feels strange, but don't be too daunted about coming down. I'll be in the kitchen and we've got cereal and toast and lots of jams and things.'

I don't reply. I don't even move. This is the longest I've ever been away from Poppy and the pain is like nothing I've experienced.

'I know this is really difficult for you, but you'll be all right, Dusty,' she says. 'I'll see you in a minute.'

She turns on the light before she leaves.

*

Rain is pouring down outside the kitchen window. Jemal is sitting at the table, his head resting on his hand, eyes weary. I think that away from this place he'd be someone with a golden aura, but in here his fire is dimmed.

He looks up at me.

'Morning,' he says.

'Hi.'

We both look at each other, silently communicating too much to say. How we're strangers, yet we're living together, stuck in this place. I wonder how heavy the weight of his story is.

'Sleep OK?' Kelly asks me, all bright, as though we're on the best holiday ever.

'No,' I say.

'It always takes a bit of a while in a new place,' she says. 'I promise it'll get easier.'

I take the bowl she passes me without saying another word.

I'm alone in the bathroom. There's no curtain across the frosted window, the rain hitting against it. I spit the toothpaste into the sink and turn on a tap I'm not used to. Even the water tastes odd.

I look in the mirror and imagine Poppy standing beside me.

'Wipe the toothpaste from your mouth,' I tell her. I don't want her going to school with anything that might make her a target for the bullies.

But she's not here and it hurts so much that I want to smash my fist through the mirror again and again, shredding my reflection into shards that cut into me so deep that I start to bleed and never stop.

They've given me a Keystone sweatshirt. It seems ridiculous that a school with six kids has its own logo, but I wear it because I figure that the more I keep my head down, the quicker I'll be back with Poppy. They can't find a new pair of trousers to fit me and don't want me to wear my old school skirt, so they let me wear my trackies.

'I'm not going!' Liv's shouting travels along the landing to my room.

'You have to.' I think it's John speaking.

A door slams. Opens.

'Get the fuck out of my room!' Liv yells.

'You're going to be late,' John says, his voice calm.

'I'm not going to be late, because I'm not going.' There's the sound of something falling to the floor. 'Which bit of that don't you understand, you thick piece of shit?'

'I'm treating you with respect,' John says. 'You should treat me the same.'

'You're the one forcing me to do something.' I didn't think that Liv could shout much louder, but she can.

'It's not me who's forcing you,' John says. 'Every child your age in the country has to go to school. You know that.'

'It's raining,' Liv shouts. 'I'm not going out in it.'

Something is definitely thrown against a wall.

'We're going to have to put you in a hold if you carry on,' John says.

'Lay a finger on me,' Liv screams. 'And I'll twist your fucking nuts off.'

There's a stomping down the top stairs and Cooper appears in my doorway.

'Probably best to get out of here before it completely kicks off,' he says, waiting for me to join him.

I stand up from my bed and only realise now that my legs are shaking. We have to walk past Liv's room, John standing there, hands on either side of the door frame, barricading her in. He looks over his shoulder at us.

'Get Kelly would you, Cooper,' he says.

'As if,' Cooper mumbles to me, as we go down the stairs.

In the kitchen, Kelly passes me a plastic bag, the purple beads on her wrist knocking against each other.

'I'll show you where everything is later,' she says. 'So tomorrow you can choose what you want for your packed lunch.'

I don't intend to be here tomorrow.

It's still raining, but not as much. I can still hear Liv shouting as Cooper and I go outside. Alfie charges in front of us, across the patio, up some steps and along a path. I don't hurry, but tip my face up to the clouds and wonder if it's raining back home and if Poppy is getting soaked on her way to school.

'Dusty!' Alfie is running back and he grabs my sleeve, pulling me with him to a building at the bottom of the garden.

Inside, he takes the plastic bag from me, opening a door to a tiny kitchen on our left, where he shoves the bag into the fridge. It's like he's swallowed a Grand Canyon of sugar and he's bouncing off the walls, pointing to a door.

'Staff office in there.' And he pulls me past it, into a room on our right.

This is school? I can imagine Poppy's face if she saw it.

Cooper stands leaning against a wall, picking grapes from a bunch in his hand. Casey sits small in her seat, hair plastered to her face. Jemal's sadness seems to have multiplied, but he still makes the effort to nod at me.

'Welcome to part two of the madhouse,' he says.

'You can't call our wonderful school that.' There's a woman in a blazer and a disgusting flowered shirt.

'I just did,' Jemal tells her. Poppy would appreciate his deadpan skills.

'You must be our new student,' she says to me. Her lipstick is so red it looks like someone has just punched her in the mouth. 'I'm Sarah, one of the teachers.'

What's the point of me knowing your name, I want to say, *when I've no intention of staying.*

‘She’s called Dusty.’ Alfie goes to hug her.

‘Personal space, Alfie,’ Sarah says, moving him gently away.

Alfie’s little face looks dejected and I wish I knew him better, so I could circle my arms around him and squeeze him tight.

‘Nice to meet you, Dusty,’ a man sitting at the table says. ‘You’re very welcome.’ I can tell by his Scottish accent that he’s a long way from home too. He’s massive, but not in that scary way. Probably because his smile actually seems like a genuine one. ‘I’m Rick.’

‘You can call him Pine-Cone-Head.’ Alfie is laughing again.

‘Too early for jokes, Alfie,’ Sarah says, at the same time Rick pulls a face that makes even Jemal smile. ‘Where’s Liv?’

‘She doesn’t want to get her hair wet,’ Jemal says.

‘Can I show you now?’ Alfie asks, pulling on Rick’s sleeve. He doesn’t wait for a reply, opening his hand to reveal a pair of earrings in his palm.

‘For your mum?’ Rick asks him.

Alfie’s smile stretches around the room.

‘I’m leaving school twenty minutes early so I’m not late for her.’

‘You need to have a good day, then,’ Sarah says. ‘So we let you leave on time.’

‘Shall we put the earrings somewhere safe?’ Rick suggests.

Alfie closes his fingers over them. ‘I’ll hold them.’

And the hope and despair and the love and the pain wraps so tight around him that it almost crushes me as well.

This place is too weird. I'm sat next to Cooper, with Jemal next to him, even though he's not in the same school year as us, and the teacher, Sarah, is standing by a screen, with a PowerPoint up about *Macbeth*. She doesn't seem to know much about the play, because she can't remember one quote without looking it up in the book she's holding.

Cooper nudges my arm to show me something he's written.

She's really a geography teacher, it says.

I pick up my pen.

She's really crap, I write and he laughs, showing a gap between his front teeth that's surprisingly cute.

'This isn't one of Shakespeare's comedies,' Sarah tells him, her red lips tight like a knot in a balloon.

'My life's a fucking comedy,' Cooper says, 'but without the laughs.'

Jemal snorts.

And then we're all laughing, except for Sarah, who looks a mixture of bored and annoyed, her hand pointing towards a picture of Macbeth's crown dripping with blood.

Seriously? PE inside this small classroom because it's raining? There's a different teacher, an older one called Brent, his hair in a greasy ponytail. And we haven't had a break from Sarah, we even had to eat our lunch with her. Alfie and Casey are with us, but Alfie is so wired that I think he'll spin through the roof.

Brent puts on a fitness video. There's no way I want to join in, but I'm not going to use my usual *I've got my period* to get out of it.

Cooper sits on a desk, busy with a Rubik's cube, his hair's fallen over his eyes, but I can still just see the black dots he's drawn.

'You've got to participate, Coops,' Brent says. 'Do a bit of exercise.'

'I'm exercising my brain,' Cooper replies. 'And my name is Cooper.'

Outside, water smashes against the window. It's the same feeling I've got inside me, a constant battering against my bones.

Everyone, apart from Cooper, starts to do sit-ups, even the teachers. Cooper stands marooned on his island, separate to us all. It's actually good to do the exercise, to feel a different pain in my stomach. I could carry on, crunching the muscles, but we stand up and jog on the spot, while on the screen, the man tells us how to breathe. He's in his beautiful garden, attached to his beautiful family home and I want to smash my fist through the glass and punch him.

'Put the earrings down for the press-ups, Alfie,' Sarah says.

'No,' he replies and his press-ups are mangled, one

hand, one elbow on the floor, his face coloured with determination. Casey, beside him, strains to even manage one on her stick-thin arms. Jemal does ten, counting them aloud before I barely start.

'OK, a circuit now,' the beaming screen man says and we start to jog around the small room and I think that if Poppy could see me now, at least she'd laugh at this craziness I've been dropped into.

'Stop swinging your legs, Cooper,' Brent says, his slimy ponytail bouncing between his shoulder blades as he jogs past.

Cooper is sat on the desk, his legs narrowly missing us as we run in our demented circle. He twists the Rubik's cube, but I know he's paying more attention to us, his legs avoiding us within millimetres.

Brent jogs past him again and grabs the Rubik's cube.

'What did you do that for?' Cooper jumps up.

'I asked you to stop and you didn't,' Brent says.

'I'd almost solved it.' I can see Cooper's anger building, limb to limb.

'Well, now you haven't,' Brent says.

I'm boiling hot from the exercise, but tension freezes the air. Cooper grabs for the Rubik's cube, but Brent is taller than him, holding it too high, getting right in Cooper's face. There's a moment of raw fear in Cooper's eyes, before he backs away, swings out his arm and swipes a row of books from the shelf.

‘Fuck you, man,’ Cooper says.

Casey scuttles under the teacher’s desk, curling into herself, her hands over her ears.

‘Go next door to calm down,’ Brent tells Cooper, his own neck pulsing with anger.

Cooper jerks back his elbow and sends a box of Monopoly flying from the shelf.

Brent is so quick that I barely have time to register what he’s doing, but he’s dragging Cooper from the room, physically pulling him away from us.

‘Get your hands off me,’ Cooper says, his voice steady. He’s not resisting, he’s going with Brent. I’d be kicking the man’s legs from under him. I’ve never seen a teacher manhandle a student like this and I look around at the others, waiting for someone to say something, to intervene.

In the space outside the classroom, I see Cooper yank his arm free.

‘Don’t ever touch me again,’ he says, standing straight, staring at Brent. The fear in his eyes is so damn clear that you could cut paper with it.

‘Are you threatening me?’ Brent asks, looming over Cooper.

‘No,’ Cooper says. ‘I’m telling you.’

Brent grabs Cooper’s wrist, turns him and twists his arm up behind his back, ramming Cooper into the wall.

‘Rick,’ Brent shouts and I see Rick rushing out of the other classroom. He’s massive, even compared to Brent.

'Motherfuckers.' Cooper's voice is muffled, Rick closing the door this side so we can't see them any more.

I look at Sarah, waiting for her to tell me that this is some kind of wind-up. I'm waiting for the door to open and Cooper and Brent to run in laughing, telling me that they've fooled me again, like when I was told to say grace at dinner. But the door stays closed and beyond it there's banging and scuffling and the sound of Cooper shouting.

Jemal stands by the books that Cooper knocked from the shelf. He shrugs when I look at him, but I can tell there's something deeper in his eyes.

'Did that just happen?' I ask Sarah. She's crouched down, gathering the Monopoly pieces back into the box.

'We've a duty to keep you all safe,' she says, standing to put it back on the shelf.

'I didn't feel threatened by Cooper,' I say. 'At all.'

'Look what he did to Casey,' Sarah says, pointing to where Casey sits beneath the desk, her head on her knees.

'Brent did that,' I tell her. I'm trying to keep my voice steady, but I feel like I'm being pushed to the edge of a cliff.

'Putting a student in a hold is never nice for any of us,' Sarah says, beginning to pick up the scattered books. 'If we let Cooper get away with behaviour like that, we'll be letting him down.'

'What about Brent's behaviour?'

'Cooper didn't leave him any choice,' Sarah says.

I want to say more, but I'm terrified that she's going

to grab me and I'll be slammed into the wall. So, all I do is stand and watch, as Alfie puts a book on the bookshelf. He only uses one hand, his other curled in a fist around the earrings for his mum.

We're back in the kitchen of the house, with Brent and Sarah. It seems they do a summary at the end of every school day.

'Don't eat that yet,' John tells Jemal, stopping him reaching for a plate of biscuits. Jemal breathes out heavily, making a noise through his lips. Cooper sits biting his nails, on the chair furthest from the door where Brent and Sarah stand.

'Dusty had a great day,' Brent says. 'She settled in really well.'

I stare at him, adrenaline still flickering through me.

'Alfie was quite hyper,' Sarah says. 'But that's to be expected.'

'He went off with Rina on time,' Kelly says.

'Unfortunately, Cooper was really uncooperative in PE,' Brent says. 'He became violent and abusive, so we had to use an RI.'

Cooper looks only at the table, the fingers of one hand tapping his lips, the other tracing a flower on the plastic cloth.

'Seriously, Cooper?' John asks him. Cooper keeps tapping at his lips. I can't read the expression in his eyes. 'So, you lose your privileges at the weekend.'

'But we're going go-karting for my birthday,' Jemal says.

'You'll be going without Cooper,' John says. 'And Liv.'

Liv. I'd forgotten about her. She didn't turn up at school all day.

'OK, we'll be off, then,' Brent says. He looks at me. 'Well done for today, Dusty. See you all on Monday.'

Sarah waves and they're gone.

'It wasn't exactly what they said,' I tell Kelly. 'With Cooper.'

'No one does a hold for no reason,' John says.

'Can I eat now?' Jemal asks and Kelly pushes the plate of biscuits towards him.

'Cooper didn't do much,' I say. 'He only knocked a couple of books from the shelf.'

'And that's OK?' John asks me.

'It's not exactly violent,' I say.

'What would you call it, then?'

I look at John and I can't answer. There's violence and then there's violence.

'Can I go and call Jen?' I ask.

John glances across to Kelly. 'When you've had your snack,' he says.

I stare at my plate and leave it empty.

The phone rings and rings, but Jen doesn't answer.

I know I should be in a calmer mood when I speak to Poppy, but I need to hear her voice, to know she's OK. I dial her number and think about how much I'm going to tell her, what I'm going to leave out. I'll tell her to hold on, that I'll see her soon. The phone rings and I imagine her scurrying away to find somewhere quiet, as far from Sue as she can get. It keeps ringing. I wait and wait, that ringing sound grinding sand into my veins.

'Answer the phone,' I shout into it, but Poppy doesn't and I run from the bedroom and down the stairs, still holding the phone to my ear. I only turn it off when I'm in front of Kelly, who's watching TV with Casey.

'I need to speak to my sister,' I tell her. 'My social worker isn't answering and I don't know where my sister is.'

'OK.' Kelly stands up, her hands motioning for me to relax, but it only makes me angrier.

'It's not OK,' I say. 'I need to speak to Poppy, or Jen, now.'

Kelly walks out of the room, so I have to follow her, away from Casey and her terrified eyes.

'Is there a specific reason you need to talk to them?' Kelly asks me.

'She's my sister,' I tell her, beginning to shout. 'Do I need another reason?'

'Is there anything in particular you're worried about?' Kelly asks, keeping her voice smooth like she's in some yoga video.

'I don't even know if she's all right.' I'm trying and failing not to cry. The only way to stop it is to shout louder. 'You've got to find a way to speak to my social worker.'

'OK,' Kelly says. 'Rina,' she calls into the kitchen.

'Keep an eye on Casey for me.' She turns to me. 'Wait here. I'll use the office phone.'

'Do you have her number?'

'It'll be in our file.' She hurries through the door and closes me out.

I sit down exactly where I am, in the hallway, my back against the wall. Kelly is ages, but when she comes out of the office she looks so apologetic that I want to hurl her through the front door.

'What's wrong?' I ask, standing up.

'Everything is fine. I didn't get to speak to your social worker, but I got through to her colleague who said that if anything was wrong with your sister, then we'd definitely be told.'

'That's it?' I say.

'Poppy is fine, which is what you wanted to know.' Kelly touches me on the arm. 'Do you want to come and watch TV with us? You could choose what goes on next?'

I'm caught between my anger exploding and feeling so tired that I don't think I can move.

'Or I could bring some cocoa to your room?' Kelly suggests.

I look at her, at the two small crosses in her ears, the tiny piercing in her nose. I know she's being kind, but a savage feeling is scratching at my lungs.

'How the hell is cocoa going to get me to see my sister?' I shout.

I push past her, barging her shoulder with my arm, but she doesn't tell me off for it. I want to stamp up the stairs so hard that my feet crack the wood beneath the carpet, but I haven't the energy. With each step I'm disintegrating.

Cooper is sitting at the bottom of his stairs, opposite my open bedroom door. I haven't seen him without a sweatshirt before and he's got words written all up his arms.

'Need to talk?' he asks me.

I'm tempted to slam the door so hard in his face that it rips from its hinges, but he's probably the only person I can cope with being around right now, so I nod and he goes inside before me. I shut the door and he sits on the beanbag.

'I know it doesn't help,' Cooper says. 'But it's true what Kelly said, that if your sister wasn't OK, they'd let you know.'

There's something about him that helps me calm right down.

'Do you have a sister?' I ask him, sitting on the bed, needing this furious anger within me to settle. Cooper looks for a moment as if he can't hear the question.

'A younger brother,' he says. 'Casper. He's five.'

'Where is he?'

'He still lives with my mum,' Cooper says.

So his mum has kept his brother, but not him.

'How do you feel about that?' I think I might be taking him too close to a line he won't want to cross.

'Conflicted,' he admits, picking at something on the

beanbag. 'I'm happy for Casper that he doesn't have to go through this. But then I worry if he's safe.'

'Do they let you see him?' I ask.

'It used to be once a fortnight,' Cooper says. 'But since I moved here, I'm lucky if it's twice a year.'

Twice a year? We once learned in biology about marrow, the bit that sits in the hollow of our bones. Missing Poppy hurts so much that I feel the pain stuck deep in there and I don't know how Cooper copes with that for months and months.

'Do you get to speak to him?'

'Not much. My mum often forgets when we're meant to have a call.'

'That's really bad, Cooper.' My words aren't strong enough for what I want to say. I'd tear the world in two if I were him.

'I send Casper letters through my social worker, so he'll never think I've forgotten him.'

It's strange to look into the eyes of someone I hardly know but totally understand.

'What's written up your arm?'

'Eliot,' he says. 'T.S. The greatest poet who ever lived.' He holds up his arm. '*Violent souls,*' he reads. '*But only as the hollow men.*'

'You haven't got a violent soul, Cooper.' But I don't know if he's really hearing me, he's just looking at the ink on his skin. 'Are you meant to not get angry? Sit like a puppy in a corner, while they separate you from your brother and then fucking pin you down?'

There's a knock at the door and Kelly walks in.

'I thought you'd like these,' she says, putting a sketchbook and pencils on my desk. 'We could go shopping tomorrow and buy more paints and brushes like you asked.'

She sees Cooper on the beanbag.

'Keep the door open if there's more than one of you in here,' she says, wedging the doorstop in place. 'Sorry, but you know the rules, Cooper.'

He salutes her as she goes, but it's clear to us all that he's using his middle finger.

'You like to draw?' Cooper asks me.

Just seeing the sketchbook is like a balm. It's like listening to the most soothing music the world ever invented.

'Mostly painting,' I say.

'Why paints?'

No one has ever asked me that before and I stumble on my answer.

'I'm not really sure,' I say. 'I like how the paintbrush feels when it touches the paint. It always feels different, like acrylic is really satisfying and with watercolours you don't really notice it.' I'm rambling, but he genuinely seems interested. 'Then when you put them on the paper, it feels different all over again.'

'I've never thought of it like that.'

Damn, his smile is beautiful.

'And being able to put what I see on to paper,' I say, trying hard to concentrate, to think only of paints. 'There's no right, or wrong. Everyone sees things differently, so everyone will draw and paint the same thing differently. No one can tell me that it's wrong, because it's mine.'

'Trust me,' Cooper says. 'My art is definitely wrong.'

'That's impossible,' I tell him. 'It'll just be your way of seeing the world.'

'Then the world I'm living in is some crazy-arsed place.'

'Fact,' I laugh. 'Do you want to do some?'

'Painting?' Cooper asks. 'Now?'

'Only drawing,' I say. 'That's all they gave me.'

I get up and take a page from the sketchbook, keep that one for me and pass Cooper the book and a selection of pencils.

'What shall I draw?' Cooper asks, sitting straighter on the beanbag, arranging the pencils on the floor in a neat row.

'Anything in this room that interests you,' I tell him.

He looks around. 'The kicked-in door?'

'Anything that speaks to you,' I say. Cooper pulls a face at me. 'Seriously,' I tell him. 'There'll be something in this room that you notice. That gets to you for some reason.'

'Sounds weird,' Cooper says.

'It's not,' I assure him. 'When you find it and you know you have to get it on to paper, it's the best thing ever.'

'Better than nachos?' Cooper picks up a pencil and begins to chew the end of it.

'Yes,' I say. 'Far better. Don't chew the end of the pencil.'

'Lead poisoning is a myth,' he says, but he stops all the same.

'It disrespects the art.' I'm smiling, but I do actually mean it. I feel the same way about people chewing pencils as Poppy does about folding pages in a book.

Poppy. I haven't thought about her for the last few minutes and now I feel guilty. But I know it's best not to think about her, if I'm going to survive this place with my sanity intact.

'I try not to think about Casper,' Cooper says, somehow reading my thoughts. 'If I do, it's the quickest route to losing my mind.'

He's right, I know he is. So I concentrate instead on the feel of the pencil in my fingers, the smooth paper beneath the flat of my hand. I look around the room, at the cupboard handles, the window glass, the corner of the bed, shapes and contrasts I'd normally be desperate to recreate, but there's nothing at all in here that speaks to me, even in a whisper.

Cooper's feet rest beside my suitcase, next to his orderly line of pencils. It's a nice mix, the straight lines knocking up against the curve of the sole of his shoe, where he's tipped his foot to the side. I sketch an outline, a realistic one at first, the loop of his laces, his sock barely showing between his jeans and the top of his trainers.

Already I'm calmer, the pencil leading me. With the

shape finished, I swap the pencil for a blue one. I make scratch marks with it one way, going over them in the other direction, then roll the edge of the point to make a faint blue wash. This is my favourite bit, the building up, the turning it into something else.

I don't look at Cooper's face, even though I want to. I don't talk to him, even though I've so many questions I want to ask. About his brother, Casper. About how he manages to keep putting one foot in front of the other when his heart is caving in.

I pick up the purple pencil to colour the bits of earth caught along the edge of his trainer, layer it with green until it's how I want it. I know when it's finished, because the feelings inside me have turned from dark, to light.

I hold it up in front of me.

'You done?' Cooper asks.

'Yes,' I say.

'Can I see it?'

I turn the paper to him and there's a change in his face. He looks from it, to me and back to my picture again.

'Right,' he says. 'So, you're really good.' He leans further forward on the beanbag. 'How did you learn to draw like this?'

I turn the picture to look at it again. 'I know it sounds weird,' I say, 'but I kind of just hold the pencil steady and it does the rest.' I glance up at Cooper. 'I've never told anyone that before.'

I expect him to laugh, but he nods.

'You did look like you'd zoned out when you were drawing.'

'You were looking at me?' The tiniest wings knock against my stomach.

'I was drawing you,' Cooper says. 'You told me to draw something in the room that was speaking to me and you were speaking to me.'

I smile at him. 'Can I see it?'

Cooper turns the paper and for all I've told him that his art can't be wrong, I'm finding it really hard not to laugh.

'It's bad?' Cooper asks. He's drawn me as a stick figure, but must've changed his mind half way through, giving me proper hands and feet and a scribble of the weird school sweatshirt and my trackies.

'It's not bad,' I say. 'There are famous artists who draw stick figures and make millions.'

Cooper passes me the sketchbook.

'You can keep it. Sell it, buy your own house and get out of this shithole.'

I prop his picture on the desk so I can see it.

'My social worker told me I wouldn't be here long.'

Cooper looks at me and there are too many things I understand from his expression. I wonder if, deep down, I believed what Jen said. Did I really think I'd only be here a couple of days? 'How long have you been here?'

'Two years too long.'

Two years? My mind slams shut at the thought. There's no way that's happening to me.

'Whose room was this before?' I ask.

Cooper straightens the pencils on the floor again, moving the red next to the grey.

'Oslo's,' he says. 'They left a message for you.'

'They knew I was coming?'

'They knew someone was,' he says. 'They engraved it into the bed with a broken bit of biro.'

I stand up and pull the bed away from the wall.

'Not there. You have to lift the mattress,' Cooper says and I do and there it is. One word. *Run.*

I exhale noisily.

'Short, but sweet,' he says. 'Typical Oslo. They liked to keep things simple.'

'Where did they go?' I ask.

'No idea.' Cooper scratches the material of the beanbag, as though there's a deep mark there. 'No doubt, they're trying to run away from the next place as well.'

I push the bed back hard against the wall.

'Have you ever tried it?' I ask him. 'To run away?'

'A few times,' Cooper says. 'I didn't get very far.'

I look at the black dots beneath his eyes, at the gulf of sadness they can't hide.

'Next time, I'll come with you,' I say.

Cooper smiles at me. 'Deal,' he says. 'Next time I go, we'll go together.'

Chapter Seven

'Mine weren't all bad.' Cooper begins to plait his fringe. 'The best one I had lasted four years. I thought they wanted to keep me, but then they moved to France and didn't take me with them.' He shakes his fringe loose and plaits it again, tighter this time. 'They sent birthday cards for a couple of years and then they stopped.'

I feel the deepest ache beneath my ribs.

'All my placements went downhill from there,' he says.

'I swear our last ones were secret drinkers,' I tell him. The thought of Poppy still being there spins my mind into panic. I breathe steadily from my stomach, the way Jen taught me.

Cooper laughs, but it's not funny. 'I had someone like that,' he says. 'But not so secret.'

'The only good thing about them was their dog,' I say.

Cooper looks at me and I know he gets how much this hurts.

'What's it called?' he asks.

'Rex.' My throat scratches on his name. 'They didn't let me say goodbye to him.'

Cooper looks at me. 'They really did that?'

I nod. It's the strangest thing having someone who completely gets it, who I don't have to explain to, or excuse what I'm thinking and feeling.

But it doesn't bring Rex back. I'm never again going to have him look up at me when I come through the door and bound over telling me *I love you, I love you.* He's been added to the long list of things I'm meant to just forget.

'How do you stop yourself falling apart?' I ask Cooper. 'Like, painting is my thing. It's like oxygen.' I study his face, but don't see any sign of him thinking this is weird. 'It helps me breathe.'

'My guitar,' Cooper says.

'You play?'

'Badly,' he replies.

I look at him sitting there, with his blue eyes shaded by the longest lashes. 'Do you realise that you put yourself down a lot?' I tell him.

He shrugs and doesn't say anything and I'm worried that I've messed up.

'Do you have your own guitar?' I ask him.

'Yeah. But I don't like to take it out of my room.'

'Will you teach me to play it?'

The front door downstairs kicks open. I hear it slam

against the wall. A scream rattles through the house, shaking the air between me and Cooper.

'Fuck,' he says. 'It's Alfie.'

He jumps up, knocking my legs with his feet as he leaps over me. I follow him, but he's miles ahead, bounding down the stairs.

'Hey, Alfie,' I hear him say and coming down the stairs I see Alfie smashing his fist into the wall, his wail piercing to my core.

A woman steps towards Alfie, but Cooper brushes her away.

'I've got this, Rina,' Cooper says, putting his hand between the wall and Alfie's forehead. 'Alfie, I'm here.'

But Alfie is thrashing and clawing.

'What happened?' Cooper asks Rina, as John appears from the office. Anger snaps across Cooper's face. 'Let me calm him down.'

'She didn't show up,' Rina tells John.

The words seem to collide with Cooper's stomach. I see them upper-cut him. Alfie was meant to be seeing his mum, but she obviously didn't turn up. His hands are clenched into small fists and I'm sure he still holds the earrings he chose for her. I've never heard anyone cry like this.

Alfie is still trying to smash his head into the wall and John steps towards him.

'We'll take over, Cooper.'

'He'll calm down in a minute,' Cooper says, with Alfie thumping his arms.

'It's not safe,' John says.

There's a glance between the adults, a silent communication and suddenly both of them step towards Alfie, hands locked on either side of him. Alfie screams and kicks, his trauma a black mist that thunders towards me, but all I do is stand and watch as they force him to sit, their size swamping him. Fury fires from Cooper's skin, his shoulders tense, his body primed to fight.

'You bastards,' he whispers, kicking the wall, storming through the kitchen door.

I'm stuck watching the adults pin Alfie down and it unravels a terror of my own, splinters of memories slipping beneath my skin. The full force of a fist to my face, the ringing in my ears that bleeds into my nightmares.

The atmosphere at dinner is stretched taut. My lips sting, where I've been biting them. Alfie sits between Jemal and Cooper, manic laughter spinning from him. Liv's volume has gone up even more and she's telling Kelly about a new T-shirt she wants to buy and a band I've never heard of and she doesn't draw breath. It feels like I'm being squeezed into a narrow passage and the space is getting tighter and tighter and there's no way out.

Cooper keeps his head bent over his plate, shovelling

in the food so quick that he barely chews it. The chicken makes me want to vomit, coating the top of my tongue and the roof of my mouth.

'Dusty,' Liv shouts across the table. 'You coming to town with me next time I go?'

'Maybe,' I say. It's obviously not the answer she wants and she glares at me, her expression switched to disdain. I don't bother to tell her that I won't be setting one foot out of this shithole until I've spoken to my sister.

Casey sits quiet as she always does, eyes alert, startling at the smallest sound. The windows to the garden are open as far as the safety lock lets them. The rain has stopped and left a sting of hanging heat.

Kelly serves up sticky toffee pudding, Alfie gets up to hand round the bowls. His eyes are still bloodshot. In my mind I draw him, the outline of his child's face, skin fragile as tracing paper. I drag my paintbrush through silvers and golds and begin his soul again with the colours of the sun.

Chapter Eight

Sitting on the bed, holding my phone, I try Poppy's number, but still she doesn't answer. Kelly stands in the doorway. I've made her try both Sue and Simon's phones, but there's no answer from them either.

'We'll try again tomorrow,' she tells me. 'I know it's tough, Dusty, but you've got to try to sleep now.'

I'd like to see her try to sleep when she's drowning.

Sometimes I cover a whole page in just one colour. I've done it since forever, a challenge to myself to make it look like I haven't lifted the pencil. A block of red, or blue, or grey, or whichever, with no emotion in it, no story behind it. I've never managed it, though. There's always a glitch of darkness in one bit, where I've pressed too hard.

I choose purple, Poppy's favourite colour, and tell myself that if I manage to make it perfect, then the next time I phone her, she'll answer. I should sit at the desk, but I need the cocoon of the duvet. I begin the gentle strokes across the paper, the pencil my anchor, holding me to my sister.

The fire alarm is so loud that my arm jerks across the page, my picture ruined and my nerves simmering. There's no way it'd be a drill in the night, but I don't move. If I get caught in a fire now, how many people would care? One. And Poppy's love for me might fill my universe, but it's still only one. The thought smothers me with thick black tar. It covers my bones, my spine, my neck, until I can't move.

The alarm is still going. Does a funeral with one person there even count as a funeral? If it were Poppy dying, I hope that Sue and Simon would go to hers. The tar inside me rises to my throat. It coats my tongue, collides with my teeth and sinks into my gums. It doesn't fill my ears, though. All that fills my ears is that piercing sound, one note fragmenting and scattering around the room.

The door opens. Kelly sees me sitting in the bed, the light on.

'Try to ignore it,' she says, disappearing down the corridor.

Somewhere amongst it all, Liv is shouting. I wrap the duvet around me and walk with it out on to the landing, to see Liv kick Kelly and run down the stairs. Cooper appears, his hair creased with sleep, and he goes past me into Alfie's room and I only realise now that Alfie is screaming, but it's being swallowed by the alarm.

It turns off as suddenly as it started. A breath of complete silence, only the vibrations of where it was. From the kitchen there's the sound of breaking glass.

Huddled in the duvet, I go into Alfie's room. He's on the floor in the corner, his arms over his ears. Even though he's tiny, his Spider-Man pyjamas are too short on his legs, showing the skinniest ankles. Cooper crouches beside him.

'It's stopped now,' Cooper says.

But Alfie shakes his head over and over. I go to them, take the duvet from me and wrap it around him. I want so much to hug him, but I don't know how he'll react. Poppy hates strangers touching her.

'I'll be back in a second,' I say and race from the room, grabbing my sketchbook and a pencil, going back to kneel in front of Alfie. 'See this.'

He doesn't look at me. He's been dragged too far into a dark place and we won't be able to reach him for a while. Downstairs, Liv is crying, begging to be let go.

I begin to draw. I'm better at copying actual things, but I manage to make it look like Spider-Man his mask peeled off and Alfie's face beaming beneath. Alfie scales the side of a building, swings his web and catches a spaceship.

'What's a UFO doing there?' Cooper asks.

'It's easier than drawing the Green Goblin,' I reply.

Alfie's eyes begin to clear.

I draw aliens escaping from the web, circular blobs that float down to bounce on the ground.

'See how they can roll away,' I say and Alfie is watching how one of the aliens rolls along the street, hitting the door of a shop and sliding beneath.

'Uh-oh,' Cooper says. 'That shop's in trouble.'

'It's a shoe store,' I say. Alfie moves his arms away from his ears. He looks at what I'm drawing, he sees what I'm seeing, how the alien pops into a shoe. 'Ready for the customer.'

Alfie laughs.

'I would not put my foot in that,' Cooper says.

'Better not shop there, then,' I tell him.

'Where did the rest of the aliens go?' Alfie asks, his innocent voice shooting a steel-tipped arrow through my veins.

'The others went into a bakery,' I say. I sketch the alien orbs lined up among a row of doughnuts, their eyes going wild.

'To eat the cakes?' Alfie asks.

I shake my head. 'To eat the customers.'

'And this,' Cooper laughs, 'is Dusty's idea of a soothing story.'

Rina appears in the doorway.

'OK, you lot,' she says. 'Drama's over.'

'Did Liv break a window?' Alfie asks her.

'There's nothing for you to worry about,' Rina says.

'But someone could come in, in the night,' Alfie says.

'We'll board it up. No one is going to get in.'

'Apart from customer-eating aliens,' Cooper says.

I can imagine him calming Casper like this and it bruises my heart when I think how he'd be the best brother if they just gave him the chance.

'Bed for you two as well,' Rina says, standing back, indicating for us to move. 'I'll stay with Alfie for a bit.'

'I want Dusty to stay,' Alfie says.

'Dusty needs to sleep,' Rina says.

I feel Alfie tense beside me and I know this could end badly. I stand up and take my duvet from him and hold out my hand.

'If you get into bed, I'll put my pictures under your pillow,' I say. 'For protection.'

Alfie's hand feels like a toddler's. It's hard to believe he's the same age as Poppy.

'I'll be scared without you,' he says, not moving.

'Enough now, Alfie,' Rina says. 'It's late and we're all way too tired for this.'

I want to tell her that however tired I am, I can stay here for him, but I know it'll make the situation worse.

Rina steps towards Alfie, the sudden movement into his space making his little legs kick out towards her.

'Alfie,' Cooper says, his arm around him. 'You're OK. We've got you.'

But he starts to scream, his face turned towards us, terror ringing again in his ears.

'Kelly,' Rina shouts into the landing. I know what's

coming, we all know what's coming and it escalates Alfie's fear.

'Come on, mate,' Cooper says, tension firing along his arms.

I stroke Alfie's hair, but he's rigid and screaming.

Kelly runs in. She looks shattered, but somehow her just being here makes the air feel calmer.

'I'll take over,' she says.

'He's not settling,' Rina tells her.

'He is,' Cooper says.

'It's all right, Alfie.' Kelly kneels beside him and looks into his eyes. His scream turns into a pitiful wail. 'Not the nicest way for you to get woken up, was it?' She picks up my drawing. 'Look at this. Here's a face I recognise.'

'It's Alfie,' I say.

'Being a real hero,' Cooper says.

'Because he is one,' I say.

'He is,' Kelly adds.

Rina lingers in the doorway, but we all ignore her.

'The aliens went in the bakery.' Alfie is so quiet that I'm not sure if Kelly can make sense of it.

'Not a place where they belong,' she smiles.

Her words soothe him more, his shoulders relaxing enough for Cooper to take his arm away.

'I think even the aliens are going to sleep now,' Kelly says.

'You OK if we go?' Cooper asks Alfie.

I wonder how often he has to do this. How many nights

are fractured in this home, where we're all meant to just carry on unaffected.

'I'll tuck you in,' I say.

Alfie gets up on his unsteady legs and lets me lead him to the bed, where he climbs under the duvet and I tuck it around him. My heart aches at his innocent face looking up at me and it makes me miss Poppy so much that I don't know how I don't disintegrate.

'We'll see you in the morning,' Cooper says.

Alfie nods. He doesn't take his eyes from us and I feel them on my back as we leave him.

I watch outside my window as the police arrive. They take Liv from the house in handcuffs, still in her slippers. She doesn't fight them, a police officer holding her elbow, guiding her down the path. They put a hand to the top of Liv's head and perhaps they're helping her, perhaps they're pushing her into the car. They close the car door and Liv stares straight ahead. Her face looks crafted from nails, a mask of toughened stone. But she's alone and I know she's terrified.

Chapter Nine

The new day is sunny, but it doesn't feel like it. Cooper hasn't said it's OK to go up and see him, but I can't sit alone another minute in this bedroom, with so many thoughts battering my skull.

There are two rooms at the top of these stairs. One has the door slightly open, the end of a bed neatly made, a chair straight in front of a desk. I turn to the other door and knock.

I'm ruffling my fringe as I wait and the door opens, but it's Jemal standing in front of me. Behind him is a total mess, clothes everywhere, boxes of Lego stacked and fallen.

'Dusty?' I probably look as confused as he does.

'Sorry,' I say. 'I thought this was Cooper's room.'

Jemal jabs his thumb in the direction of the other room and slams his door shut.

I go and knock and wait, but there's no answer, so I push the door further open and peer round it. Cooper is sitting on a stool, headphones on. Behind him, words are written in neat lines all over the wall. He's looking down at the guitar he's playing, his hair falling forward, and he doesn't know I'm here.

'Cooper?'

He looks up and sees me and smiles, with that gap between his teeth that does something to my knees. He takes off the headphones and rests them around his neck.

'You OK?' he asks.

'Not really.' I step into his room. It's empty of everything apart from the bed, a desk with one book on it, a chair and the stool he sits on. 'Where's all your stuff?'

'In the cupboards,' he says. 'Did you speak to your sister?'

'She's still not answering,' I reply, sitting on the bed. 'And my social worker doesn't work weekends and Kelly says I can't phone the emergency social worker, as there's no emergency.'

Cooper nods and hooks his hair behind his ears. His eyeliner is different today, a deep black smudge of it making his eyes shine even more blue.

'Their idea of an emergency is entirely different to ours,' Cooper says.

'Liv isn't back from the police station yet,' I say.

'She will be,' he says. 'They won't keep her in for two nights.'

'Have they ever called the police on you?' I ask him.

‘A couple of months ago. At the same time as Oslo.’

And now Oslo is gone.

‘Are they going to get rid of you too?’ I ask.

‘Probably soon,’ Cooper says.

‘It’s making me so fucking angry, Cooper. Like I want to destroy everything.’

‘This place specialises in generating fury.’

‘And then arresting us for it?’

‘See why I want to run?’ Cooper says.

‘You think you will again?’ I ask.

‘It’s either I go on the streets myself, or they kick me on to them.’

‘Is there nowhere else other than here?’

‘I’m sixteen,’ Cooper says. ‘Probably a secure unit.’ He runs his fingers lightly over the guitar strings, creating notes that appear and fade.

‘Liv looked really scared,’ I say.

‘Yeah,’ Cooper says. ‘She would’ve been.’ He strums a different note.

‘What’s with all the writing?’ I gesture towards the wall.

Cooper holds up his arm. ‘Same poet,’ he says.

From here I can read some of the words.

More distant and more solemn than a fading star.

‘My foster carers who went to France?’ Cooper says. ‘The dad used to read Eliot’s poems to me and his kids.’ He points towards the desk, at the book there. ‘That’s the actual book he gave me.’

I don't ask if I can look at it. I can already tell that it feels kind of sacred.

Instead I look at the wall again. Line after line of tightly packed words.

In the mountains, there you feel free.

'So, no one ever taught you to play guitar?' Cooper asks me.

'I've always stuck to art,' I tell him.

'This is art,' he says. 'What do you see when I play this?'

The chord ripples through the room.

'Water,' I say. I didn't even need to think. It's the stillness on top of a lake, the reflection caught in it.

Cooper closes his eyes and he begins to sing. I stare at him. It's ridiculous how beautiful it sounds, like the lake has turned into the ocean, and the sun and the stars and the moon are caught together on its surface. I didn't think people our age were meant to be able to sing as good as this.

He opens his eyes and smiles at me, but he doesn't stop singing, his fingers swift over the strings, his foot against the stool, his song wrapping me in a safety that I didn't even know could exist.

Chapter Ten

'I swear to fuck, I'm going to kick off,' I tell Kelly. 'I haven't spoken to my sister in three days and you need to do something about it.'

'It's Monday tomorrow.' Kelly's voice is so calm that I want to rip her voice box out. 'We'll definitely be able to sort it then.'

'I'm not waiting until tomorrow.' I'm trying to match her unflustered attitude, but it's not working. 'Poppy needs me. I need to speak to her today.'

'I'm really sorry, Dusty, but I don't think that's going to happen,' Kelly says. Simple as that, like she can wash this problem down into the sewers and not have to think about it.

Alfie sits beside her on the sofa. I know I'm interrupting the film he's watching, but it's not that I'm worried about. He hasn't recovered from his mum not showing up. He's too fragile and my rage might break him. One day he'll splinter so much that no one will be able to put him together again.

I kick the door frame hard as I go out and storm into the kitchen.

'I need to go in the garden,' I tell John. He's stirring dough mix in a bowl and barely glances up at me.

'There's no one to supervise you,' he says.

'I'm old enough to go into the fucking garden on my own,' I tell him.

I pull on the door to check, but of course it's locked.

'I'll be done in twenty minutes,' John says. 'I'll come out then.'

'I want to go out there now,' I say. 'On my own.'

I'm suffocating. I need air.

'You'll have to wait.' John sieves some more flour into the bowl. 'I won't be long.'

I don't pause, but it doesn't seem like me who's doing it. I step forward and whack the bag of flour from him. It turns the room white, covering John's hair, his face, his clothes. There's a snapped moment of stillness, before I run.

In the bedroom, I jam the chair under the door handle and lean my weight into it, but I don't hear John storming up the stairs. I don't hear anything, apart from the rumble of the TV below. I definitely did it, though, because I've got flour on my hoodie and jeans and I try to rub it off, but it leaves smears of white.

My phone rings. I look down at it to see a number I

don't recognise. I wipe my hand on my sleeve and answer it, nearly drop it as I put it to my ear.

'Is that Dusty?' A woman's voice, someone I'm sure I don't know.

'Yes,' I say.

'I'm Jen's colleague, calling you with an update on your sister.'

A pebble drops in my chest, rippling fear through me.

'What's happened to her?'

'She's fine,' she says. 'But we've had to find an emergency placement for her.'

'They kicked her out?' I can't find my breath.

'The relationship became irreparable, yes,' she says.

'Where is she?'

'She's right here,' the woman says. 'Would you like a word?'

She's there with her. Poppy.

There's a mumbling, a pause.

'Dusty?'

It's definitely her voice.

'Prim. Where've you been?'

'Where've *you* been,' she says in a fake American accent and I know she's trying to make me laugh, but I can tell that she's crying.

'What happened with Sue?' I ask.

'They kicked me out,' Poppy says.

'What did you do?'

'Are you mad at me?' she asks.

'No,' I say. 'I'm mad at them.'

'I tried really hard, because I thought that if I was good, then they'd let you come back. But Simon told me to stop talking about you, so I got the kitchen chair, the one with the cat on it and I threw it through the window.'

I shouldn't laugh, but the thought of my timid sister and the look on Simon's face.

'Prim,' I say, as stern as I can.

'That was just the start of it,' she says and I realise that she's not laughing at all. She's heart-crushingly sad.

'Have they moved you to a residential, or a family?' I ask her.

I never pray, but right now I beg God that a family has taken her in. That it's a mum and a dad as beautiful as she deserves.

'One older woman, with four other kids.'

'Are they hers?'

'No. None of them.'

'Do you like her?' I hope she does and I hope she doesn't, which is a mixed-up way to feel.

'I'm not sure,' she says.

'Whereabouts is it?' I ask.

'Newcastle,' I think she says, but she's either got her hand over the phone, or has turned her head.

'Newcastle?'

That's miles and miles away.

'Are you remembering to brush your teeth?' I ask.

'Sometimes.'

'Poppy,' I say. 'You've got to do them, twice a day, or they'll rot.'

'I'll try,' she says. I wish I could be like Elastigirl so I could be beside her before she even finishes her sentence. 'My eczema isn't too good.'

'Has she got the right cream for you?' I ask her.

'I haven't got much left,' Poppy says.

'You've got to tell her and she can get you more.' I want to slam the phone against the wall. The foster carer should know. She should've checked the tub and not expect my twelve-year-old sister to remind her it's running out.

Poppy doesn't pretend to hold in her tears any longer. She's sobbing so hard and I grip the phone, my chest burning.

'I don't want to be here,' she says.

'It's going to be OK,' I tell her, my words so far from the truth. 'It won't be for long.'

Poppy is struggling to breathe normally and there's a knocking sound.

'Dusty?' It's the woman again.

'We need to be together,' I tell her.

'We're working on it.'

Always, they're working on it.

'When can I see her?'

I can still hear Poppy crying. It's taking every speck of control not to scream at the woman.

'I'll talk to Jen tomorrow,' she says. 'We'll see what we can organise.'

'How will I get to where Poppy is staying?'

'It's not ideal,' the woman admits.

Speak the truth, I want to yell at her. *You know it's going to be a long time until I see her.*

It feels like bricks are being lowered on to my chest. Piles of them, cracking my ribs.

'You need to hug her from me,' I tell the woman. I'm going to have to hang up, so that Poppy can't hear me crying.

'I will do,' she says and her kindness sounds genuine, but it pushes a flat palm to the bricks, sinking them deeper.

'Tell her that I love her,' I say. 'And to tuck in her shirt. Prim always needs to tuck in her shirt.'

'Her shirt?' the woman asks.

'Poppy will understand,' I say.

My sister will know. It's our language, our shortcut. It's about the only thing they can't take from us.

My thumb is shaking as I press it over the red button and cut her voice from me.

I didn't think it'd be possible to laugh, but my stomach cramps from it and I'm grabbing on to Cooper, but he's making it worse. It's not even that funny, the Homer Simpson voice he's doing, but Jemal is creased over and his laugh is the snort of a demented pig. It's literally like we're passing the laughter between us and it gets bigger each time.

We're trying to stack cards in the patch of carpet between Cooper and Jemal's rooms, but we're not getting very far.

'I've got it,' Jemal says, wiping his eyes and shuffling on his bum into his room. It's like we're small kids again. If Poppy were here, it'd be perfect.

He comes back dragging a box piled high with Lego.

'If we surround it with this,' he says, 'then it won't fall.'

I haven't held a piece of Lego since Mr Evans' Year 5 class, when Poppy and I lived in Norwich with Guy and Chris. It's a good familiar, the feel of it in my hand, and it drops me right back in the middle of that classroom with its smell of bottled paints and basil plants.

We sit in silence for a bit, concentrating on our build. Cooper nudges his hair from his face, his eyeliner smudged from laughing.

'There's this building,' he says, 'in Nevada, that literally looks like it's melting.'

The cards I'm stacking are leaning and Cooper reaches out to help me steady them.

'In ten years' time,' Jemal says, 'we should meet there.'

'At a melting building in Nevada?' I ask.

'Yeah. Wherever we are,' Jemal says, 'we make our way there. On April thirtieth.'

'April thirtieth?'

'My birthday.' He smiles. 'Now you'll never forget it.'

He holds his hand above the card structure. 'You have to swear to it.'

I place my hand on top of Jemal's. 'I swear to it,' I say.

Cooper reaches over his hand and puts it on top of mine.

'If I'm still alive,' he says, 'I'll be there.'

Chapter Eleven

The school day is a waste of time. No disrespect to Liv, but she can't read very well and so can't understand what's on the board or the worksheets and so causes mayhem instead. Cooper spends the entire history class writing poetry up his arm.

I'm clock-watching until I can speak to Poppy again. I want to know if they've got her a place in a good school. One that she'll be starting without me.

'I need to phone my social worker,' I tell Kelly, as soon as I'm back in the main house.

'School debrief first,' John says, patting the chair beside him as though I'm a dog.

There's no point arguing with him, as I know he won't budge, but I feel a switch flick deep inside me, a door open a crack to let anger trickle through. I choose a different seat, next to Alfie.

'Dusty has had another good day,' Sarah says from

where she stands beside the table. I pull my hair at the back of my head until it hurts.

'I learned jack shit,' I mumble.

I thought I was quiet enough, but Alfie giggles and shifts to crouch with his feet on the chair, stuffing sliced strawberries into his mouth. He's a bolt of electricity. I swear if I touched him now, I'd get an electric shock.

'Is there something you want to add?' John asks me.

I zone them all out, look instead at the robin outside the window, on the top step by the grass, watch it peck around and fly off.

'See you tomorrow.' Rick lifts his hand to wave at us, but Sarah is already gone.

I stand up.

'Have a snack first,' John says.

'No,' I reply.

I know I'm dropping little bombs of tension around the table, but Poppy is the only one I want to protect and she's not here.

Kelly gets up. 'Tell you what, let's use the office phone, so you can get a bit of peace and quiet.'

I follow her from the kitchen and we go through the door off the hallway that I haven't been through, into a room with a table along the length of the wall, a massive whiteboard on the wall filled with some sort of timetable, paperwork everywhere. I'm not necessarily a tidy person, but this much clutter does my head in.

'Take a seat,' Kelly says. 'I'll find her number.'

She gets a file from a shelf, my name on the side of it. I feel the weirdest feeling as she flicks through papers that are my life. I'm reduced to print-outs in a file and she could pause on any of them and read details about me that I don't want anyone to know.

'It'll be in here somewhere,' Kelly says.

I know Jen's number, I could tell her it, but all I can think is that I'm naked for all the world to see and there's nothing to cover me. I want to rub out everything in that file and start it all again.

Kelly runs a finger down a page and stops. 'Here it is.' She leans over and picks up the phone, dials the number and passes the phone to me.

'Can I talk to her in private?' I ask.

Kelly shakes her head. 'I'd prefer to stay here, in case she needs to talk to me.' The sympathy on her face makes me want to punch her.

I turn my back as the phone rings.

'It's Dusty,' I say, as soon as Jen answers. 'When can I see Poppy?'

'Dusty. How are you getting on?'

'Poppy is in Newcastle,' I say.

'She is,' Jen says. 'We've found her a temporary place, with a very experienced foster carer.'

'Is there room there for me?' I'm glad that Kelly can't

see my face. She'd be able to tell that my heart has a hammer slamming into it.

'No,' Jen replies.

No. It's the smallest word, but it fills the room, pushing against me, inside me, until it's all I can hear. My life reduced to a stream of negatives.

'When am I going to see her?'

'It's difficult, Dusty. It'll have to be a time when an adult can accompany you half way and coincide with someone else, perhaps me, being able to drive Poppy to meet you. It's not something that will happen weekly. I'll try absolutely everything I can to make it work, but it might be more like every month, maybe two.'

Her words come to me from a dark tunnel, too slippery to hold.

'Dusty?'

'That's impossible,' I tell her.

'It'll hopefully only be temporary,' Jen says.

She's lying. I know how these things work. Once we're in a placement, even if it's not a great one, they stop trying to look for somewhere else.

'I'll get together with Poppy's new carer and see if we can sort out a date that suits the adults at your end too.'

I close my eyes and imagine holding a match to her words, watch them go up in flames.

'She's in a really good place, Dusty. There are four other

children around the same age. Two of them go to the local school, where Poppy will be starting on Friday.'

I won't be with her to check she eats breakfast, to do her hair right.

'It's got a really good reputation,' Jen says, but I hang up on her and will never know what else she wanted to say.

Anger overwhelms that door inside me. It knocks it from its hinges and spills in a torrent through my blood. I scratch my palms and try to breathe slowly, but each breath is adding fuel to the fire.

'Dusty,' I hear Kelly say behind me, but I don't want her here, I don't want to see her, I don't want to hear her. If she stops speaking, I can pretend I'm not here. That instead I'm in an office at my school, that Tessa B goaded me too far and I finally snapped.

Kelly touches my shoulder and I push her away.

'Don't touch me,' I warn her.

'OK,' she says. 'It's OK.'

'It's not OK.' I'm not shouting, but I'm close, the frayed ends of my anger dipped in petrol.

'What did your social worker say?' Kelly keeps her voice calm.

The debris of my life stacks up inside me. I'm too small for this. I can't hold it all.

'Let's go and get a snack,' Kelly suggests.

'You think food can fix this?'

I kick the chair towards her and see fear cross her face.

'Try to calm down, Dusty. Just tell me what Jen said.'

But I don't need to stay calm, because Poppy isn't here to keep safe. For so many years I've had to breathe and breathe and breathe through my anger to try to protect my little sister and stop us being separated. All these years I've played by their rules and they took me away from her in any case.

Black tar smothers my bones.

'What's the fucking point?' I shout and grab my file. I begin to rip out all the paper and all the notes they have on me, about my crappy mum and my AWOL dad, my failures in foster care, my failure in school, my fucking failure that follows me everywhere. I shred it all.

I hurl the empty file at the wall. I pick up a computer keyboard and throw it across the room as John comes in, and I pick up the nearest chair and throw it at him.

'Dusty,' John says. 'We're here to help you.'

'It's OK, John,' I hear Kelly say, but she's so distant, as if in a different room. 'I can deescalate this.'

Years and years of hurt have become a boiling river that burns my insides. I scream because it's agony and I'm caught in a current I can't swim against.

I grab another chair and slam it against the table. Its leg buckles and I slam it again. I launch the chair towards John and reach for the computer, but my arms are yanked back.

‘Take the other side of her,’ John tells Kelly, his voice strained. She hesitates, but now her hands are locking me down too.

‘Get off me,’ I scream, but they grip harder, their fingers bruising.

It fires a memory right at me, my stepdad’s strength, and the thought triggers a brutal wall of fear that falls on me. I’m buried in terror, but they won’t let go. I’m kicking them, trying to get them away.

John moves behind me, but I can’t twist to see, he’s too strong.

‘You’re hurting me,’ I cry. These people, who are meant to protect me.

I’m forced on to a chair, bile blocking my throat. Kelly kneels next to me, her hands still gripped tight to my arms.

‘The quicker you calm down, Dusty,’ she says. ‘The sooner we can stop.’

I kick her, my foot ramming into her shoulder.

John presses harder on my arms, his big, male fingers in fists around me.

‘It’s hurting,’ I say and I’m crying, but he doesn’t let go.

I’m seven years old again, my stepdad pinning me down.

‘Please,’ I cry, but they don’t listen.

There’s no fear like this. It’s a darkness that smothers the earth. It sweeps through me, a tornado wrecking everything in its path, until all that’s left of me is my empty skin that falls limp into hands that were never meant to do anything other than catch me.

Cooper sits beside me on the bed, the door to the room open.

'Would it help to draw?' he asks me.

I shake my head. I don't want to hold a pencil in my hand when I have bruises under my arms. The memories will leak on to the page and I won't be able to cope with seeing them in colour in front of me.

My phone rings. It's Poppy, but I don't answer it. How can I tell her that we're going to be OK, when the world is exploding from the inside out into a thousand burning stars?

I have to sit at the kitchen table in the evening with the others. Kelly sits two seats away from me. She tries to speak to me as though nothing has happened, but hearing her voice kick-starts the adrenaline that I'd managed to get down to a simmer.

I don't want to eat, but I have to. I chew the lamb curry and swallow it, the spice leaving a trail against my tongue.

I'm shaking as I put my plate and fork in the dishwasher.

'Do you want ice cream, Dusty?' Kelly asks.

I shake my head and walk away, leaving my half-drunk juice on the table, my fingerprints on its glass the only proof I was there.

*

I sit on Cooper's bed, listening to him playing guitar. It's the only thing that can come close to soothing me right now. I read the inked lyrics written all up his arms and they somehow hold me from spinning into the darkest void.

Poppy, you'd really love this boy, I tell her. I sit and wait for a reply, listen so hard for the sound of her voice, wait for her to come tumbling up the stairs. But she isn't here.

'Cooper,' I say. 'You know when you said we could run away together?'

He stops playing, puts his guitar on his knees and looks at me.

'Yes,' he says.

'Did you mean it?' I ask.

'Of course,' he says.

'I need to go and find my sister,' I tell him.

'We can do that.' Cooper makes it sound like the easiest thing in the world.

'How, though?'

He glances towards the door and looks back at me. 'I've got money.' He's lowered his voice to a whisper, because we're only ever allowed a small amount of cash at one time. 'In one of my homes I had a job with the farmer next door. We pretended I was just helping him out, but he paid me for the work I did.'

'No one ever found it?'

'They never search because they don't expect me to have it.'

'You really think we can do it?' The thought lifts some of the bricks from my chest.

'We might as well try.' Cooper picks up his guitar again, brushes the strings with his fingers. 'In the words of the best poet ever, we've got to dare to disturb the universe.'

Chapter Twelve

'You've eaten all the peanut butter,' Liv shouts at Jemal. 'What am I going to have for breakfast now?' And she slaps the back of his head.

'Leave it, Liv,' Kelly says.

Jemal doesn't retaliate. I watch him take it in and dull his eyes. It's impossible, I think, for anger to go nowhere. It'll be storing up inside of him, whether he likes it or not.

Liv shrieks and storms off up the stairs, Kelly following her.

'You OK?' I ask Jemal.

He shrugs and he's blinking quick. I didn't think I'd feel guilty about getting out of this place, but right in this moment I do. We'll be leaving Jemal, without telling him. I'm just adding to the long list of people who've let him down.

I don't know if he notices that I fill four bagels with cheese and ham and that Cooper has taken a tub of pasta from the fridge. I put two bananas and an apple into a plastic bag, fill my water bottle and head to my room.

There's nothing in here I'll miss. I've got my phone, my Katniss socks and my sketchbook and pencils in my old school rucksack and that's pretty much all I need. I stuff in a hoodie, underwear and my trackies.

So, this is it. I stand by my door and can hear John singing in the kitchen now. I'm hoping Kelly is still watching TV with Alfie and Casey.

Cooper appears, his rucksack on his back. He smiles, holds up the house keys he stole ages ago, and points to the stairs, without a speck of fear. We go down and I know we've only moments to get this right. The sitting room and kitchen have people in and we need to get to the front door, Cooper get the key in the lock and get out of here before they see us. My heart is banging, but it's different to what I've known, a good feeling, that blooms excitement in my bones.

We're on the bottom stair, but there's someone on the landing above us.

'Cooper?' We look up at Liv. Cooper waves to her silently.

I think she'll shout, but she stands dead still.

'Good luck,' she mouths.

We walk past the sitting-room door. I don't look in, only concentrate on Cooper's hand as he puts the key into the lock.

There's a noise behind us.

'Hurry,' I whisper and he turns the key with one hand, grabs the handle with the other, as John comes out of the kitchen, tea towel over his shoulder.

There's a split second where he stares at us confused, but he's running towards us and I see Liv charging down the stairs, throwing herself at him. And Cooper and I are outside and we're running, down the front path, going right at the end. John is shouting and I know he's chasing us, because his voice isn't fading. But we're younger and we're faster. Cooper grabs my hand at the end of the street and pulls me down another road and I'm running. There are mums and kids going to school and we run past them and I don't look back, but I'm sure John is still there. Cooper and I leg it down the road and along more pavement and we keep running, my rucksack knocking against my backbone, Cooper's hand in mine. It's quieter and I can't hear footsteps behind us, so I chance a look back. John is there, but he's far behind and he's slowing.

'Unfit bastard,' Cooper calls to him and we laugh and keep running.

We turn another corner and the streets are in a blur, until Cooper stops.

'Where is it?' he asks.

The taxi he ordered isn't here. Our plan is already falling apart.

'We're probably early,' I reassure him.

Cooper looks back down the road. Any moment, John

could appear. Or Kelly could've got in the car and be driving along trying to find us.

We crouch down beside a car, but we look suspicious. The last thing we need is some mum calling the police on us.

'What do we do?' Cooper asks me.

'We wait,' I tell him, standing up. 'It'll be here.'

He nods. 'Or we could walk to the station?'

'It's too far. If they realise where we're going, they'll get there before us.'

A car turns into the street, but it's not a taxi.

'Shit,' I say. My heart is battering to get out.

'It'll be here.' Cooper repeats my words.

I watch the end of the street. I can't see John.

The sound of another car. Cooper looks towards it and smiles.

'Right on time,' he says, and this boy I hardly know, but know I like, steps out into the road to flag down the car that'll take me closer to my sister.

I hadn't thought the train station would be this busy, but it's good I guess, as it's easier to hide if they search here.

'That's the departures board,' Cooper says, his eyes barely settling on all the names and times flashing above us. I realise that we didn't plan this far ahead. 'It's too confusing.'

'Let's just get the first one,' I say. 'And figure out the Newcastle bit later.'

Cooper adjusts his rucksack on his back. 'Bolton?'

‘Is that far enough away?’ I ask him.

‘Not really.’ Cooper studies the board again. ‘Blackpool?’

Most of the seats in the train are reserved, but Cooper and I find two together, even if they are facing backwards.

‘We can watch hell getting smaller in the distance,’ he says, as I sit next to the window.

We don’t put our rucksacks on the shelf above us, keeping them on our laps. Cooper gets out a bucket hat, pulling it low over his eyes.

‘It’s my disguise,’ he says, all jittery, glancing up at everyone who walks past.

He finds his book of poems and opens it, his hands fidgeting.

On the platform beyond the window, there’s a screen that says the places the train will stop and how long until it’s leaving. Two minutes. It’s a strange world we’ve stepped into, filled with commuters and luggage and noise. There’s no sign of John, or Kelly, or any of the adults from Keystone.

But there’s a police officer. Two of them. Walking towards one of the train guards.

‘Cooper,’ I say and he stops reading and sees them too.

One of the officers says something, the other one looking around.

‘Don’t look at them.’ Cooper speaks so quietly I can barely hear him.

I lean my elbow against the window and rest my head in my hand, so from the outside you wouldn’t be able to see my face. But now that means I can't see what they're doing, if they're coming this way. And I can't see the clock to know how long we've got.

'There's no way they'll be searching for us here,' Cooper whispers. 'If they're looking anywhere, it'll be around the streets near the house. Runners usually end up in the park. Or Maccie Ds. That'll be the first place they'll look.'

I count in my head and get to twenty-six when a whistle blows. I look at Cooper and smile. A few more seconds. The platform begins to move. I look out of the window and see the two police officers still standing there, one has her arms crossed and she's laughing at something the train guard must've said. Posters on the platform go by too fast for me to read, until they're not there at all. And the only thing that's outside the window now is vanishing buildings, their colours blurring into each other.

I unzip the front pocket of my rucksack and get out the first pencil I find. It's an orange one and I hold it tight in my hand to calm me.

The fact that we've really done this hits me the moment that the buildings are replaced by fields and trees. The last time I ran away, the only real time, was trying to get back to Chris and Guy's. I was ten and couldn't understand why they didn't want Poppy and me to stay. I knew they were temporary fosters, but I thought they'd change their minds, that there must've been some kind of mistake. Poppy and I slipped out of our new carer's back garden, along the path that ran behind the houses and we just started to walk. All I really remember is trying to stop Poppy's coat from dragging in the mud and the police car pulling up alongside us and Poppy was crying and the guilt and confusion I felt. That I was meant to be saving her, but I'd ended up making her sad.

'Cards?' Cooper puts his book back in his rucksack and pulls down the small flip table attached to the seat in front.

He takes the cards from the packet and starts to deal. I pull down the tiny table on my side, and now there's hardly enough room to move with my bag on my lap. I don't need to ask what we'll be playing, as it'll be the same game we've played over and over with Jemal.

'Will Jemal hate us for going without him?' I ask Cooper.

'He wouldn't have wanted to come,' he replies, making two neat piles of seven cards. 'He's got too much to lose.'

Jemal is desperate to get back to his mum. It's all he thinks about and he's sure he won't be allowed to if he messes up.

'Will his mum be able to stay clean for him this time?'

Cooper passes me a pile of cards. 'No.'

It's too hard to think about. It's easier to just rearrange the cards in my hands, to put the numbers together, the suits in a row. I feel my shoulders relax as we begin to play, the familiar sound of the cards placed on the pile, the feel of their soft edges when I pick up the next one.

‘Do you think they’ll guess we’re going to find Poppy?’ I ask, not meaning to disturb his concentration.

‘Probably,’ he says.

‘So, they could have people waiting for us at Newcastle station?’

‘Possibly.’ Cooper puts down a card, but changes his mind and swaps it for another.

‘Perhaps we should stay in Blackpool for a bit, then,’ I say.

‘Makes sense.’ Cooper says it as though it’s normal, us choosing to go where we want, with no one to stop us.

I don’t see her until she’s beside us. A woman, older, leaning towards Cooper. I feel him tense, am terrified that he might lash out.

‘It’s rare that young people play cards these days,’ she says.

‘It passes the time,’ Cooper replies, smiling that smile.

‘It’s nice to see,’ she says and touches Cooper on the shoulder, before she carries on walking down the carriage.

Cooper doesn’t move for a moment. The last time I saw an adult’s hands on him, they were pinning him down. A shrill memory rattles along my spine. I can still feel the bruises under my arms and they trigger a ripple of deeper memories that swarm as bees. I stare at the cards in my hand. If they weren’t Cooper’s, I’d rip the queen’s head clean from her shoulders, drop the king beneath my feet and grind his face to oblivion.

Chapter Thirteen

Cooper throws his arms wide and begins to run across the sand, taking the hat from his head, his hair caught by the wind. He looks back at me and smiles, turns and keeps running.

I stand where I am. The sky above us is still morning blue, more pastel than eye-wateringly bright. The sea lies back beneath it, all the way until that perfect line of the horizon. All I smell is the ocean, that ancient water turning.

Cooper looks small by the shore. I see him kick off his trainers, pull off his socks and roll his trousers to his knees. With his rucksack on his back, he wades into the sea.

I sit where I am and take off my trainers, tuck my socks deep inside them, right up to the toes, holding them both in one hand as I walk to where Cooper waves to me. The sand is already warm, each footstep pressing through to the cooler grains below. It's the strangest thing, being free. To be able to walk with no one watching, only a friend near the shore. I keep expecting hands to grab me, but there's just the faint salt wind against my skin, the sounds of the sea circling me.

Cooper kicks water in an arc, his face so happy. The water is freezing and I step into it laughing, hopping from foot to foot, holding my trainers high. He's saying something, but I can't hear until I'm closer and I'm sure he's reciting lines from his poet.

He puts his palms flat to the surface and before I realise it, he's holding his hands either side of my face, laughing as my eyes widen at the cold. I scoop water and throw it at him and he stumbles back, nearly falling completely into the sea.

'Truce,' he says, scrabbling to get away, but I keep chasing him. 'Truce,' he shouts, turning to splash the whole of my front. He holds his hands up in surrender.

'Seems a bit uneven,' I say, his clothes are pretty much dry.

'I'll buy you an ice cream,' he says.

'A double one.'

'A double one,' he repeats.

'Deal.'

I wade deeper than Cooper, my shorts short enough for the water to touch my thighs. The waves are small, but still I go on tiptoes each time they move.

We sit on the sand eating our lunch in silence, side by side. The cheese in my sandwich is squashed warm, but here it has a different taste. The bread keeps sticking to my gums and I work it free from my teeth.

'We've definitely got enough money to get us to Newcastle?' I ask Cooper.

'Definitely. I'm keeping it safe in my pocket.' He throws his last bit of sandwich in the air and catches it in his mouth.

'You could earn a bit for your skills,' I laugh.

'I'd be a millionaire.' Cooper smiles at me.

How could I have been forced from my sister and blasted into the orbit of this boy?

'Do you think they've already told Poppy I've gone?' I ask.

'I don't know,' Cooper says. 'Their logic is pretty screwed most of the time.'

It's so wrong that she's in a place I've never seen, with people I've never met. It makes my stomach turn and I look to the straight line of the horizon to try to stop my anger from exploding. More than anything, I want to speak to her, but I know I'll worry her if we haven't got more of a plan sorted.

'When did you last see Casper?' I ask Cooper.

It feels safe to ask him here about his brother, that if his emotions rip through his skin, there's no adult to pin him down and force them back in.

'Ninety-six days,' he says.

'You count them?'

'Every single one.' Cooper picks up sand in one hand, lets it fall through his fingers to his other palm.

It feels like all the sorrow in the world has been scooped up and forced into him, filling him so full that I don't know how he doesn't fracture. I want to take his pain and rip it into pieces so small that it'll never be able to find him again.

'There's an artist who makes these incredible pictures out of salt,' I say. 'He makes them to feel connected to his sister after she died.' I know that Cooper is listening, even though he's not looking at me. 'They're massive, all over the floor, of waves and forests.' I remember the first time I saw a picture of his work, it felt like my stomach filled with stars. 'And at the end of every exhibition, he sweeps them up and takes the salt back to the sea.'

Cooper turns towards me and pushes back his hair with sandy fingers. 'Can we go and see them one day?'

'He lives in Japan,' I tell him.

'We can make it to Japan,' he says.

Chapter Fourteen

MISSING PERSON/RUNAWAY REPORT

Department of Public Safety

Investigating Officer: DCI Sania Zadeh

(Underline those that apply) Adult <u>Juvenile</u>

(Underline those that apply) Missing Lost Suspicious Endangered <u>Runaway</u>

Incident Location: Keystone Children's Residential home, Bolton

Missing Person Information:

Name: Dusty Delaney

Nickname(s): N/A

DOB: 29/11/2008

Age at Disappearance: 16

Race: White British

Sex: F

Height: 5ft 7

Hair colour and style/length: Dyed blonde, straight, to just below chin. Pink fringe.

Eye colour: Hazel

Complexion: Fair

Build: Slim

Scars, birthmarks, moles, tattoos, other identifying marks: None

Piercings: One in right ear, two in left. Stud in nose.

Teeth, including gaps: Straight teeth, no gaps or braces

Eyewear: None

Clothing worn at time of disappearance: Blue denim shorts, dark blue T-shirt, white trainers

Jewellery: Unknown

Medical, mental and physical condition: Dusty was new to the children's residential home, having recently been moved out of foster care due to a permanent breakdown in the placement. Although she seemed to have settled at Keystone, she was upset to have been separated from her sister and there's a possibility that she'll be heading to Newcastle to find her. Officers have been positioned at Newcastle train station and CCTV is being monitored.

MISSING PERSON/RUNAWAY REPORT

Department of Public Safety

Investigating Officer: DCI Sania Zadeh

(Underline those that apply) Adult <u>Juvenile</u>

(Underline those that apply) Missing Lost Suspicious Endangered <u>Runaway</u>

Incident Location: Keystone Children's Residential home, Bolton

Missing Person Information:

Name: Cooper Lawson

Nickname(s): N/A

DOB: 01/10/2008

Age at Disappearance: 16

Race: White British

Sex: M

Height: 5ft 11

Hair colour and style/length: Black, scruffy, chin-length

Eye colour: Blue

Complexion: Fair

Build: Slim

Scars, birthmarks, moles, tattoos, other identifying marks: Approximately one inch scar, above right eyebrow

Piercings: None

Teeth, including gaps: Small gap between two front teeth. No braces.

Eyewear: None

Clothing worn at time of disappearance: Blue jeans, white T-shirt, black trainers

Jewellery: Ring on (possibly) right hand

Medical, mental and physical condition: Cooper has been increasingly anxious in the home, recently displaying signs of violence within the school environment. He's been more unsettled since a previous resident was moved on. Staff describe his behaviour as unpredictable.

Chapter Fifteen

The smell of sun cream takes me straight to Poppy, to her scrunched-up face when I put it as close to her lashes as I can, making sure all her skin is protected. It reminds me how the last time we were on the beach together, I forgot to bring it. *Tell him you think he's Jude Bellingham.* Her words flare bright enough to incinerate me, because she's not here for me to show her that I've remembered it this time and to tell her that I'll never let her burn again.

I thought I knew what it was like to miss someone and now I realise I had no idea. I close my eyes to rub the sun cream on to my own face and only open them again when I'm sure I've built my wall up high enough to stop any emotions getting through.

'Is it all done?' I ask Cooper, my face tipped up towards him. He looks so carefully at me that for a moment everything else in my world blurs at the edges.

'Yeah, all good,' he says and I'm not sure if it's me, or the sun that's put the red on his cheeks.

He squeezes way too much of it in his palm and smudges it across his face, rubbing it as though he's in a shower.

'Done?' he asks me.

'Almost,' I say.

I lean towards him to smooth the rest of it into his skin. He sits still, my fingertips sweeping over the arc of his cheekbones.

'There,' I say.

'Thanks,' he says, opening his eyes.

I don't know if he can feel it, this *this*, drifting like smoke between us.

'Shall we go to the pier?' he asks.

I don't reply, only nod, wiping my hands on the back of my shorts.

There must be speakers everywhere, music blaring between candyfloss and pink sticks of rock.

'This place is a sensation overload,' I say, holding the straps of my bag. I don't admit to Cooper that crowds aren't really my thing. Too many people make my ribs feel broken, even when no one's actually touching me.

I look down at my feet, see the slats split with glimpses of sea beneath us. My stomach tells me it's unsafe, but at the same time I want to smash through the wooden planks and see what it feels like to fall.

Poppy would hate it. I imagine her refusing to budge, refusing to walk and I'd have to lift her up and carry her over the worst parts. It's getting more difficult to give her piggybacks these days, but even when I'm eighty I'll find a way.

Cooper gets me the double ice cream like he promised and we sit on a wooden bench at the side of the pier to eat them, the cold taste helping to calm the chaos around me.

'Do you think it's possible to paint sound?' I ask.

'How would you do that?' Cooper asks.

'I think I could,' I say. 'Every painting is a feeling.'

'You've lost me.' Cooper bites the end from his cone and holds it above him until the ice cream drips on to his tongue.

'There's no way I can look at a picture and feel nothing,' I say. 'I reckon if they cut me open when I'm studying a painting, they'll definitely see feelings there.'

'You saying that feelings are a physical thing?'

'Well you can *feel* them, can't you?'

'But you can't actually touch them.' He bites another chunk of his cone and has to shove loads more into his mouth, the ice cream melting everywhere.

'I reckon they're like bubbles. Loads of them, growing and popping.'

'Sounds a mess,' Cooper says.

'Feelings are,' I say, swallowing ice cream too quick and for a moment it gives me brain-freeze.

A girl skips backwards in front of us and she falls, and

when she's picked up by her mum, I hate that I feel jealousy. And I hate that I keep watching how her mum brushes her elbows and kisses each of her palms and runs her hand over the child's hair. Envy swells like burning bubbles inside me. I need to put the longest needle down my throat and pierce them one by one.

'Which ride shall we go on?' Cooper asks, passing me a biscuit from the packet he took from Keystone's kitchen this morning. Only this morning. Time is warping today.

'You've got enough money?'

'Tons,' he says, which makes me think he probably doesn't. 'What about the waltzer?'

'I just think my head might spin off,' I say.

'I'd pay to see that,' he laughs, moving out of the way of a man who looks about one hundred.

We stand beside the bumper cars, swamped by a smell of fudge. The two girls next to us are talking about a boy they like and about a party they're going to. I don't know if Cooper is listening to them too, and whether he feels the same as I do. Their words salt poured into a cut within me that never heals.

I tune out their voices and head us towards a ride where someone is strapped into a harness and flying.

'That one,' I say, pointing to it.

'You say no to the waltzer and you choose that,' Cooper says.

'It's different,' I say, touching his arm. 'You up for it?'

'I've always wanted to fly,' he says.

'Have you never been on a plane?'

The only time I went on one was after Chris and Guy. But my heart was too wrecked to enjoy it.

'What do you think?' His words sound a bit harsh, but I don't think he means them to be. 'Planes are saved for the lucky people,' he says, stopping by a ticket booth.

I watch him pay and don't tell him that standing beside him makes me feel like one of the lucky ones.

'You can't go on with your bags,' one of the ride attendants tells us.

'Can't I wear it on my front?' Cooper asks him.

'Afraid not. You can leave them here. Lots of people do.'

'Will they be safe?'

'Never had a problem before.'

Cooper looks at me. 'You think we should?'

'If it means we can fly? Definitely.'

We put our bags on the floor inside the fenced-off area, Cooper squashing them together to try to make them as small as he can.

'Will your cash be safe in your pocket?' I ask him, imagining it falling out for people to catch below.

'It's not going anywhere,' he says, wedging it deeper.

They put these padded bibs on us, long enough to touch our knees, with straps across them and a bar each to hold.

I look ridiculous and I shouldn't feel self-conscious that Cooper is seeing me like this, but I do.

We follow the woman up some steps and she's attaching us to a contraption and I think I'm definitely feeling regret. It's all a bit serious up close, with straps and locks and the wind is blowing into us before we even start.

'OK?' the woman asks me.

'Thanks,' I hear Cooper say and the gate we're attached to lowers, taking us with it, stopping when we're lying flat on our fronts, floating just above the platform.

'Is it too late to back out?' I ask Cooper.

'You serious?'

'I'm not sure,' I say.

I'm about to shout and ask them to stop, but we're being lifted up.

Cooper links his arm through mine. 'I've got you,' he says.

We're lifted higher than I'd expected, even though I saw exactly how high we were going to go. This wasn't a great idea. At least with the waltzer, if anything had snapped, we wouldn't have been hurled high into the air to crash into the sea.

'It's safe,' Cooper shouts, but I can't look at him as he walks in and out of my mind. 'They wouldn't let us do it if it wasn't.' His voice is shaking a bit, like he's trying to convince himself as much as me.

We're dizzy high, everything tiny below us. It's how life makes me feel sometimes, that I'm at a distance, an outsider looking in. And no one can hear me, apart from Poppy. *Next time we're here*, I tell her, *we'll go on this together.*

'Ready?' Cooper says, his smile terrified.

I nod and he must pull the bit that he's been told, because we're falling, the wind taking my stomach and throwing it to the sun. We fall and fall and fly up and we're screaming and Cooper is laughing like a maniac, saying something I don't hear, squeezing my hand until I'm sure my bones will break. But I don't care, because my bones will repair and I'll be forever left with this feeling.

The world drops and we're flying backwards, the pier beneath us appearing. And we're lifting again. I'm only this. A movement, a scream, adrenaline flooding me to swamp all other hurt. I'm alive, I'm dying and Cooper is with me, our hands locked together, raised against the speed of the wind.

The rise again, the drop. The sea beneath us, Cooper yelling to the sky. Perhaps I do want our harness to actually break free, so we can keep flying together. But we slow, swinging lower and there's no one to wave to and I wish that Poppy was here, that she's waiting. Cooper lets go of my hand, my legs finding it difficult to stand.

'That was amazing,' Cooper says to me and to the woman who unhooks us, to anyone who can hear. His eyeliner dots have smudged even more and I lean over and wipe my thumb beneath them. There's a bolt of electricity in my arm. I tell myself that it's leftover adrenaline, needing somewhere to go.

We find our bags exactly where we left them, as the ride attendant said we would.

Cooper picks them up and looks at me. 'Where do we go next?'

'Anywhere,' I say.

Chapter Sixteen

I hold that feeling of flying and try to trap it inside me, wanting to tell Poppy how it felt. As though the sky had made wings just for me and Cooper, fastened them on our backs and mistaken us for birds.

We walk down steps beside the roller coaster and here the gaps beneath our feet are way bigger than the normal walkway. It's like a giant mesh of metal squares and if I was really tiny, I'm sure I could slip through. Beside us, there's the never-ending track of the ride, close enough to almost touch.

'Not the most fun place to be,' I say, holding on to the edge.

But Cooper is climbing on the railings.

'Don't, Cooper,' I say.

He's already jumped down the other side and is standing with a carriage full of people on the roller coaster rattling above him.

'You coming?' he says.

'You're not going to try to get on it?' I ask him.

'I'm not that stupid.' Cooper crouches low and crawls beneath the track. 'It's always good to see life from a different angle.'

'I think you are that stupid,' I shout over to him.

'The awful daring of a moment's surrender,' he shouts back laughing, lying down, facing up to where the carriage will soon rush over the top of him.

'It's not a time for poetry,' I say, tempted to join him now I know he's safe.

'Always a time for poetry.' Cooper looks towards me. 'Quick!' he shouts. 'Before it comes round again.'

'You're a nutter,' I say, climbing over.

'No, you're a nutter,' he laughs, moving up to make space for me.

And I'm lying next to Cooper, beneath the crashing sound of the track and it's actually more terrifying than it looked, because it's really loud and I can see the carriage rising and falling and it's getting closer.

'Ready?' Cooper asks, reaching for my hand.

'Always,' I say.

And I don't mean to scream, but it's hurtling above us, so quick that it rips my nerves along with it.

Somewhere through the noise, someone is shouting, and Cooper and I crawl from the space and we're up and running. Cooper nearly falling as we scramble over the fence, two men behind us now.

We fly up the steps, past a blur of people, not meaning to barge into them, my bag jolting against me, past rides and music, the colours of rusted steel smashed together with gold. Straight to the exit of the pier and we have to slow for a moment, a family blocking the way.

'Sorry,' says Cooper. 'We're in a rush.' Pushing past them, me grabbing his elbow, letting go.

We dart down a road to the right, away from the beach, take the first left and there's hardly anyone here, so it's easier, but there's also nowhere to hide. We probably don't even need to keep running, but we do, because we're free, we're hunted, we're together and it's brilliant.

Down more streets, until my chest feels like it'll explode. I only stop when Cooper slumps to the ground, one arm slung over his stomach, his hair stuck to his face.

'We're not exactly the best criminals,' Cooper says.

'I never set out to be one,' I say.

My heart isn't settling. I'm waiting for someone to appear and grab me.

'Where to next?' Cooper holds his hand towards me and I pull him up. We both step away from each other at the same time. 'Shall we get food?'

'I need to phone Poppy first,' I say.

Cooper nods. 'You won't tell her where we are, though? Not yet, until we're in Newcastle.'

We find a wall to sit on, small enough to keep our feet on the ground. I get out my phone, but don't dial Poppy's number.

‘Have I let her down?’ I ask Cooper.

He does that thing where his eyebrows crease towards each other. ‘No, Dusty, you haven’t.’

‘But what if they stop me seeing her?’

‘They’ve stopped you seeing her in any case,’ Cooper reminds me.

I type in her number. We’re in the shade here and I only realise that I’m feeling a bit cold when the phone rings.

‘She not answering?’ Cooper asks.

‘Hello?’ It’s Poppy’s voice, close enough to be beside me, but she’s too far away.

‘Prim?’

She’s crying again, because of me. That’s all I ever seem to be able to do. I’ve changed from being her protector to her tormentor and I hate myself for it.

‘It’s OK,’ I tell her, but it’s not. Nothing is.

‘Where are you?’ she asks, her words broken up by her tears.

‘I’m having a few days away from the home.’ I won’t tell her that we’re on our way to see her.

‘Where, though?’

I’ve never held anything back from her. Never lied to her.

‘Somewhere more fun than that Keystone place they put me in,’ I say. ‘How is it where you are?’

‘Can I come with you?’ she asks.

I’m letting her down again and again and again.

'I'll see you soon,' I tell her.

'Jen says you ran away with a boy.'

Cooper has got a pen out of his bag and is writing something on his wrist.

'I've got a partner in crime,' I tell her and I see Cooper smile. 'You'll like him.'

'Do you *like* him?' she asks and I sense her hurt lifting a bit. 'Is he a Peeta, or a Gale?'

The boys from *The Hunger Games*. We both thought Katniss chose the wrong one.

'Is it sunny where you are?' I ask.

'Gale, or Peeta?' she repeats, not falling for my subject swerve.

'Poppy,' I begin.

'Tell me.'

I know if I say it out loud, I'll be admitting something to myself that I can't step back from.

'Gale,' I tell her.

And for the first time since I've been speaking to her, I can tell she truly smiles.

Chapter Seventeen

Telephone conversation between Poppy Delaney (PD) and her social worker, Jennifer McKay (JM).

JM: Your carer told me you had a phone call, Poppy.

PD: Am I not allowed phone calls now?

JM: Was it Dusty?

PD: No.

JM: You've got to be really honest with me, Poppy. When did you last speak to her?

PD: I don't remember.

JM: You must be able to.

PD: I don't.

JM: Well, when you did speak to her, what did you speak about?

PD: Stuff.

JM: Stuff?

PD: Yes.

JM: You won't be in trouble if you tell us, Poppy.

Silence.

JM: Dusty won't be angry with you. You'll be helping her.

PD: You separated us. That wasn't helping her.

JM: It's only temporary, until we can sort things out.

PD: You made her run away.

JM: If she said that to you, then it's not true. She was in a place where she was safe and now she's not. Do you understand that?

PD: I'm not stupid, Jen.

JM: I never said you were. But I don't think you're understanding that we have to get Dusty back. I'm worried about her.

PD: I'm not.

JM: You're not? Not at all?

Silence.

JM: The boy she's with. He was recently violent in the home.

PD: Dusty said he's nice. And she's a good judge of character.

JM: Maybe she is, but she hasn't always got the best judgement about things she's doing.

Silence.

JM: Poppy, you need to tell us if she gives you any clue about where she is. We will find her, but we need to get to her as soon as we can.

Silence

JM: It's important, Poppy. Do you understand that?

PD: I'm hanging up now.

Chapter Eighteen

'Try one.' I pass one of my vinegar-soaked chips to Cooper.

'Nope.' He shakes his head, almost falling off the wall.

But I press it to his lips and when he laughs I shove it into his mouth.

He winces. 'Vinegar is just wrong.'

'It's so right,' I say, licking salt from my fingers. I can just see the sea from where we're sitting. 'What do you want to do, Cooper?'

'What, now?'

'No. Like, in the future.'

He unsticks one of his chips from the paper wrapping.

'I wanted to be a footballer when I was younger. For about five minutes.'

'I can't imagine that.'

'Nor could anyone else.' When Cooper laughs, it reaches his eyes, his soul lit.

'What about now?'

'Sometimes I think I'd like to translate books,' he says. 'Then I'd be surrounded by words all day.'

'Translate them into what?' I ask.

'Different languages. So they can be read in loads of different countries.'

'Wouldn't you need to be fluent in another language?'

'Yes.' He dips a chip in ketchup and bites the end off it.

'And are you?' I ask him. 'Fluent?'

'No.' He laughs again. 'What about you?'

'Am I fluent in a language?'

'No,' Cooper says. 'Your future.'

'I wouldn't mind going into space,' I say. 'Be an astronaut.'

Cooper looks at me. 'Any other options?'

'An ice skater, or one of those people who uses bows and arrows at the Olympics.' I crunch on the tiniest chip, which is essentially just burnt grease.

'You can skate?' he asks.

'I can't do either,' I tell him. 'I haven't made up my mind which I'm going to choose.'

Cooper looks at the words on his arm. He has to twist his elbow to show me the bit underneath, where his skin would be smooth if it wasn't covered in ink.

'*Time yet for a hundred indecisions*,' he reads.

'So, still time for you to learn all those languages,' I tell him.

'Always time,' he says.

*

'Could you buy us cider?' I ask the woman. 'We'll pay you for it.'

I thought I'd picked a good one, but I know as soon as she really looks at me that she won't. She doesn't say no, just walks away.

We're standing next to a corner shop. It's getting dark, but I've swapped my shorts for my trackies and I'm wearing my hoodie, so I'm not cold any more.

Cooper approaches someone a bit younger this time. She looks in her early twenties.

'Sorry to disturb you,' he says and she stops. 'I'm wondering, if I give you the money, would you mind buying me a couple of cans of cider?'

She smiles at him. 'No problem. Any type?'

'Anything is fine,' Cooper says. He hands her a fiver. 'Is that enough?'

'Plenty,' she says. 'I won't be long.'

She disappears into the shop and Cooper shrugs when he sees me looking at him.

'Some of us have it,' he smiles.

'She'll run off with your money,' I tell him.

'She won't.' But there's a flicker of doubt, which makes me feel victorious even if it will mean him losing a fiver.

The woman comes back out and passes two cans to Cooper, dropping change into his hand.

'Enjoy,' she says, smiling at me too.

Cooper passes me a can. 'Shame we didn't bet on it.'

'Well, I've nothing to give you,' I remind him, as we begin to walk to find somewhere to drink them.

It's the time of day when the shadows pop out, the time I love to paint. People see grey and black, but there's so much more. There are bottled rainbows hiding in corners.

We stop in a car park behind some shops, with a small bit of grass next to some bushes, by a wall. The bins next to us stink a bit and I'm glad I've changed out of my shorts, with the grass being so dry and stubby.

Cooper opens his can, the sound of a knuckle crack. Froth fizzes up and on to his fingers and he licks them quick, before it spills down the side. He pulls a similar face to the one with the vinegar.

'Not good?' I laugh.

I tap the top of my can, because that's what Roseanna told me to do, when we'd shared some cider in the toilets at break time, in the school before my last one. Thinking of her brings a crunch of missing in my ribs. She's the only friend I made who I wish I'd kept in touch with.

I try to be casual, slipping my fingernail under the ring pull and opening the can. The cider smells OK, so I take a swig. And another one, swilling the fizz around my teeth, before swallowing.

'Do you like it?' Cooper asks me.

The pop of cold slides down my throat. 'Not really,' I laugh, drinking more.

Being in care makes you feel like you've got belts

tightening over your whole body, even over your mouth and your face. But here, with Cooper, in a car park marked with bird shit, I feel the buckles loosen.

'How come Dusty?' Cooper asks, eyes squinting at the cider taste.

'How come what?'

I'm getting more used to the cider now. It doesn't make me want to retch any more.

'Are you named after Dusty Springfield?'

'Who's that?' I ask, although I know it's the same person that people always say.

'A singer,' Cooper says.

'Is she as old as your poet?'

'Is she as dead as him?' Cooper drinks. 'No.'

'It's Dusty Baker,' I tell him. 'My uncle loved American baseball and I'd watch it with him. Dusty was the manager of his favourite team and apparently I'd chant his name as I pretended to smack the ball.' I stretch out my legs and move a bit, so my bum isn't so numb. 'It's not my real name.'

'So, what are you really called?' he asks me.

'No one gets to know,' I tell him, tipping back more cider.

'Ever?'

'Before he was a manager,' I say, 'Dusty used to play for the Atlanta Braves. He's my life mascot.'

Cooper points towards the ugly car park. 'Not sure he's done a great job so far.'

'He's been slow getting started,' I admit, 'but he's kicking into gear now.'

Cooper knocks his can on to mine. 'Here's to gear kicking,' he says.

'Here's to Dusty Baker finally coming good and sorting out my life.'

We drink together, looking at each other and, even with his can mostly obscuring his mouth, I can tell that he's smiling.

'So, will you never tell me your name?' he asks.

'If you guess it right, I might,' I say.

'Jasmine?' Cooper asks.

'Nope. That's one guess gone,' I say. 'You only get three a day.'

'Three?'

'That's plenty.'

'Do I have to do them all in a row?' Cooper asks. 'Or can I do one now and the others later?'

'However you want.'

'Will you tell me what it starts with?' he asks.

'No,' I say.

'Scarlet?' he asks.

I shake my head. 'That's two wrong.'

'I'm going to save the third,' he says, 'so I definitely get it right.'

'Good luck with that,' I say, drinking another mouthful of cider.

Cooper puts down his can and makes his fingers into a square, looking through them.

'If you could paint anything in this car park right now,' he says, 'what would it be?'

'Your eyes,' I say, without thinking.

Cooper lowers his hands. 'My eyes?'

'Yes.' I shrug. I want to tell him that it's because I realise in this moment that there's no one in the world with more beautiful eyes. 'Perhaps just one of them.' I press my arm flat to the wall. 'One massive eye on this wall.'

Cooper pushes my rucksack towards me.

'Can we use your pencils?' he asks, talking quicker than he normally does.

'To draw eyes?'

'No, we have to draw our best memory.' His arms expressive. 'And whoever does the worst one has to do a dare.'

I stop opening the pencil box and look over at him.

'Poppy and I do dares,' I tell him.

'See.' He smiles. 'We're obviously soulmates.'

'What's that?' I ask him.

He looks at me in the way that people do, when they don't understand why there are gaps in what I know.

'Someone your soul already knew,' he says.

I don't get what he's saying. 'Your souls meet before you meet in real life?'

'Yeah, I suppose,' Cooper says.

I take another mouthful of cider, the can almost empty.

'Do you think our lives are planned out before we even start?' I ask. There was an RE lesson, where Roseanna got into a row with the teacher about it.

'Maybe,' Cooper says, clicking the ring pull so it flicks down on top of his can. 'But I reckon we have choices that can change it, that we don't even know are choices at the time.'

'Well, that's a bit unfair,' I say.

'How come?'

'It's like you're in a game you don't know has started,' I say.

'But you always end up where you're meant to end up, even if you go on a bit of a winding path to get there.'

'So, I was always meant to end up in a shitty residential home?'

Cooper shakes his head and his hair falls over his eyes. He pushes it back behind his ear.

'That's not where we end up. That place is just a hole on the side of the path.'

I swirl the small amount of liquid left in my can. I like the way the cider has turned my legs into air.

'And not all choices are ours, because they won't let us have them,' Cooper says. I'm not sure he's making sense, but I like listening to his voice. 'They make decisions for us and don't care if they get them wrong.'

He looks so earnest, so sad, so angry. I want to ask him if the rules of the game say you can kiss your soulmate, but the words slip behind my lips and stay there, safe and out of sight.

'So, we need to draw a favourite memory?' I ask instead.

'Too difficult,' Cooper says.

'To think of one, or to draw?' I ask.

'Both,' Cooper says. 'It was a dumb idea of mine.'

'It wasn't,' I say. 'We'll try it.'

'So says the artist.' Cooper takes the purple pencil from the box. 'Here goes nothing.'

We sit cross-legged facing the wall, side by side, our knees touching. We don't speak and I don't look at his picture, concentrating on my own, of Poppy sat by a campfire, holding a stick over a flame. The best bit to do is the marshmallow, where it melts and browns. I still remember the taste of the crispy sweet burnt bit. Poppy had watched me as I'd peeled the outer layer, her face half lit by the flames. Me pretending that it didn't hurt my fingers, the ooze of boiling marshmallow dripping down the stick.

'Your picture is really good,' Cooper says.

I sit back to look at it. 'I'll have to tell Poppy that she's been immortalised on a wall.'

And now I see Cooper's. There's a table and two people. They're stick figures, and even though his brother is much younger than him, he's made them the same size. They both have matching party hats and smiles so wide that the pencil lines go off their cheeks. There's no sign of his mum. Just him and his brother on their own.

I feel tears so sudden against my throat that I've no chance to stop them. I know why I'm crying, but it's too massive to say.

Cooper touches my arm. 'It was a happy memory,' he tells me, yet all I can see are those layers and layers of grief in his eyes.

'So was mine,' I say, wiping my eyes and looking up to the dark sky to hold back my tears. 'You know, I'd go through all the shit again to have Poppy as my sister.'

'Exactly that,' Cooper says.

'I tell her that if there's ever a flood like with Noah's Ark, then she'll always be the one who walks with me on to that boat.'

'I hope Casper will remember me enough to go with me,' Cooper says.

And there aren't any more words, because they don't exist. There are none to describe how he's been forced apart from his brother. None to describe the life that Cooper has been left to stumble through alone.

Chapter Nineteen

This document is strictly confidential communication to and solely for the use of the recipients and may not be reproduced or circulated without prior written consent. If you are not the intended recipient, you may not disclose or use the information in this document in any way.

An incident at Blackpool's South Pier has positively identified the two teenagers Dusty Delaney and Cooper Lawson, who absconded from their children's residential home this morning. Adults within the home are extremely concerned for their safety, describing them as impulsive and vulnerable.

CCTV taken shows them running along Lincoln Street and there was a possible sighting on the corner of Cheshire Street.

Chapter Twenty

I look up at Blackpool Tower, at the columns of lights, reaching high up into the darkness. For the first time all day, I'm glad that Poppy isn't with me. I'm happier with the thought of her safely in bed, hopefully sleeping.

In front of us, beyond the stretch of sand, is the sea. There's something comforting and frustrating in the way the sound never ends.

'Do you think we'll ever feel normal?' I ask Cooper.

'What's normal?' Cooper replies.

'I don't know,' I say. 'Like everyone else?'

'Who's the guy who gets to say what we should all be like? Seriously, Dusty. Who ever thought it made sense that billions of people all different from each other should somehow all be the same?' His words rush out. 'Who you are is normal to you. And in my normal Cooper-land, you need to eat the whole chilli, or it won't be the proper dare.'

'It'll burn my mouth off.'

'Which is why I bought milk.' Cooper holds up the bottle as if it's a trophy.

'You should work in a prison,' I say, the chilli between my finger and thumb.

'No doubt I'll end up there.'

'What if I vomit?' I ask.

'The seagulls will eat it.'

'That's literally disgusting,' I tell him.

'You're welcome,' Cooper says.

I adjust my seating position on the steps, as if it'll make any difference to the heat of the chilli.

'Do you think the police are looking for us?' I ask.

'Distracting tactics,' Cooper says. 'It won't get you out of eating it.'

'If you squint at the tower, the colours are a kaleidoscope.'

'Distracting again,' Cooper laughs.

'Not me,' I say and crunch into the chilli.

It's fine for a second, but then my tongue ignites, sweeping a flame across the back of my throat. I flap my arms, my eyes watering. I'm laughing, but then I'm not, because it's really burning.

I swipe out with one hand, trying to get the milk, and Cooper opens it and passes it to me, grabbing the rest of the chilli from my fingers.

'I honestly didn't think it'd be that bad,' he says.

I pour the milk down my throat, gulping it and swirling

it over the roof of my mouth. Every breath hurts, so I drink more and the cold liquid helps.

Cooper looks like he hurt me himself. 'I'm sorry,' he says.

I try to laugh, but my tongue is melting.

'Next time,' I whisper-speak. 'You do the dare.'

I watch my feet walk in the darkness next to Cooper's, our trainers in time with each other. I don't want to ask him where we'll sleep tonight. I don't want our only option to be going back to Keystone. Mind you, it's probably too late to get a train there now, even if we wanted to.

'I know it's a different pier,' I say to Cooper, 'but they might have the same security guards?'

'We didn't exactly rob a bank,' Cooper says.

'What if they've got our faces on a central system, or something?'

'We ran too quick for them,' Cooper says. 'We'll be fine.'

The lights at this time of night are a bit much, but I guess they're quite pretty against the sky. We walk with the sea either side of us and under us, almost to the end of the pier, and go into a building, into a huge room with a stage at the end.

'Is it a show, or something?' I ask Cooper.

He looks a bit like he wants to run again.

'Blackpool's Got Talent,' a boy beside us says. He doesn't look older than us, but clearly works here, in his weird waistcoat. 'Want a go?' He passes Cooper a ticket and Cooper has it in his hand and I follow him into the room.

'This really isn't my thing,' I say.

'Our other option is to sit on the street,' Cooper reminds me.

'Fair point,' I say.

But now that we're in here, he doesn't seem to know what to do, so I walk ahead, between the tables, to one furthest away from the entrance, with a couple of empty chairs. There are four other people at the table, but I don't have the courage to ask them if we can sit here so we just do and I figure they'll tell us if we can't. They're turned to face the stage, one of the women glancing back and acknowledging us with a smile, so we must be OK to be here.

Cooper copies me when I put my rucksack on the floor between my feet and we watch a man in a shiny blue suit jog towards the stage, high-fiving people as he goes.

I move my chair closer to Cooper's. 'Can we leave?' I ask.

'I can't hear you,' he says, but I know he can.

There's a strange feeling around us, not a bad one, but one that I can feel pressing against my skin. The energy of loads of excited people. Happy people. I'm sure we learned something about it in science once, a spinning together of atoms. Or maybe they're spinning apart.

A woman on the stage starts to sing and I feel bad for her, because people are laughing. Even Cooper. The man closest to him slaps the table and starts to call towards the stage. I can't tell if the woman minds. I'm sure I see a twinge of embarrassment, but she carries on singing and at the end the audience cheers like she's just won the World Cup.

Blue Suit squeezes between the tables, his bum brushing up against people's chairs. The man at our table leans towards Cooper and says something. I don't know what it is, but Cooper replies and they both laugh and Cooper glows. I'm torn between feeling jealous, but also another level of happy, that he's being seen for the person he is. And that person is enough. The man holds out his hand towards me and it makes me feel normal, if normal does exist.

'I'm Ray,' he shouts, his palm damp. 'And this is Shona.' He nods at the woman beside him.

'I'm Dusty,' I say.

'You're here on the wrong night.' Ray raises his pint of Coke. 'Dusty Springfield was last week.' When he laughs, I can see two fillings jammed into his teeth near the back.

'She's named after a baseball star,' Cooper tells him, but Ray's reply is drowned out by cheering from everywhere.

'Either of you going up?' Shona asks us.

'Cooper can sing,' I say, regretting it as soon as I do. But he doesn't look annoyed, more kind of hopeful. Even when Shona is pulling him by the arm, getting him to stand.

And the cider we had earlier must've given him more confidence than I thought, because he's walking up to the stage alone, walking between the tables as if this is totally something he was meant to do. This should be a moment when everyone goes quiet, but they're all still too loud and I've an urge to stand on the table and shout at them all, because Cooper might look relaxed, but I know that deep down he's terrified.

He picks up a guitar from a pile of instruments at the front and holds it like it's an injured bird and he's going up the steps. The woman next to Ray leans over to me.

'Is he good?' she asks.

'Yes,' I say, but I wish now that he wasn't up there, that we'd never come here, but it's too late. Cooper is on a stool on the stage, but it feels to me like he's sitting on the edge of a cliff. And I'm sitting here on my own, seeing him adjust the microphone and brush his hair from his face, though it falls again as soon as he looks down at the guitar.

He strums a note, tightens a string and people are finally going quiet.

Cooper coughs and looks over this way, but I don't know if he can see me. When I was in a dance show in the last year of primary school, there were loads of people watching, but the lights on us were so bright that I couldn't see anyone. I could only sense them, in the dark, and perhaps that's what Cooper feels now.

He leans towards the microphone.

'This is for you, Dusty,' he says.

And my heart just stops.

Shona leans towards me. 'He's an old soul,' she says.

The best soul, I want to tell her. One that the world wants to turn its back on, pretend doesn't exist. Label with bullshit and shut in a drawer and lose the key.

The room goes so silent, with Cooper singing alone on the stage. A song about how wildflowers can survive. How they might not feel right where they grow, but that's OK. It's a song about me and Cooper and Poppy and Jemal and all the others, all the places we've been planted where we didn't belong, all the times we've been uprooted and replanted. And I think that I'd go through my whole shitty life again if it meant ending up right here, watching Cooper sing.

He finishes the final note of the song and does this small shrug and everyone goes nuts, but I just sit and watch him walk from the stage and down the steps. He gives back the guitar and he's smiling so much that it hurts my mind.

Ray stands and slaps him on the back like they're old friends.

'Was it OK?' Cooper asks, but he's looking at me.

'Bloody brilliant,' Ray says.

Cooper sits beside me.

'Yeah, it was,' I tell him.

And I swear that if he smiles any more it'll break his face, but perhaps that'd be the perfect way to shatter.

The next singer is a blur and the next. I'm beginning to worry that someone might've taken some footage of Cooper when he was on the stage and will have already posted it on social media and it could match with a photo of us on some police computer somewhere.

I reach for my bag, but two new people are up there now and they're singing the song I sing to Poppy, about how wonderful life is with her in my world. Every note is a physical ache, because she's not here and I don't know when I'm going to see her again.

'You OK?' Cooper asks me.

I shake my head.

He picks up his bag and stands up.

'You off?' Ray asks us.

'Getting some air,' Cooper replies.

We walk between the tables and I know people are looking at us. Behind me, Poppy's song throws shards of glass between my shoulder blades.

Outside, I breathe in the darkness. Concentrate on the tower in the distance and pierce each one of my tears on the top of it, letting them explode amongst the lights.

'I'm so tired of holding up my world, Cooper,' I say quietly.

'I get that,' he says.

He looks at me and I know he does. There are so few people who really do. Who know what it's like to be alone and drowning in a system that wants to pass you to the next person and the next. How tiring it is to keep starting again.

From inside, we can hear people clapping and cheering.

Cooper steps up on to the bench that lines the side of

the pier. I see him step on to the thin pole of railing. He stands there, his hands stretched wide, and if he slips there'll be nothing to stop him falling into the sea.

'Don't,' I tell him.

'I'm balancing,' he says.

'Please don't,' I say.

Maybe fear grabs him, or maybe he cares that I care, because he steps back on to the bench and lies down, his bag beneath his head.

'Looks like this is our bed for the night, then,' he says.

I mirror him, lying down, my legs bent at the knees so I can fit, my feet almost touching his. I'm feeling a bit cold now that the effects of the cider have worn off, but there are worse places to sleep. Above us, the sky is a murky black, muddled by lights. Below us, water knocks against the stilts that stop this pier from drifting off.

'How many stars are there, do you reckon?' Cooper asks.

'I've never counted them,' I say.

'I tried to once, with Casper. We were sat in the park, freezing, because I'd forgotten our coats.'

'How far did you get with the counting?'

'Not very.' In the quiet I can hear the ocean, the smallest waves that have travelled from so far away. 'It's weird, isn't it,' Cooper says. 'That some of the stars don't really exist. I can never get my head round that.'

I look up, but can't see any of the stars that Cooper must see.

‘Sometimes I think I don’t exist,’ I say. ‘That apart from Poppy, no one really knows or cares that I do.’

Foster carers and social workers and teachers and friends, we always just disappear from their lives, as though we were never even there.

‘You exist in my world, Dusty,’ Cooper says.

It feels like even the moon holds its breath.

‘And you in mine, Cooper,’ I say.

People are leaving the karaoke and someone is shouting and I can’t work out how they know our names and then I remember.

‘It’s Ray and Shona,’ Cooper says, sitting up.

‘Guitar boy,’ Ray shouts, coming towards us. ‘Best act of the night.’

‘Seriously?’ Cooper asks, his smile instant.

‘Come and sing at ours,’ Shona says, when they’re beside us.

‘A few of us are going back to the house,’ Ray says. ‘If you want to join.’

Cooper looks at me.

‘Why not?’ I say.

Shona helps me up, although if anything I’m keeping her from falling over.

‘We haven’t got a guitar,’ she says. ‘But I can play spoons.’

Ray laughs and puts his arm around her and Cooper and I are following them, all the way along the pier.

We wait on the pavement with Shona, as Ray goes to get his car, and two other people have joined us and a couple of other men. It must look a bit odd, how young we are, but no one says and I get a spark of adrenaline that we're doing this, that we're going where we want, when we want. Cooper must feel the same, giving me a wide smile. We're being accepted by people and I feel the buzz of it in my veins.

Ray pulls up in his car beside us all, another car behind him. Shona steps forward, stumbling, leaning against the door that she holds open for us. I bend down and get into a car that smells of leather and sickly air freshener.

'All good?' Ray turns towards us, his elbow on the back of his seat.

'All good,' Cooper repeats, moving along so we're sat close together.

Another man gets into the car next to us. Shona sits in the front and closes the door.

'Nathan's following,' she says.

'Let's go, then,' Ray says and we're pulling away.

Cooper and I both put on our seat belts. Ray feels like a good driver. Maybe showing off a bit, one hand on the wheel, but he's in control. He's reliving the evening with Shona and she's getting a bit annoyed as they discuss accents, and I look out of the window and watch the houses go by. I don't think I've ever been out this late and it feels different. I'd like to find more hidden colours in the dark. Like with killer whales, people think they're black and white, but they're not, they're blue and purple and green and bronze, you just have to look a bit harder.

We drive further out of Blackpool and the houses become bigger and there aren't so many of them. Cooper is talking to the man next to him about a band called Ora Violet and how their lyrics are properly poetry.

'Clean Bandit,' the man says.

'I don't know them,' Cooper says.

'Look them up,' the man tells him. And Cooper nods and I wonder how we're meant to look them up with brick phones and no access to unsupervised laptops.

Shona suddenly turns in her seat. 'How old are you both?' she asks.

'Eighteen,' I say.

'You students?' she asks.

'We're travelling about a bit before we decide what to do,' I say.

She nods and if she knows I'm lying, she doesn't seem to care, turning back to look out of the front of the car again.

We go right, down a narrower road and there are no street lamps any more, so we can only see by Ray's car lights. It's dark behind the hedges either side of us. Cooper is quiet now and I'm wondering if he's thinking that we should've just slept on the beach after all. I try to send him thoughts to tell him not to worry, because these people are grown-ups and it's a good thing, being invited to theirs.

We turn into a small drive and there's a house in front

of us, one of those bungalows with rooms in the roof. A porch light shines out as far as the fence on one side and trees on the other.

'It's a nice place,' I say and Ray smiles at me in the car's mirror.

Funny that earlier Cooper and I were talking about choices and paths and we've ended up as lucky as this.

I get out my side and wait for Cooper. There's a weird smell, maybe from a black bag stuffed to overflowing in a bin. Cooper's face looks sunburnt in the porch light and I hope I don't look as pink, though my forehead and cheeks still feel a bit hot.

Ray's key is in the door when another car pulls up and a man jumps out of the passenger side.

'Oi, oi,' he shouts, his fingers linked through a hole in a box of cans. 'Lewis is here!' He's not as old as the others, his tracksuit top zipped high up to his chin. He reminds me a bit of Zane Elgar in Year 13, who I wish wasn't handsome, because he's a bit of a dick.

Ray flicks on a light switch inside a hallway.

'Make yourselves at home. Lewis, look after Cooper and Dusty,' he says. 'I'll get the drinks.'

Cooper and I stand where we are. I hadn't really thought beyond driving here. Shona goes through a door and we have to follow her, into a room that makes me smile at Cooper.

'We've come to the right place,' I say, sounding more confident than I feel.

But he doesn't seem enthusiastic, not even when he sees the leather sofas and pool table down one end.

'Fancy a game?' Lewis asks him.

'I've never really played,' Cooper admits.

'I'll teach you.'

Lewis opens the box of cans and passes one to Cooper and for some reason it hurts my heart to see Cooper thinking about where to put his bag, choosing a place beside the wall, taking three attempts to open his can.

Shona pats the place on the sofa next to her. It feels a bit patronising, but she's been friendly up to this point, so I sit with her, the leather seat squeaking as I push my rucksack behind my ankles.

'So, you're called Dusty?' she asks me.

'Yeah,' I say.

'Did you get stick for it at school?' she asks.

'Sometimes,' I say. 'I'm over it now, though.'

Ray comes in, carrying a battered metal tray with drinks on.

'My speciality cocktail,' he says.

More people fill the room and he leans down to pass me a glass. It's cold, with ice in the top of it. The liquid has separated into two, going from transparent, to a layer of dark red at the bottom. I glance over at Cooper and he's looking at me, standing across the room with a snooker cue in his hand.

'OK?' he mouths.

And I nod, but I'm not sure I am. All my confidence has evaporated. I want to tell Shona that the drink is pretty, that I wish I could scoop the colour from it and use it to paint poppies, but my words are stuck.

'You don't sound like you're from round here,' she says, swirling a straw through her drink, clinking ice against the glass.

'We're just travelling through,' I tell her.

'Where are you from?'

I struggle to keep eye contact with her. What if Cooper and I have been on the news? What if someone has been bothered enough that two kids in care have run away, our photos circulated so that everyone is looking for us?

'Southampton,' I say. It's not a complete lie. I did have an emergency placement there for a few months.

I drink some of my cocktail, in the hope that she'll stop asking questions. It tastes disgusting, exactly how I'd expect petrol to taste, but I swallow it and smile and hope she doesn't notice my eyes watering.

Cooper is trying to take a shot at the pool table and Lewis is helping him, leaning over him, his arm against his. Even when the ball is hit, Lewis stays standing in that position, until Cooper moves to get his can from a half-empty bookshelf, swigging from it as though it's something he does every day.

Another man comes and sits on the other side of me, his shirt with too many buttons undone, tufts of chest hair sticking out. He stinks of cigarettes and really strong aftershave.

'I'm Nathan,' he says. 'Ray's brother.' Biceps bulge out from beneath his short sleeves. 'Younger brother, obviously,' he laughs.

'I'm Dusty,' I say, wishing for the first time in ages that it wasn't my name, because I don't want to make conversation about it.

Nathan's thigh presses close to mine, but in fairness to him, there's not much space on the sofa. I gulp more of my drink, but it doesn't taste any better. If anything, it makes my stomach clench more.

Shona keeps stirring the ice in her glass, the noise disappearing when someone puts on music. I see Cooper wince at the song choice, Lewis laugh at him, squeeze his shoulder.

Ray stands by the unlit fireplace, deep in conversation with two men, one of them leaning against the mantelpiece, animated as he speaks, fiddling with his earring.

'Is Ray your husband?' I ask Shona, because I can't think of anything else to say.

Her laugh is high-pitched and ends up with her coughing into her hand.

'He'd like to be,' Nathan says.

Shona dabs her mouth with the back of her hand. I hadn't noticed her rings before, one that shines enough to be a diamond, but I don't know if it's real.

‘Is Cooper your other half?’ she asks me.

I see him lining up the cue, his hair falling down, but not completely in his eyes, a look of concentration on his face.

‘He’s my better half, but not my boyfriend,’ I say and both Shona and Nathan laugh and it helps me to relax.

My legs begin to feel the same as they did after the cider. Hollow, but also full of bees. I almost laugh, the thought of them filled up with buzzing wings. Instead, I stir my straw through the cocktail, seeing how the colours sink into each other.

The kitchen is brighter than the lounge, a long tube of light right in the middle of the ceiling and one above the countertop, below the cupboards. A woman in skinny black jeans gets a bottle from the fridge.

I don’t hear what Ray says, but Cooper is laughing and the sound of that makes me laugh too. The drink I’m holding is different to the last one and I only sip at it, because my head doesn’t feel straight.

It’s cold in the garden, but Ray has lent me a coat and it’s worth being outside because the stars look incredible, almost like they can’t be real because they’re sparkling so much.

Lewis is standing next to Cooper again and he’s speaking loads, but Cooper keeps looking at me and I can’t tell if he wants me to save him, or not. It’s difficult to see how far the garden goes, because it's completely dark after a bit. I don't like the way the bushes tip.

Nathan has got a small tin on the table. It looks like one that should have toy soldiers in it, but that would be weird. He opens it and there are paper rollies and he peels one from its packet and takes a pinch of something else from the tin and crumbles it on to it. I don't mean to stare, but I do, watching him roll up the paper, his tongue licking along the line and sticking it together, stroking it to make the shape perfect.

Cooper is beside me, when he hadn't been, and up close he's even more beautiful. I reach up to touch his hair, but he moves my hand and I can feel his fingers linking with my own.

'We should go,' he says.

I should ask him to kiss me, or maybe just kiss him without asking.

'You're my better half,' I say, my words swollen and bending in the wrong way.

'Dusty,' he says. 'Look at me. Seriously. I'm going to get our bags and we're going to go.'

'I don't want to sleep on the beach,' I tell him. 'I'll be scared.'

'Don't you two have anywhere to stay?' Ray asks. 'You're welcome to crash here.'

'Thank you, Ray,' I say, unlinking my fingers from Cooper, so I can put my arm around Ray. 'You're the best.'

And I kiss him on the cheek and can feel his arm around me, which helps because I nearly fall over.

Cooper looks at me in the way he does to the adults at Keystone. Pure anger.

'I'm not one of them,' I laugh, my feet tripping over each other, so Ray has to hold tighter to my waist.

A woman, who has the straightest brown hair, replaces my drink with a glass of water, but when I drink some, I feel sick. Like when Poppy and I went on a boat to France with Chris and Guy and the waves were so big that I vomited over the side.

'I loved Chris and Guy,' I tell Cooper.

Nathan's lighter makes a flame and he holds it to the rollie in his mouth and it glows and the smoke that comes out is a thick grey and smells odd. He passes it to Cooper and he passes it straight to the next person and he looks so cute standing there with his sunburnt nose and his beautiful eyes.

It's cold on my face and I like that, but I don't like Ray's arm any more, so I move away and Shona passes me the rollie and it feels different to a cigarette, fatter, squashier and I won't look at Cooper as I put it to my lips and inhale.

Near the sofa and the music is good and my dancing is on fire and I like that people are watching. No one taught me how to dance I just knew how to do it but I haven't done it in ages and I'd forgotten how good it feels. The music steps inside me. It's water and it washes everything away. Only the sound, like clouds, like thunder, and it's loud and melts the walls and twists the pictures and I close my eyes, arms in the air, knowing that they watch me.

Someone holds me and it's better with my eyes open, my brain rocks less. I don't know him, but he's smiling which is nice. And it's good to have someone's arms around me. I miss Poppy and I love her hugs, but sometimes I want bigger arms to protect me in the way I protect her and this man is doing that. He's a bit old, but his arms stroke my back and it feels good.

He's saying something to me, but the music is too loud to hear, so I laugh, because it was probably funny. His knee is between my legs, which I don't really like, so I dance in a way that he can't do that. His face is close. I shake my head in time to the music. My arms are in the air, twirling like a mermaid and his arms stay around me.

He tries to kiss me, but I laugh and push him away. His lips are wet on my ear.

'You're really pretty,' he says and it's like he's poured melting gold through the top of my head and I feel it slide all the way to my toes.

The song changes and is slower and I don't like it, because I want to keep dancing properly. We're closer to the wall and there are more people than before. I can't see Cooper and I want to see him.

The man holding me laughs, his head back, mouth wide and it's gross how there's chewing gum sat like a mangled snail on his tongue. There's a shift in his arms, his muscles twitching and the air around me begins to split. His hand goes lower and I feel him cup my bum and I really don't like it, but people are watching and I'm cool and I don't want to make a scene.

He suddenly disappears from me, a woman yanking his arm. The one with the long brown hair, who gave me water.

'She's half your age,' I hear her say.

'She wants it,' he says and I walk away because all I wanted was to dance and I want Cooper, because he'll dance with me.

I'm sat on the toilet, my head against the wall, trying to make the room stop spinning. My knickers round my ankles, like stretched skin. I'm trying to pull up my trackies, but I fall over, straight on to my knees, one hand on the sink to catch me. I have to roll on to my back, on to a bobbly bathmat, so I can pull them up.

The lock is one of those slidey ones and the door handle is round and feels smooth. I open it and the man from dancing downstairs is in the doorway, one arm above him, leaning against the frame.

'I wanted to check you were OK,' he says.

'I'm good,' I say. 'Thank you.'

I mean to walk forward, but I fall to the side and he puts out his arm to stop me crashing to the floor.

'Tell you what,' he says and I don't know how it happens

because it's so quick, but he's picked me up and is carrying me and it's funny, but it's not.

'In the garden,' I tell him.

'Best to rest it off for a bit,' he says. 'You'll feel better then.' He pushes open a door with his knee and all I see is a bed and he puts me on it. It's really soft, but I don't want to be here.

'I'm going to find Cooper,' I say, trying to sit up.

'You're best off in here.' His hand is on my shoulder and I don't like it there.

'No,' I say and try to move off the side of the bed.

'You can't be all tease and nothing else,' he says, but it's mumbled, because his face is in my neck.

'I was dancing,' I say and it's embarrassing because I'm crying, but he doesn't do anything to comfort me. He rolls on top of me and he's so heavy and I can't breathe and I push my hand into his face, but he laughs.

He's suddenly light, falling, Cooper beside him. The man yells, turns on his back and Cooper knees him between his legs. I see the man double over, his spit on his lips and I think I'm going to be sick, but Cooper is grabbing my arm and pulling me from the bed and out of the room. He has both our rucksacks in his other hand and I nearly fall down the stairs, but he doesn't stop.

We're outside and running. I'm crying and it's cold. I don't look behind me, but I can smell that man and his skin and a wave of terror crashes into me.

My tears are burning my chest and my breath is strips of light that I can't reach.

'I can't run.'

'You can,' Cooper tells me.

He's pulling me fast past hedges. We're on a bigger road and we run across it, down another street where cars are parked.

Cooper stops by a wall and my breathing is speeding round my body, shaking my legs so I have to sit. Cooper is on his phone, holding a piece of paper with a number written on it. He's peering round, saying a street name. I curl my head into my knees, feel Cooper by my side.

'He hasn't followed us,' Cooper says and I nod, but don't lift my head. 'Did he hurt you?' Cooper is sitting close, but not touching me.

I shake my head. But he did. He hurt every part of me, pulling the trigger on a different pain.

'I'm sorry,' I whisper.

'You're not the one to be sorry, Dusty.' Cooper's face has the same anger I saw on him earlier. 'I should've stayed with you.'

'It's not your fault,' I say.

But still I won't look up. Shame floods me and I press my eyes into my knees to stop it spinning too deep into me.

'I couldn't find your hoodie,' Cooper says, 'so I grabbed this on the way out.'

He puts something across my back. I don't move.

'Is it his?' I ask.

'No,' Cooper says.

I pull it closer over my shoulders. It feels like a long, fluffy cardigan. My heartbeat begins to slow. I can't hear it in my whole body any more.

'The taxi is here,' Cooper says and I look up to see him standing in the road and waving at a car. There's a man in the driving seat.

'I don't want to,' I say.

Cooper crouches in front of me. 'We need to get in it,' he says. 'It's taking us to the station.'

I let him help me up. The cardigan is a long one that reaches to my knees and I keep it clasped around me. We sit in the back seat and the taxi driver eyes me in the mirror. I stay close to Cooper as we're driven away.

The train station is deserted. It's a big, echoey place and it hurts my eyes, but when I close them the floor rocks more and I knock into Cooper.

'Where are we going?' I ask.

He's still holding my rucksack, his own over his shoulder.

'On the first train,' he says, looking up at the board. 'But it's not for a couple of hours.'

I focus on the laces in my trainers, to stop me falling over. There's a twist in one that shouldn't be there, but when I bend down to fix it, I topple.

'Fuck's sake, Dusty.' He's pissed off and I don't know how to put it right.

'You're my best friend,' I tell him.

We go to a ticket machine and he's pressing letters and numbers.

'You're very clever,' I say and it's true, he's the cleverest person I've ever met and the nicest.

Tickets flick out of the machine and Cooper gets them and puts them in his pocket.

'I don't feel well,' I tell him.

'Are you going to vomit?' he asks and I nod.

He doesn't look annoyed any more, just worried and I'm walking alongside him, but the floor won't stop sliding.

There's one of those machines with bottles of drink and Cooper chooses and slots coins in and there's a thud. He opens a bottle of water and passes it to me. I shake my head.

'You'll feel awful if you don't drink it,' he says.

The top of the bottle hits my teeth. I swallow some water and it clashes in the pit of my stomach.

'I'm going to be sick,' I say.

'OK,' he says and he's pulling me with him.

He pushes open a door and we're in the toilets and there are the cubicles and I don't want him to see me vomit, but I haven't time to close the door. I have to touch the toilet to steady myself and there's piss on the rim and I retch. I'm so embarrassed about the sound, but I can't stop it and my back curves up and there's a string of bile from my mouth and I can't hold it back and sick comes up all liquid and soaked bits of crisps and when I see it I vomit more and close my eyes and feel it pour past my throat and splash into the water. It's disgusting and it hurts and it stinks and I know Cooper is here, seeing me like this. I want to tell him that I don't want him to look, but my words are wet with saliva.

Cooper is beside me, squashed next to the toilet, holding my hair back from my face.

'You'll feel better now,' he says.

But I can smell the sick and can still feel the slime of those cocktails in my throat. I retch again. Only red liquid comes up and I spit at the end of it.

My shoulders hurt and my stomach hurts, but I think I'm done.

'We've got just under two hours until the train,' Cooper says.

He lets go of my hair and it falls on to my cheek. He passes me some toilet paper and I wipe my mouth and hands.

'I want to phone Poppy,' I say and I'm finding my bag, but Cooper takes it from me.

'Not now,' he says. 'It's the middle of the night.' He looks annoyed and I don't want Cooper to be annoyed with me.

'I want to sleep,' I say, but the words come out as a mess.

Cooper stands up and I shuffle down and rest my head on his trainers. I swallow and my throat burns and I put the memories of that bastard at Ray's house into a burning pit and send him to hell. His hands, the weight of him, the smell of him. I cut him up, piece by piece and he screams as I feed him to the flames.

'Dusty.' Cooper is nudging my shoulder.

We're somewhere weird, but I don't know where. A smell of detergent and stale air hammers through my skull. I sit up and we're in a toilet and I remember, the train station. My cheek hurts.

'Your feet were my pillow?' I ask, looking up to where Cooper stands with his back against the cubicle wall.

I'm wearing a cardigan that isn't mine and I feel a violent rush of all the things I need to forget. I sit and take it off and leave it on the floor.

'You'll probably need that,' Cooper says.

'I'm not cold,' I say, standing up.

'We've got to get the train.' His eyes are bloodshot, his head too heavy for his shoulders.

I ache all over, mostly the bones along my right side. And my throat. And my head. I open the door and wash my hands and face in the sink. I rinse my mouth through with water, which I need to swallow because I'm so thirsty, but I don't want to drink the water in here.

The station has a few people around, but not many.

'Where's platform three?' Cooper looks like he wants to punch a window. I link my arm through his, to calm him down and lead him where we need to go. Away from here. To find Poppy.

'Will it take us all the way to Newcastle?' I ask him.

'No. I'll figure out where we change.'

This train looks exactly the same as the last, but on this

one we've got a proper table and there's air conditioning blasting all over us. Maybe that's good, so it can turn last night into a frozen block. Trap that bastard so he can't reach into my mind.

I pull my feet on to the seat and look out of the window, because I don't want Cooper to see me cry. Normally when I feel like this, I'll find Rex and curl up beside him and put my hand over where I can feel his heart beating. He's never judged me. He's never made me feel like a piece of shit. I wish I could trap those good feelings in a bottle and carry them with me everywhere.

'I really, really miss my dog,' I say.

Cooper looks at me with eyes that get it.

'Fuck them,' he says, this boy who loves his words.

He begins to take his arms from the sleeves of his sweatshirt, pulls it over his head and passes it to me.

'No,' I tell him. 'You'll be freezing.'

'I don't need it,' he says.

It smells of Cooper. Of safety. I like the way it's too big for me, how the sleeves go almost to the tips of my fingers.

'Suits you,' he smiles.

'Suits you better,' I say, but I think I don't ever want to give it back.

'Do you need some water?' he asks. 'Or will it make you spew again?'

'It wasn't me who did that,' I say, taking the bottle from him. 'It was a hologram.'

I wish it had been a hologram at Ray's house, on that bed. An imaginary figure, with no feelings and no soul to scar.

'He won't know where we are,' Cooper says. I swear his mind is wired to mine. 'He can't hurt you again.'

The train begins to move. Cooper is sat next to the aisle, so anyone who comes along will have to get through him first to get to me. I reach for his hand and this time I don't let go.

Chapter Twenty-One

S35 Data Protection Act - CCTV request

Form for completion where CCTV footage is requested under S35 of the Data Protection Act. Information required by law or made in connection to legal proceedings.

Details of the person making the request

Name: DCI Sania Zadeh

Organisation: Bolton Central Police

Address: Scholey Street, Off Manchester Road, Greater Manchester

Postcode: BL2 1HD

Tel no: 0161 872 5050

Email address: SaniaZadeh@boltonpolice.co.uk

Date/Time of the incident

N.B. *CCTV footage is only held for 14 days before it is overwritten on our systems.*

Date of incident: 29/04/2026

Start time 08:35

End time 08:42

What incident the footage captured (please provide as much information as possible)

Two teenagers are seen disembarking the train on Platform 6 at Newcastle station. Female, wearing dark tracksuit trousers, a black sweatshirt, white trainers and carrying a rucksack. Male, wearing blue jeans, light-coloured T-shirt, black trainers and carrying a small grey rucksack. Next seen crossing the concourse and exiting by the main doors of the station, leading to Neville Street.

Chapter Twenty-Two

It's weird, freedom. For years, I've ached for it. A physical feeling that sometimes becomes all I'm made of. And now Cooper and I are standing outside Newcastle station, overflowing with freedom, and I don't know what to do with it. All I really know is that we have to find Poppy. And when my brain sorts itself out, there'll be a clearer path to getting to her.

We sit on a wall and I feel empty and full and confused with it all.

'Do I look as shit as you?' I ask Cooper.

He smiles, but it turns into a yawn. 'Worse,' he says.

I punch him on the arm, when in actual fact I wish I was linking mine through it.

It's still quite early, but the day is already warm. I could give Cooper his sweatshirt back, but I keep it on.

'Food would be good,' Cooper says.

'I feel like I'm eating sand,' I tell him.

He gets the bottle of water from his bag and passes it to me. There's not much left, but I drink all of it and pass it back to him empty.

We stand up again and I feel tiny in this place of huge buildings and everyone seems to know where they're going apart from us. I'm trying to look confident, to blend in, so no one can suspect that we're not meant to be here, but my stomach is a mess. It's easier when we turn down a quieter street.

'How about there?' Cooper suggests.

Across the road is a cafe with a red-striped awning above two tables out the front of it.

'You sure?' I ask him, aware that we've already used a fair bit of his money. 'We could just get a sandwich, or something?'

'I'm sure.' Cooper is heading towards it, avoiding the only car that's driving down the street.

There's a bell that sounds over the door and the smell of greasy butter and coffee makes me realise how hungry I am.

There are only a few tables and we sit at one in the middle, against the wall, with its chequered tablecloth and squeezy bottles of ketchup and mayonnaise. The girl who gives us the menus doesn't look much older than us, her hair scraped back into a high ponytail, a few strands escaping.

'Thanks,' Cooper says and she smiles and looks at him a moment longer than she looks at me, before she goes away.

'It's a bit expensive here,' I tell him.

'I'm loaded,' he replies.

I watched a film once called Bugsy something, about a load of kids pretending to be adults and that's what it feels like now, that Cooper and I are practising at being grown-ups. I'm expecting the waitress to come back and kick us out, but she stays there behind the till, folding paper napkins over cutlery.

'I might've done something a bit stupid,' Cooper says, his voice too quiet for her to hear.

'No change there, then,' I say.

Scrambled eggs on toast looks like the cheapest thing on the menu. I feel bad asking Cooper if I can have a drink as well, but I really need to have something fizzy.

'I might've taken his wallet,' Cooper says.

I look at him above the menu.

'Whose?'

'The man at Ray's house.'

'Which man?' I ask, but he doesn't reply and I know from the feeling of lead in my stomach who he means. 'Tell me you didn't do that.'

'I didn't do that,' Cooper says.

'But you did?'

'Yeah,' he says. 'I did.'

'Fuck, Cooper.'

'When I punched him,' Cooper says, 'his wallet fell to the floor. So I picked it up.'

I glance towards the door, expecting that bastard to have somehow found me here.

'I wanted to get back at him.' Cooper looks confused and angry and protective all rolled into one. 'Are you mad at me?'

'Is there any cash in it?' I'm trying to sound casual, but my heart is battering my ribs.

'I haven't checked.'

He gets a small, leather wallet from his bag. It makes me feel sick, just seeing it.

'I don't want to know his name,' I say. 'If it's on anything in there, don't tell me.'

Then he won't be real. Just a figure in a nightmare that I can wake up from.

Cooper nods and opens it. Even from here, I can see a couple of notes. He grins as he takes out two tenners and puts them in his pocket.

'That piece of shit is paying for breakfast,' he says.

'I hope he pays for it in hell.'

'You don't sound like you're from round here,' the waitress says, writing the food we want in a small notepad.

'We're just visiting,' I tell her. Cooper looks panicked and I don't know why. He stares down at the menu he's still holding, studying it as though for clues. 'Can you recommend places for us to see?' I ask, needing to sound authentic.

The waitress leans over him and points to one of the

tourist places advertised in the margins. 'You can't come to Newcastle without seeing the Victoria Tunnel,' she says. 'And the Hatton Gallery –' she drags her nail across the menu to a picture of a building – 'is meant to be really good. I've never been there, which sounds bad as I live here.'

I'm sure she's waiting for Cooper to say something, but he doesn't even look up.

'I like your tattoo,' I say to her.

'Thanks.' The waitress tucks her notepad under her arm and rolls her short sleeve higher so I can see the pattern that swirls up and over her shoulder. 'My friend Daisy did it. I'd really recommend her. She did this one too.' She turns away from us and holds up her hair. There's the smallest dragon breathing fire on her neck.

'I really like them,' I say. Cooper doesn't add anything. Maybe the fact she's so pretty has stumped him into silence.

After we've finished eating, she comes back with the bill and I'm glad that Cooper got out the money from the wallet earlier, so I don't have to see it again.

The waitress brings him his change on a little metal plate, along with a napkin that she's written on.

'If you need somewhere to stay,' she says, 'the Albatross Youth Hostel is pretty good. And I've put Daisy's address on there too, in case you want a tattoo. Tell her Kinsa sent you.'

It's the first time that Cooper actually looks at her and smiles.

Chapter Twenty-Three

I'm stuffed full from breakfast and my headache has gone. I won't try to phone Poppy yet, as she should be in school now, so we've time to go to the gallery that Kinsa recommended.

'Can you at least tell me what your name starts with,' Cooper says.

'Somewhere from A to E,' I say.

'Is that all I'm getting?'

'Yes.'

'Progress, I suppose,' Cooper laughs. 'Is it Ava?'

'No,' I reply, but I'm distracted by a woman across the road, crouching down to speak to a toddler in a pushchair. She reaches into the back of the buggy and it must be food she gets, because the girl puts it into her mouth.

'Ella,' Cooper guesses again.

The woman begins to push the buggy in the opposite direction to us. Perhaps she doesn't know that her jeans are tucked into her sock on one side. I don't know why it makes me sad.

'No, not Ella,' I tell Cooper.

'Am I close?' he asks.

'Well, it's a name,' I say. 'One of billions of others.'

'Will you ever tell me?'

'It's on a need-to-know basis,' I say. The sky is so blue, the sun bouncing off shop windows.

'Well, I do need to know,' Cooper says.

I link my arm through his and I feel him go awkward, so I pull away.

'There was a boy when I was about ten and he called me Lusty Dusty. I thought he was saying Lastly Dusty, like *and lastly, the one we've all been waiting for.*'

'Lusty Dusty sounds like a porn star's name,' Cooper says.

'Thanks for that.'

A blush colours up his neck, but doesn't reach his face.

'I didn't mean you should be one, or anything,' he says.

'Are you having rude thoughts about me, Cooper?' I laugh.

'No.' He says it too quickly and I have to keep my smile stuck in place, when all I want to say is *I think I might be having them about you.*

I swear, as soon as I step inside the gallery, I can feel it. Like in that film about that boy who does ballet. Electricity, but not in wires. A low hum in the centre of my bones.

I look at Cooper, but I don't think he notices it.

'Where do you want to go first?' he asks me.

'All of it,' I say.

I reckon it's the same thing that people get when they've got a home that's theirs. Like I belong here. And the building is so beautiful, all high ceilings, with a dome window right at the top. The massive columns and echoey floors make me think I'm in some really rich person's house.

The first room is huge and open and filled with abstract art. It's never been my thing, but I understand why people get it.

'I could do these,' Cooper says, his face stuck on that confused expression he gets.

'You couldn't.' It seems wrong to speak in here, like we're in a sacred space. 'Look at the lines. The colours.'

Cooper peers closer to a painting, in a way that would annoy a teacher.

'I'm looking,' he says.

It's actually annoying me a bit and I don't want to have that feeling about Cooper, so I walk through the room, breathing in the colours, whispering a silent sorry to the artist that I didn't stay. These pictures would've taken years of their life, dragged up from their guts and I'm pretty much ignoring them, drifting past as if they don't matter.

We're in a room with strange sculptures at one end of it. I've only tried pottery once and I was rubbish at it, but

I loved it. I walk towards them and can remember the feel of wet clay in my fingers, how it let me sink my thumbs into it, but wouldn't do what I wanted it to.

'These are just weird,' Cooper says.

'Talk quieter,' I tell him and feel a bit bad, because he looks hurt.

'We're the only ones in here,' he points out.

But I can sense the artist, their eyes and hands and heart, pulsing at the edge of the room. We're close enough now to see it all. The chair with what might be a baby, but it hasn't got a head and is held down by a belt strap. Beside it, not too close, a melting form that can only be its mother. I feel it right in the centre of my stomach, the force of a punch, but a gentle one.

There's a strange, bird-like form, bent towards the ground. The texture ruffled and smooth all at the same time. A rope keeps us from getting too close to them, but it's overwhelming, my need to step over it and touch the sculptures, to step inside them, to become part of them.

Cooper starts to giggle beside me.

'Not sure what that's meant to be,' he says, pointing to a mound of blue. 'It looks like a steaming pile of crap.'

Whistle-quick anger flares in me.

'If you don't like it, you don't have to stay,' I say.

But he's proper laughing now and I don't even know if he hears me. A woman comes into the room and I'm so embarrassed. That we look like dumb kids, who don't get it.

I go as far away from Cooper as I can get, but he stays with me, trying to hold in his laughter, making stupid snorting noises.

'I actually want to be on my own for a bit,' I tell him.

He wipes under his eyes. 'I'm better now. Honestly. I've stopped.' But he's got a smile he can't hold back and I'm surprised that I want to shout at him.

'I'll meet you at the entrance when I'm done,' I say, guilt blazing when I see the confusion in his eyes. 'Come and find me there then.'

And I walk away from him and it's hard, because I feel something pulling me towards him, that any second I'll hurtle back, like on an elastic band, but I make it to where the room ends, leaving Cooper behind.

I thought it was what I wanted, but I feel lost. I've somehow gone from being whole, to half of me, without Cooper. Leaving him has made me miss Poppy even more and knowing that she's not here with me makes it difficult to breathe. I should sit down, but I have to keep moving. I need to find a way through this aching.

I go through a room of paintings of buildings and don't get me wrong, they're amazing, but they don't walk into my soul.

I feel small, going up the stairs. There are more people here and it seems like I'm shrinking, when I don't want to be. This is my place. I should be able to grow and fill it, until there's no way anyone can get me out and I'll have to stay here forever.

At the top, I go into a smaller room and I can tell, instantly, that this is the one that'll blow my mind. It's all black and white, so I'm surprised the effect it has on me, but the drawings are insane. I stand in front of the first one, not too close, because I want to see it all. The spider's web is so detailed and although you can tell it's been done with a pencil, my brain is taking a while to understand that it's not a photograph.

I want to tell Cooper that they remind me of the salt artist, but he's not beside me and I feel a lunging hit of regret. He was only laughing. That was his way of reacting to the art and surely that's what every artist wants, to make people feel something. Like here, with these pencil drawings, it's hard to explain, but I can almost taste the lead. It sounds mad, but looking at them makes me feel it's in my teeth. I wish I could tell Cooper, even though I know exactly what his face would look like.

'They're beautiful, aren't they?' I hadn't noticed the man come in. He's much older. I can imagine the pencil artist drawing the fine lines on his face.

'Yes,' I say.

'It's my favourite room in the gallery, at the moment,' he says, his eyes on a drawing of the surface of the sea.

'They're so real,' I say, 'but they're also not.'

He nods. 'I think you're right.'

I'm right. I don't think anyone has ever said that to me. It gives me an unfamiliar confidence, like this old man is opening a door to a new world for me, letting me step through.

'You can feel it, the water, the sound of the waves.' Somehow I don't feel stupid saying this. 'But when I notice the pencil lines, something stops me.'

He looks at me now, like he's really interested.

'Not many people can explain it in quite such a way,' he says.

I'm scared to say more, as I don't want him to realise that I'm only dumb old Dusty, but he's the first person I've met who I think will understand. Not even Miss Grajek, the best art teacher I had, could make me open up like this. Maybe this is what freedom is.

'I feel like I'm drawing it with her,' I say. 'That it's a shared process.'

'Symbiotic,' he nods.

'Yeah,' I say, though I've no idea what he means.

'There are very few artists who do that to me,' he says and I move with him in front of a drawing of a night sky. The darkness and the stars. 'Mary Cassatt, definitely. Perhaps Vermeer, to a lesser degree.'

I look up at him. Because Mary Cassatt is who I studied in Year 10. I wanted to choose someone different to everyone else.

'*The Fitting*,' I say, relieved and proud that I know one of her paintings.

The man looks at me and I'm sure he's surprised. '*The Fitting* is one of my favourites.'

'Although I'm not a massive fan of pastels,' I admit.

'You prefer strong colour?'

'Yes.' It's terrifying and amazing having him really listen to what I've got to say. It does something funny to my lungs, but it's a good feeling.

'Yet you're moved by these pencil drawings?'

'It's out of our control, isn't it?' I say. 'Chemistry between things.'

'Are you an artist yourself?' he asks me.

I laugh. In a universe not yet invented, my paintings would hang on this wall. 'I wish.'

'Do you paint?'

I look at him and I'm trusting him.

'It's one of the only things I live for.'

He puts his hand on my arm, as I'd imagine a granddad might. 'There's always something worth living for, however small,' he says. 'You're lucky, you have the driving force of art. For you, there'll always be another picture that needs to be painted.'

He takes out his wallet and for a moment I think he's going to give me money, but he passes me a card with a name written on it, in the centre of squares of colour.

'If you ever want a gallery to work in,' he says. 'Get in touch.'

The card is smooth and solid and fragile in my fingers.

'I'm Terence,' he says. 'It's been a real pleasure to meet you.'

He pauses for my name.

'I'm Dusty,' I tell him.

He smiles. 'That's a name I'm not likely to forget.' He holds out his hand for me to shake. 'Well, Dusty, I hope our paths cross again.'

He turns and goes and there's only the sound of his shoes on the shiny floor. I listen to them, until I can't hear them any more.

Cooper is sitting on the steps outside the museum. Even though I've been ages, he's still waiting for me. He's got his eyes closed and maybe I shouldn't disturb him, but I'm so happy to see him again and I want to have that feeling when he looks at me. I stand so that I'm blocking the sun, my shadow on him, and he opens his eyes.

'Hey.' He smiles.

'Hey,' I say.

I move a bit and the sun spills across his face and he puts up his hand to shade his eyes.

'I'm sorry.' He says it more like a question.

'Me too.' I sit next to him and it's so good to be this close to him again. 'Did you see any other rooms?' I want to tell him about the gallery owner I met, but I don't want him to think it sounds creepy, when it wasn't anything like that.

'A few,' Cooper says. 'Then I went shopping. I bought myself a hoodie from a charity shop, courtesy of the bastard's bank card.'

'It worked?' I ask.

Fear of that man creeps in from where I've tried to keep it in the shadows.

'I used my own money to get you this –' Cooper opens his rucksack and pulls out a big plastic bottle of salt '– so you can do a picture like that salt guy.'

He passes it over and everything else melts away, because it might just be the nicest thing anyone has ever done for me.

'What's our plan, then?' Cooper asks.

I'm not sure if I should tell him that I don't really know.

'First, I'm going to call Poppy,' I say, putting the bottle of salt in my bag and getting out my phone. It's always a bit embarrassing using it in public, because I'm sure people must see it and wonder why I haven't got a proper one.

There are four missed calls from Jen, but I ignore them and dial Poppy's number. It rings and rings. I glance up at Cooper, as if he can magically get her to answer.

'No reply?' he asks.

I let it ring some more, pushing it hard against my ear.

'Maybe she's still in a lesson,' I say, which is a good thing, but my chest hurts when I think of her alone in a new school, walking down strange corridors, girls being nasty without me to protect her.

It takes every effort to hang up.

'I've got a load of missed calls from my social worker,' I say.

'She'll only be asking where you are,' Cooper says, 'but you should check them in case.'

I nod and listen to the first one. Cooper's right, it's Jen waffling on about me coming home. *Home?* She's joking, isn't she? I hope in most homes there aren't adults ramming you into the wall just because you piss them off. The next message from her sounds angry, saying she needs to speak to me and the next is more panicked. None of them are about Poppy, so I delete them all.

'We'll have to find something else to do until I speak to her,' I say.

'We could go to the angel,' Cooper says.

'What angel?' I ask.

'There's a massive metal one by the road,' Cooper says. 'I didn't realise it was near Newcastle.'

He's not making sense to me, but because it's Cooper, I don't mind.

'Do we walk there?' I don't tell him that I'm too tired and would prefer to find a park to sleep in.

'Taxi,' he says. He waves that man's wallet in front of me. I get a horrible, swooping feeling that knocks from my neck to my feet. I want him to chuck the wallet, so I never have to see it again, but there's also a part of me that wants to drain the bastard's bank account.

I stand and hold out my hand to pull Cooper up. And amongst all the wrong, nothing has ever felt more right than this.

'Let's go find our angel,' I say.

Chapter Twenty-Four

AFFIDAVIT - FRAUDULENT USE OF A CREDIT OR DEBIT CARD

Privacy & Confidentiality notice

The information in this document is intended for the information of GM Police only.

Investigating officer: PC John Gerrick

Case number: VT 29/04/26/3462

Credit card/ATM card/**Debit card**

Complainant/Victim: Brandon Wright

Incident: Debit card stolen from 16 Sheldon Road, Blackpool, at around 0200 hrs on 29/04/2026 Debit card used to purchase two chocolate bars from Clayton News, Clayton Street, Newcastle, and a sweatshirt from Oxfam on Percy Street, Newcastle.

Date of report: 29th April 2026

CCTV from Clayton News shows a young male, white, approximately 6ft, dark hair, slim build. Wearing blue jeans, white T-shirt, black trainers, carrying a grey rucksack. Details circulated.

Chapter Twenty-Five

The taxi drops us in a small car park on the side of the motorway. The sound of cars melts away though, when we turn the corner and see the angel, standing on its small hill, with its massive arms stretched wide. I know what he's been talking about now. I've seen pictures of it.

'It's enormous,' Cooper says.

'I didn't realise this is the one you meant,' I say.

It gets bigger as we get closer, its rusting colour cutting through the blue sky above it. At the bottom of the hill, we stand and just look at it. It's so huge, but shrinks into me.

A woman races with two children up the path through the grass, their laughter catching and falling. Cooper and I watch them and I'm sure he'll be thinking the same as me, because I doubt we'll ever be able to see a mum and her kids without thinking it.

The angel looks down on us as we go up towards it. There's something really protective in its wings.

‘We could live here,’ I say to Cooper.

‘On a hilltop?’ he laughs.

‘There are worse places,’ I say. We could set up camp, and bring Poppy and Cooper’s brother to live with us. In the angel’s shadow where no one could hurt us again.

Cooper starts to walk round it, but I walk the other way, as I need to phone Poppy. The base of the angel has metal ridges big enough to stand between and I hide myself in one, with no room to move. I look out at the grass and the trees and the road and the sky, at the tops of the buildings of Newcastle carving their own way. All those lines that hold all those places that hold all those people. People I’ll never know and who’ll never know me. Or Cooper. I can’t imagine anyone’s life without Cooper in it.

Poppy would love this. She’d stand in the indent next to mine and I bet she’d start to sing, out of tune and beautiful. I know I don’t usually believe in God, but I whisper a prayer to the angel to keep Poppy safe. I get my phone from my pocket and crouch down, cocooned by the statue.

There’s the ringing tone and this time she answers, her voice so close.

‘Prim?’ I ask.

‘I thought it’d be you,’ she says.

She sounds a bit happier. ‘Who else is going to phone you?’ I laugh.

‘I’ve got loads of people wanting to speak to me,’ Poppy says.

'One day, they'll be queuing down the road for you,' I tell her.

'No, there really are people wanting to talk to me. About you,' she says. 'Like the people from the home you were in. And the police.'

My skin goes cold. They're looking for us.

'Don't worry, they won't find me,' I tell her. 'Katniss is impossible to catch.'

'Jen keeps harassing me to tell her where you are.'

'Ask me where I am, then,' I say.

'Ask me first,' Poppy says.

'I know where you are,' I say. 'Newcastle.'

'No,' Poppy says. 'They moved me on.'

She's not here?

'After one night?'

'I guess that's the meaning of temporary.'

The wind picks up and catches me on the neck.

'But I've come to find you,' I say. 'In Newcastle.'

Poppy is so silent, for such a long time, that I think she's gone.

'I'm not there,' she says.

And it feels like I've been forced away from her all over again. That I was holding on to her, but I've lost my grip.

'Where've they put you?'

'With a woman called Amira.' She's whispering now.

'Where?' I ask her.

'Sunderland,' she says.

'Where's that?' I ask.

'Jen said she tried to tell you.'

'I didn't answer when she called.'

'Amira's coming,' Poppy says. 'I've got to go.'

'Message me your address,' I tell her.

'I will.'

'Is she good to you?' I ask.

'Yes,' she says.

And her phone is silent.

Cooper appears and he looks so sad that I don't want to tell him about Poppy not being here. He sits down beside me and he looks up to the sky where a bird flies without moving its wings, it just kind of glides. I wonder if it can see Poppy, or whether Sunderland is too far away to have us both in its sight.

'I had a sister,' Cooper says.

I think I must've misheard him. 'A sister?'

'Cira,' Cooper says. 'She was my twin. She died when we were seven.'

The clouds, the sun, the earth all stop. My heart too. Cooper had a sister? A twin? For a moment I disappear into a hole so black and resurface to see him pushing up the sleeve of his hoodie, showing me words written in a tight scrawl.

'A heap of broken images, where the sun beats,' he reads. 'Eliot feels like a link to Cira, you know? When I read his poems, it's like she's talking to me.' He brings his knees up to his chest. 'Is that weird?'

'No,' I tell him honestly. I want to say that it's beautiful, but there's no beauty in his sister not being here. And I want to ask him how it can be that she isn't, but I know there's a reason he's kept her hidden, that talking about her could be what finally drowns him.

'They never told me where they put her ashes.'

Cooper looks at me and a crater has crashed through the candle in his eyes.

'They wouldn't let me know, in case I tried to run away to find her.'

I can't find the right words to comfort him. They're too far out of my reach, swamped by the avalanche of wrong decisions that adults have made. Cooper breathes in, fills his lungs with the angel's air, as though he's trying to get it to take the space of all his hurt.

'When we were younger, we had our own language,' he eventually says. 'No one else understood it and we didn't really either, but I always knew what she was saying.'

I think of Cooper, with his sister, and I know what he means, because I can read Poppy's mind just by looking in her eyes. The thought of never doing that again makes panic flood me, yet that's how Cooper must feel every day.

'We used to do that thing,' he says, 'where people would ask Cira to think of a number or a colour and I always guessed it, because we'd spend hours planning the answers. Colour?

Yellow. Number? Seven, unless it was up to a hundred and then it was fifty-six. I still go through our list when I can't sleep.'

'Do you imagine her answering it with you?' I ask.

'Always,' Cooper says. 'It keeps her alive.'

I think of her here, curled up beside him.

'What food is she thinking of?' I ask.

'Ice cream.'

'Animal?'

'Orangutan,' Cooper laughs.

'Orangutan?'

'We had to have some that were unusual, to make it seem real.'

'Country?' I ask.

'Canada,' Cooper says.

'Sound?'

There's another silence.

'I don't know,' he says. 'We never did that one.'

I want to tell him to ask her, but I'm worried that she won't reply.

'Perhaps the sound of a seagull?' I suggest.

But if he hears me, he doesn't say. I stay as silent as I can and hope that he can hear Cira.

We look out over the grass and I reach for Cooper's hand and hold it so tight, make myself an anchor for him so that his grief doesn't lift him away. There's the lightest wind on my face and I wonder if Cira is here. I imagine her running around this angel with Cooper, laughing in their language that only the two of them can understand.

'Apparently, there are memorials in the trees here,' Cooper says. 'Can we leave something for Cira?'

'We can do anything we want to, Cooper,' I say.

I get up, still holding his hand, helping him to stand. Down the hill and into the trees. Deeper in, I see things hanging from branches and closer still, there are teddies and old candles tucked between the roots.

'It's like a church,' I whisper. There's silence and thoughts and prayers, under a ceiling of leaves.

Cooper kneels down beside a little wooden box. Inside it, there's a plastic red jewel, on top of a folded note. Cooper closes the box and looks up to a string of beads attached to a low branch. They've obviously been here a long time, their colour dampened with mildew.

'I'm going to leave a letter for Cira,' he says, 'but I don't want anyone reading it.'

'We'll have to get it on to the highest branch we can,' I suggest, taking my rucksack from my back and getting out a pencil and my sketchbook. 'You can use this.'

I can't imagine it, if the only way to speak to my sister was leaving a note, with her never being able to reply.

Cooper takes the paper and pencil and goes on his own to sit on the ground, leaning against a tree. If I painted him now, there'd be so little colour.

I stand away from him and see all the memorials people

have left here. There's so much loss gathered in one place, pressing against my chest and my face. It makes me think of my mum, yet there's no space here for my own hurt and it's different in any case. I lost her, but she didn't die. Somewhere, she exists. But I don't know what words I could write to her to hang from a tree.

I use my feet to clear a patch of earth. When it's big enough, I crouch and sweep it with my hand, my fingers brushing roots. The trees are dense enough to block out the heat, to create that damp smell of a time before I even existed.

I pick up a thin stick and it reminds me of a picture on a Christmas card that my second Year 5 teacher, Miss Edwards, gave me, of a robin with its twig-like legs and footprints in the snow. For a while, it was my most precious thing, until they made me move home again and I ripped it into the smallest squares and threw it from my bedroom window.

I snap the stick in half and start to draw and I don't mean to draw my mum, I really don't, but now she's here, lying on the earth in front of me, her outline the same as when she'd been sleeping on the kitchen floor and me stepping over her and I remember the taste of the only milk left, lumpy and sour and I wanted to spit it into the sink, but I had to drink it.

I drag my hand hard over the picture. Push her further into the ground. Burying her, because it's the safest place for her to be.

Cooper is beside me as I stand up and kick leaves over the space, as though it was never there.

'Shall we hang your message to Cira?' I ask him.

Cooper wipes his eyes and under his nose, his face raw.

'I could go on your shoulders,' I suggest.

'Will you be OK with that?' he asks.

'Trapeze is my middle name,' I say.

He smiles his Cooper smile. 'What's your first name, though?'

'Good try.' I smile back at him. 'You need to go really low and stay close to the trunk, so I can steady myself.'

Cooper crouches right next to the tree, holding the trunk to give himself balance and I sit across his shoulders, my legs either side of his neck, my feet still on the ground.

'You sure?' he asks.

'Never been surer,' I say and he begins to stand, wobbling. I can still touch the tree with my hand, but hardly at all, so it's not going to be much good in stopping me falling.

'OK?' Cooper asks.

'You sound like I'm really heavy,' I say.

'You are,' he says.

'Oi.' I swipe at him with my foot, but it makes him sway to the side.

'Dusty,' he says, all serious.

Cooper stands straight, trying to stay on the same spot. There's a branch not far above me and I grab for it, pulling it down to my level. It helps me feel more secure, even though it's bendy and will most likely snap if I lean on it too much.

'Pass me your letter to Cira,' I say and Cooper has to let go of one of my ankles to give me the piece of paper bunched in his palm. 'Stay still.'

'I'm trying,' he tells me.

'I'm going to have to pierce it slightly,' I say. 'You OK with that?'

'She won't mind,' Cooper says.

I'm determined not to break through any of his words, so I get the corner of the paper and push it carefully on to the smallest part of the branch. I imagine it piercing through Cooper and through Cira, joining them together again. I hope that wherever she is, she knows we're doing this. I hope she knows forever how much her brother loves her.

'Done?' Cooper asks.

'Yeah,' I say. I take my hand from his message and it unfolds enough for me to see the word *sorry* written in Cooper's messy, beautiful handwriting.

Chapter Twenty-Six

The entrance to the hostel has a light broken, so the only one working shines directly on to the front desk. The boy sitting behind it glances up from his phone.

'I'll be a second,' he says, thumbs rapid fire across his screen.

The desk has lost most of its varnish and there's not much on it, apart from a computer and a bell to press, which I want to ping, but I don't. On the wall, a plastic display thing is stuffed full with leaflets, the ends of them curling over themselves. I glance at Cooper. He hasn't said a word about Cira since we left the angel.

The boy swears and drops his phone on to the desk.

'Sorry,' he says. 'Bad timing.' He's got a circular earring in his ear that's rammed right into the lobe, stretching the skin.

'Do you have a room?' I ask.

He leans over to the computer and types on to the keyboard.

'We've got a bunk in the dorm,' he tells us. 'Happy with that?'

'Is there a shower?' Cooper asks.

'A shared bathroom,' he says. I want to ask him if he ever takes out his coin-shaped earring and if it leaves a massive hole. 'How many nights?' he asks us.

I look to Cooper. 'One?' He knows now that Poppy isn't in Newcastle any more. Sunderland isn't too far, so we just need to figure out what we do next.

The boy behind the desk lifts the card machine, taps buttons on it and faces it towards us. Cooper takes a bank card out of the bastard's wallet. He won't look at me as he presses it to the top of the machine.

'Other way, mate,' the boy says and Cooper turns the card.

The boy looks at the screen. 'That didn't work,' he says. 'Hang on, you can try it again.' He presses the buttons. 'Perhaps with your pin this time?'

'The pin number?' Cooper asks.

'Or try tapping again?' the boy suggests.

Cooper presses the bank card to the top of the machine and I'm trying to look as casual as I can, when inside I'm a swirling mess.

'No, sorry, mate,' the boy says. 'It's still not working.'

'That's OK,' Cooper says, putting the card back into the wallet. 'I'll pay with cash.'

He takes notes from his pocket. His fingers are shaking,

but I don't know if the boy notices as Cooper counts the correct money. The boy takes it from him and slips it into the till and gets a set of keys.

'Keep the noise down after eleven. Bathroom is a couple of doors down the hall from you. Separate toilet. It's all obvious, there are signs. You're on the second floor, last door on the left. Sorry about the view.' He passes the keys to Cooper.

'Thanks,' I say.

The boy picks up his phone. 'Stairs and lift round the corner,' he says, pointing to an archway.

Cooper and I follow his instructions and step into the lift. I look up into the corners and don't see cameras, but I can't trust that there aren't any, so can't tell Cooper yet about the fear that's creeping in, that the police might be tracking the bastard's card and that they'll be able to find us here.

We play-fight each other for the buttons, reaching for normal, when inside me a black cloud is looming and waiting to break.

There's the sound of the lift doors opening on the second floor and we're in a narrow corridor that smells of waxy cleaning stuff. We walk past the toilet and the shower, to the door at the end.

But Cooper's confidence is a thin layer and it takes two attempts for him to get the key in the lock. He swings open the door and two people look at us, from where they sit on the floor playing cards. I check the door number. This is definitely eight, like we were told.

'New room-mates.' The woman nearest us has a strong accent, Australian I think. She's got to be at least ten years older than us, her red hair coiled on top of her head with strips of ribbon. She looks amazing, like a maypole.

'Come in,' the other one says. Her hair is cropped so short that I can see her scalp. 'You're not disturbing us.'

'We're on these two bunks,' the red-haired woman pats the bed beside her, with its tangled sheet and a pillow leaning against the wall. 'You can have any of the others.'

'Be warned, though.' The one with the crew cut picks up a card and puts down another. 'The top bed feels like you could crash through at any moment.'

'I'll have this one, then,' I say, moving into the room, swinging my rucksack on to a top bunk.

'You want to fall through the bed?' Cooper asks me.

'I'd prefer to be the one crashing through, than crashed on,' I tell him.

The crew-cut woman laughs. 'I like your thinking.' She lays her cards in a fan on the floor, face glowing with victory. 'Want to play?'

'I'm going to shower first,' Cooper says. He looks at me and I know we need to speak alone.

'I'm going to make a phone call,' I say, climbing up the bunk's ladder to get the phone from my rucksack, leaving the bag where is.

I don't know whether I'm meant to say *we'll be back in a minute* to these strangers who won't care whether we are, or aren't.

The panic on Cooper's face is instant, as soon as we close the door behind us. He doesn't seem to know what to do, so I walk towards the shower room and we go inside. There are two cubicles and I check they're both empty.

'The bank card didn't work,' he says, 'so he must've reported it's been stolen.'

'Can they tell where we are when you just tried to use it?'

Cooper leans back against the sink. 'I don't know. Maybe?'

The smell of bleach in here is making me feel sick. 'Shall we go and stay somewhere else?'

Cooper begins to bite the skin around his thumbnail. 'We'll run out of money if we have to pay for somewhere else tonight.'

I put my hand on his arm, can feel the shudder of adrenaline in his veins.

'Maybe they won't know where we are yet,' I tell him.

His eyes look into mine and ground me and spin me all in the same breath.

'Perhaps he doesn't want the police involved,' he says, 'after what he did.'

Or perhaps, I think, our faces are pinned up on police noticeboards all across the country. They'll find us and separate us, send Cooper to a secure unit because he's got no chances left.

'So, our options are to stay here,' I say, 'or sleep on the street.'

Cooper nods. 'Let's stay here for tonight.'

'And leave tomorrow morning,' I say. 'When we've found out exactly where Poppy is.'

'OK,' Cooper says, more settled.

'Right,' I say. 'I'm going to phone her again.'

In the corridor, I stay in sight of the shower-room door. The phone rings only once before I hear Poppy's voice. She's in a different universe, too, too far away. The sound of her crying reaches inside me to twist my guts.

'What's happened?' I ask her.

'I miss you,' she says. 'I don't want to be here on my own.'

'I'll find you,' I tell her. 'I asked a taxi man where Sunderland is. It's not far. Cooper and I can get a bus.'

'When?' she asks.

'Tomorrow,' I tell her, hoping it's a promise I can keep. 'We'll come and get you.'

'OK,' she says.

'Did your new carer get some more eczema cream?' I ask her.

'Yes,' she says, sounding happier.

'Good. And what about school?'

'Jen says she's getting it sorted.'

I feel such a violent rush of anger that Poppy will be

starting in a new school without me. That she'll be walking down corridors I've never seen. That she'll have no one to speak to at break when she's feeling terrified.

'Are you eating all your greens?' I ask, needing to calm myself, to find a sense of normal.

'No.' I'm sure she's smiling at the thought of me always hiding broccoli under the cheese on her pizza.

'Wearing clean clothes, though?'

'Yes,' Poppy says. 'And how's Cooper? Do you still *like* him?'

She manages to gather my anger in her angel wings and turn it into laughter.

'He's nice,' I say.

'Nice?'

How do I tell her that he's all the best words? That Cooper gives me his sweatshirt when I'm cold and writes poetry on his arms. That I think I want to kiss him. And that I swear his star has been hurtling towards mine since the day we were born.

I feel miles better after a shower. I stood under that warm water and let it run over my face and down my body and tried very hard not to think of Cooper. I didn't have a towel and so shook myself dry as much as I could, wiping the rest of the damp with my T-shirt.

My hair is still wet, but the bedroom is warm. Cooper and I sit with Orla and Sancha in a circle, our knees almost touching. I've laid the cards exactly how they told me, but I still don't really know what's going on.

'What does an ace do again?' Cooper asks, his rucksack still on his lap.

'It's a wild card,' Sancha tells him.

Orla picks a card from one of her piles, but groans and collects the ton of cards from the middle.

Sancha leans across Cooper and he lets her look at his cards. 'Do that one next,' she says.

'Kind of cheating,' Orla says.

'Kind of needed.' Cooper puts down a seven of clubs.

'So, how long have you two been travelling for?' Orla asks us.

'Only about six weeks,' I say, calm as anything.

'What do you both do?' Sancha asks.

'Travel.' Cooper laughs.

'You must need to work along the way?'

'Not at the moment,' Cooper says. 'We've got enough.'

'Lucky for some.' Orla rolls and unrolls a blue scrap of ribbon in her hair, looking at the three cards in front of her. She turns the middle one over. 'Yes!'

'What's Australia like?' I ask them.

'New Zealand,' Sancha corrects me.

'It's on our list to visit,' Cooper says.

I'm way out of my depth now. My geography is rubbish, so if they ask us whereabouts we want to go, then I won't have a clue.

'I'm out,' Sancha says, slamming down her last card on the pile.

'On that note,' Orla says. 'It's time to go out. You two want to come?'

'We're going to start at the Old George Inn,' Sancha says. 'It's the oldest pub in Newcastle.'

She stands up and pulls Orla to her feet. There's an ease between them and I wonder how long they've been together, how they met. I want to tell them that they've no idea how big their world is compared to ours.

'I'm a bit tired,' I say *and we'll get kicked out the pub in any case.*

'Yeah, me too,' Cooper says, his bag still tucked close to him. 'Let us know if it's good and we might go tomorrow.'

I ache to have their choices. To be able to go out the door and just keep walking, not worrying that there are eyes on my back.

'I'm going to get a tattoo.' Cooper's voice drifts up to me from the bottom bunk in the half-dark. 'Kinsa, the girl in the cafe, I'm going to go to her friend.'

'It'll hurt,' I tell him.

'I'm good with that,' Cooper says. 'I'm going to have Cira's name.'

I pull the thin duvet around my shoulders, even though it's too warm in the room.

'That's a beautiful thing,' I say.

But it fills all the hollow parts of me with sadness.

'Will you design it for me tomorrow?' Cooper asks.

'I'd like that,' I say. I touch my hand to the wall, the same wall that touches against Cooper below me. 'What was Cira like?' I ask.

There's a silence, but it's not a bad one. It's like Cooper is leaving a space for his sister to exist again.

'She was the other piece of me,' he says. 'The better part, though. She was quiet, but she was funny.'

I can't imagine there being a better part of Cooper.

'I never stop missing her.' He says it so quietly that I'm barely sure he's spoken. 'One minute she was there and the next she wasn't. It was only a friend's dad who tried to make sense of it for me. He told me that Cira was gone, but that she'd still always be with me.'

I think of the note he wrote her, attached now to a branch in the dark amongst those trees.

'Why did you say sorry to her, Cooper?' I ask him.

He doesn't answer.

'I didn't look at it on purpose,' I say.

The room becomes too heavy, blocked with my thoughts and his thoughts that usually match, but now it feels like they're avoiding each other, looking for cracks to disappear through.

'Because it's my fault she died,' Cooper says.

My mind spins, falls.

'Our mum's boyfriend was beating us,' Cooper says.

'And I shouted at Cira to run. He was hitting her and I got between them and I screamed at her to go.'

'That's a good thing, Cooper. A brave thing.'

'She ran out of the house and across the street without looking. There was a car, going too fast.'

I don't want him to fill in the gaps. I never want him to relive what he must have seen.

'It wasn't your fault, Cooper. You've got to believe that. You're not the one who did something wrong.'

'I did everything wrong,' he says.

'Did you make her laugh?' I ask.

'Yes.' Cooper sounds confused.

'And she knew you loved her?'

'More than anyone.'

'Well, that's enough,' I tell him.

'But I didn't keep her safe.'

The room feels darker.

'That wasn't your job, Cooper,' I say. 'You only had to love her. And you did that.'

I turn over on to my side and hang my arm over the edge of the bed. Light from the street outside is pushing through the curtains, showing me how he reaches up to put his hand in mine.

'What do you think happens when we die?' Cooper's words fill the room, sudden and too bright.

'I don't know,' I say, his touch pulsing through me. 'I hope we go somewhere.'

'How would that even work?' he asks.

'In RE once, we were told about an experiment where they weighed someone just before they died and then just after they died and they were lighter. So they must've had a soul that left their body.'

Cooper doesn't reply, but I'm sure if I could see into his mind, I'd see his thoughts spinning.

'I believe in ghosts,' I say. 'Too many people have seen them for them not to be true.'

'Some souls get stuck here?'

'Maybe they choose to stay,' I say.

Someone shouts out on the street and laughter spirals up. I think of Cooper's grief that he carries, needle sharp, cutting through the skin of his heart.

'For ages, I was convinced Cira wasn't dead,' he says. 'That they were hiding her from me. Or that she didn't want to see me for some reason.'

I feel his hurt within me, sticks lit between my ribs, the burn spreading.

'We could go to that big church tomorrow,' I say. 'The one we went past with the really tall spire. We can have our own funeral for her.'

I can hear Cooper breathing. 'I'd like that,' he finally says.

And in the silence, he doesn't let go of my hand.

Chapter Twenty-Seven

I wake in the morning light, turn on my back and stare up at the ceiling. I wish I'd never found out how Cira died. I know that's selfish, because Cooper has to live with it every second of every day, but I can't get the image out of my head. Of Cooper trying to save her. Of his sister running from hell into a nightmare worse than any I can imagine.

So, I do what I always do. Package the sorrow in a box, store it away where I can't see it, move my mind to a brighter place. I sit up, the bed squeaking, take my hairbands from my wrist and tie two spiky ponytails, my point of contact for lightning.

There's a rush of movement from the bottom bunk and Cooper jumps out of the bed. I try to ignore how good he looks in his T-shirt and boxer shorts.

'Have you got my bag?' he asks me.

'Morning to you too,' I say, beginning to climb down the few rungs of the ladder.

‘I’m serious, Dusty. My bag’s not here.’

‘Did it fall under the bed?’ I ask.

Cooper kneels down and looks beneath the bunk, and I feel a crazy jolt of electricity seeing his naked legs.

‘It’s not there.’

We both look to Orla and Sancha’s empty beds at the same time.

‘Have they gone?’ Cooper asks, even though it’s obvious they have. There’s absolutely nothing of theirs here.

‘You think they picked up your bag by mistake?’ I ask him.

‘I kept it in the bed with me, Dusty,’ Cooper says. ‘Closest to the wall.’

‘Did you sleepwalk with it?’

Cooper doesn’t even pause to look at me. ‘I don’t sleepwalk.’ He searches under their bed, pulls back their duvets. He yanks on his jeans and is still doing them up when he runs out of the room and I follow him, down the stairs that he jumps three at a time, landing by a door that he charges through. There’s a girl sitting behind the desk.

‘They stole my bag,’ Cooper tells her. He goes out the front door of the hostel in his bare feet, looking up and down the road. ‘They’ve gone.’ He’s back at the desk. ‘They stole my bag.’

‘Who did?’ The girl doesn’t look much older than us and slides her chair slightly further away.

'Orla and Sancha,' Cooper says. 'We shared a room with them last night.'

'One's got a shaved head,' I say. 'The other has lots of hair and ribbons.'

'They checked out a couple of hours ago,' the girl says.

'But they've got my rucksack,' Cooper tells her. I put my hand on his arm to try to calm him.

'We'll have their details on the system,' the girl says, softening towards Cooper.

'We can track them down and get it back?' Relief spills through him.

'The police will hopefully be able to.'

I've still got my hand on Cooper's arm and I feel him tense.

'Did you have your wallet in it?' the girl asks. She looks at the screen and then writes something on a piece of paper. From upside down I can see it's Orla and Sancha's names.

'No,' Cooper says. 'I slept with my wallet in my pocket.'

'Anything valuable in the rucksack?' She moves the mouse, clicks it and looks up at Cooper.

'A letter for my brother,' he says. 'And my poetry book.'

Wings beat inside me. *His book.*

'You're a poet?' The girl sits up straighter, starts to smile.

'No,' Cooper says.

'It's his most important thing,' I say, but immediately wish I hadn't, because Cooper's book is more than can be explained to a stranger. How the pages hold the breath of a person who gave him hope. A foster carer who gave him a reason to keep living, to keep fighting.

'Was your phone in the bag?' she asks.

Cooper nods. He doesn't tell her that it's a shit brick one.

'Shall I call the police?' the girl asks, looking uneasy again.

'We'll do it,' I say and pull Cooper with me.

We walk in silence up the stairs and to the room, stay silent as we go inside and don't speak as we search it again. I go to check in the shower and the toilet, but Sancha and Orla haven't left the bag there.

Cooper sits on the floor, his back against the bed frame.

'It's really gone, Dusty,' he says.

I sit in front of him and he's searching my eyes for a different truth, but I can't give it to him. His poet's words sneak in faded ink up his arms, almost washed away from his shower last night.

'The worst thing,' he says, his voice falling into the shadows inside him, 'is that they'll probably throw it away. It won't be any use to them.'

'Then maybe we'll find it?'

'It could be anywhere, in any bin in the whole of Newcastle.' Cooper's laugh doesn't have a speck of happiness.

Orla and Sancha have no idea that they've taken a sledgehammer to his soul.

Chapter Twenty-Eight

I wish I could sit right here on the pavement and draw a picture of the church to show to Poppy, but Cooper has been shattered by his stolen poems and I'm going to stay by his side.

The doors are open and the heat follows us in, but stops short of the first benches. And normal sound doesn't come inside either. There's the strangest quiet, how I'd imagine shrinking and entering an atom would be.

'Cira loved castles,' Cooper whispers. 'I reckon if she's stuck around, then she'll be here.'

The ceiling is so high, the sunlight joining with the glass colours in the windows, spilling into patterns along the columns of stone and across the floor.

'Where do you think the candles are?' Cooper asks me.

I choose to walk left, I suppose because it's clockwise, and we go behind the benches and down the thinner aisle alongside them.

‘How come my trainers are squeaking, when yours aren’t?’ I ask Cooper.

His smile makes me think he’s forgotten, just for a second, about his book.

‘I’m a hollow man,’ he says. ‘It’s why I’m silent.’

His poet’s words. So, not forgotten at all.

We go past brutal paintings of Jesus being nailed to a cross, and right at the front there’s a small room, not closed off, but with wooden arches carved with berries and leaves. Beyond it is a statue of a woman holding a child and next to it, tons of tiny, flickering candles.

‘Do we just go and light one?’ Cooper asks.

I look around, but there’s no one to tell us. And no one to stop us if it’s wrong. ‘I guess so.’

There’s not much light in here and no window and the carpet makes us even quieter than before. We have to go up a step to the candles and Cooper picks one up and tips it, unlit, towards the wick of another’s flame, holding it steady until the flame transfers to his.

If I were to capture Cooper in paint, in one moment, I think it’d be now. The reflection of the light on his face, his mind travelled far away.

I step from him, to leave space around him for Cira.

In the corner, near the start of the wooden arches, I crouch and take the bottle of salt from my bag. The nozzle on it is difficult at first, but I crack it open and keep it almost shut, so only a bit of salt will come out. And I begin to pour it so slowly on to the carpet, creating a heart, with a *C* inside. It's difficult to do and a bit messy in places, so I tidy it up using the edge of my little finger.

From Cira's heart, I make a trail of salt drops leading along the side of the wall, towards the candles. Footprints for her to follow, to find her way to Cooper. He looks over at me and doesn't need to ask, because he knows. He turns his back to the candle flames.

'She's here,' he says.

'She'll never leave you, Cooper,' I tell him.

He nods and I reach up to wipe away his tears.

Chapter Twenty-Nine

From: JohnGerrick@westdivisionblackpool.co.uk
Sent: 30th April 2026 12:49
To: SaniaZadeh@boltonpolice.uk
Subject: Fraudulent use of debit card

Hi Sania,

As requested, an update on the fraudulent use of Brandon Wright's debit card.

There was an attempt to use the card at the Albatross Youth Hostel, 51 Grainger Street, Newcastle. The card was declined. CCTV footage is being analysed, but we have a description of the person attempting to use it: male, possibly mid to late teens, dark hair, wearing jeans, carrying a grey rucksack. Accompanied by a girl, possibly mid to late teens, blonde hair with a fringe, also carrying a rucksack. Both were relaxed and friendly and gave no indication of either anxious or threatening behaviour.

If I can be of further assistance at this stage, let me know. I will keep you updated of the outcome of the CCTV and any further developments.

Regards,
PC John Gerrick

Chapter Thirty

I didn't feel comfortable getting the bus to Sunderland, too many people who could be looking for us, with no chance of escaping if anyone got us on the actual bus. But we made it and we're here early, waiting by a massive bit of grass, with football goals either end.

There are houses close by, so we sit by some trees around the edge, even though I'm convinced there could be cameras here. Perhaps I'm just nervous that Poppy won't be where she said. Or that we'll get to the house and there'll be a police officer waiting outside.

I pick up a leaf from the ground and stick its stalk into the earth.

'Do you wish you'd brought your guitar when we left Keystone?' I ask Cooper.

He's writing poetry on his arm, remembering every word from his stolen book.

'Yeah. I don't feel right without it.'

A bird appears above us and disappears.

'If you got to meet one singer,' I say, 'who would you choose?'

'Do they have to be alive?' Cooper asks.

'No.'

'That'd be a one-way conversation.' He writes the end of a word, pressing the biro in deep, almost enough to puncture his skin. 'The person I'd choose is alive and her lyrics are insane. You know when you can't imagine that a song never existed?'

'Not really,' I admit.

'Well, she's good-looking as well,' Cooper says.

'So, that's the real reason?'

'Probably,' he laughs.

And I wonder how we managed to walk into each other's lives. That he's the thing I can't imagine never existed.

'Can you draw a hollow man for me?' he asks.

'How do I draw that?' I ask.

'Whatever you imagine him to be like.'

'Do I have an option?'

'No,' he says, pushing the pen into my hand.

'I'm not very good if I don't have something to copy,' I say.

'Better than me.'

'Where shall I put him?'

'Here.' Cooper points to words that follow a line, from

the back of his arm to the back of his hand. *This broken jaw of our lost kingdom.* The last word, *kingdom*, wraps around his thumb.

I start to draw a square. 'This isn't going to be good,' I warn him. 'This is his body.' And I draw two legs, so that the hollow man is walking from letter to letter.

'He's headless,' Cooper points out.

'Not for long.' And I draw a big, square head, with no eyes, or a nose, but a smile that curves all the way from one side of his face to the other.

And I begin to fill the hollow man with so many things. With music notes and a guitar and the word *hahaha* round in a circle.

'He's not very hollow now,' Cooper says.

'That's because he's never really been hollow. He's stuffed with brilliance.'

'Can you draw a hole for him to fall into?'

'Nope,' I say, passing the pen to him.

Cooper holds up his arm to look at my drawing, his hand reaching beyond the shadow of the tree and into the sunlight. I know I shouldn't be thinking it when he's so sad, but he's so damn beautiful. It's like, if you wanted to draw a perfect face, you'd draw Cooper. And the maddest thing is, he has no idea.

He looks at me and sees me watching him. He reaches out for my arm and he's touching me and I think the world will stop spinning and I'll fall off. He's going to kiss me and

I'm not ready and I am ready, but instead he begins to write on my skin.

I start to laugh. 'It tickles,' I say, and my reaction is to pull away, when all I want is for Cooper's hands to be touching me.

He writes an *L* and an *O* and keeps writing, but it's upside down and hard to read. He's concentrating so hard, looking only at my bare arm, turning my skin meaningful with his poet's words.

'Which poem is it from?' I ask.

'"The Waste Land",' he says. 'The bit about a hyacinth girl.'

'What does it say?'

'*Looking into the heart of light, the silence.*'

I know that paintings are my thing, but this melts me. Maybe it's because I'm so close to Cooper and his fingers are on my wrist, but the ink sinks into my veins and I swear I taste the words.

'There,' he says. 'Done.' He puts a full stop at the end, but keeps his hands there and I'm the one who pulls away, which is ridiculous and I don't know why I do it. My body just did something that I didn't want it to do.

'That's cool,' I say.

And Cooper begins to write on his arm again, tiny letters to fit in as many of his poet's words as he can, before he forgets them.

*

We're walking towards Southside Gardens when I see them. Poppy, with a woman who must be her foster carer. It takes the strength of the universe not to rush towards them, but I know Cooper and I can't be seen.

I pull on his arm to stop him.

'That's Poppy,' I whisper.

We watch them. I see how they're chatting, Amira walking slowly by my sister's side. She looks kind, like Poppy said. Older than I thought, wearing a chunky blue cardigan even though it's warm, and she's got Crocs on her feet. She looks at Poppy as they talk, really paying attention to her.

We can see them until they turn the corner and disappear.

'You OK?' Cooper asks me.

'Yeah,' I say, although seeing Poppy has created a mess of love and chaos in my stomach.

'She looked happy,' Cooper says. And I nod. 'She might've got a good one.'

'I hope so,' I say.

'Shall we follow them?' Cooper asks.

'No, let's wait,' I tell him. 'We've only got one chance to get this right.'

Cooper and I walk along the street where Poppy now lives. It's everything I'd hoped she'd get. There are houses and each one of them has a drive and most have a car out front. I'm scared, though. Scared of cameras hiding where we can't see them. Scared that there'll be police waiting to jump out on us. That I'll find my sister, but they'll separate me from Cooper.

'Do you think they've got the house under surveillance?' I ask him.

'We're not that important,' he says, but his eyes aren't settling easy on anything and he's scratching his finger with his thumbnail.

'What number again?' he asks.

'That one,' I say.

We're almost in front of it and we slow to a stop. I get my phone from my bag and text her. *We're here.*

'Should we hide behind the car?' Cooper asks.

'It'll look too suspicious,' I say. Houses line up on the other side of the street and anyone could be watching.

'What if her carer comes out with her?' Cooper asks.

'Then we run,' I say. 'And if Jen is here, we double-run.'

Cooper squeezes my hand. 'I'll be with you,' he says.

The front door of the house opens and he lets go and Poppy looks so small and out of place standing there, in a stranger's doorway, in a street I've never been in. She sees me and stops.

I wave at her and her smile is the sweetest thing and she runs over and throws herself at me. I just want to stand here like this, holding her so tight that neither of us can breathe, but she's left the front door open and so I pull her and Cooper to sit with me on the ground, hoping that if any neighbour sees us, they won't suspect a thing.

'This is Cooper,' I say.

'Hey,' he says and Poppy grins at him, all goofy and gums and he smiles at her. The world's most precious people both together by my side.

'We better get out of here quickly,' Poppy says, 'before Amira sees that I've gone.'

It's only now I realise that she's got a small rucksack with her. Panic almost winds me.

'You can't come with us, Poppy,' I say.

I might as well have hit her.

'But you said.'

'Not yet,' I tell her. 'I just need to figure a way.' I stumble on my words.

'Is your carer nice?' Cooper helps me out.

'Yes.' Poppy nods, eyes Bambi-wide at him.

'And you feel safe?' he asks.

'Yes,' Poppy says.

'That's good,' Cooper says.

'But I want to be with you two.'

'You will be,' I tell her.

'What if they stop paying for your phone?' she asks. 'How will I get in touch with you?'

'They won't.' I'm confident in this. Jen wouldn't risk cutting off contact with me.

'You sure?' Poppy asks.

Someone is calling my sister's name.

'Is that Amira?' I ask her.

Poppy nods again. 'But I want to come with you.'

I think of that man at Ray's house. Of the dark streets. Of the fact that we've got nowhere to sleep tonight.

'It's not safe,' I tell her.

'So, it's not safe for you either?' She holds so tight to my hand.

'We're fine.' Another lie. They're stacking up. 'We'll come and see you tomorrow. We'll have more of a plan.' There's got to be a way that we can make this work.

'You promise?' Poppy asks.

'We promise,' Cooper says.

Amira calls again from inside the house.

Poppy leans towards me and hugs me so hard that I think her arms will sear through my T-shirt and be forever imprinted on my skin.

'Cooper is definitely a Gale,' she whispers. The boy Katniss should have chosen.

She always manages to make me smile, even when my heart feels like it won't go on beating.

'I love you,' I tell her.

'I love you too,' she says, standing up and hurrying towards the house.

'Don't forget to brush your teeth,' I whisper, but I don't think she hears.

'There you are,' I hear Amira say. She's not angry. Her voice is as perfect as it should be. 'Are you all right?'

'Yes,' I hear Poppy reply.

Amira says something else, but I don't know what it is. The sound of the door closing. My sister gone.

Chapter Thirty-One

'You want to do this?' I ask Cooper.

'Definitely,' he says.

We're back in Newcastle and I feel strangely empty and alive, having seen Poppy, but leaving her behind. *Tomorrow*, I think. *I'll see her tomorrow and come up with a plan.*

I ring the doorbell, because it doesn't look like Cooper is going to. He's all wide-eyed and fidgeting from foot to foot. We wait and then there's the sound of footsteps and a lock sliding back. A girl stands in the doorway, smaller than Cooper and I, but probably a couple of years older. She holds her wild curls from her face.

'Are you the couple from the cafe?' she smiles. 'Kinsa told me you might turn up.'

'We liked her tattoos,' I tell her, Cooper not saying a word.

'Her dragon one, or the root tendril?' she asks.

'Both,' I say. 'Cooper was wondering if you could do a tattoo for him?'

'Of course,' she says, opening the door wide to let us through.

We're in a narrow hallway, with a pile of shoes stacked against one wall. The stairs in front of us have hardly any carpet left, the floorboards showing through in the middle. Someone has written *keys* on the wall, but there's only a hole in the plaster next to it, where a hook must've been yanked out.

'My tattoo equipment is cleaner than the house.' Daisy laughs and we follow her into the kitchen. 'I cleared a spot in case you were coming.'

The table is sparkling compared to the rest of the room, with two chairs sat next to it. I look at Cooper. It's not too late for him to back out.

'Right,' Daisy says. 'Cooper, isn't it?'

'Yeah,' he says and he blushes and I realise that she's actually really pretty in a way that elves are cute. She looks good standing next to him and it makes my stomach flip. 'This is Dusty,' Cooper says, touching my arm, which makes my stomach flip all the way back again.

'So, have you got a picture for me?' Daisy asks.

'It's in my sketchbook.' I find it in my bag and turn to the right page. 'Cooper told me what he wanted and I drew it for him.'

Daisy takes it from me. 'Cira,' she says. 'Pretty name.'

She looks at Cooper, but doesn't ask. It wouldn't take a genius to see the sadness covering his skin.

'Where do you want it put?' Daisy asks him.

'Over my heart,' Cooper says. 'Is that OK?'

'That's fine,' Daisy says. 'But you'll have to lie down for it.'

'Here?' I ask.

Cooper is way too long for the table and he can't go on the floor.

'We'll have to go in the other room,' Daisy says.

'Have you cleaned in there?' Cooper asks and Daisy laughs.

'No,' she says. 'But all my equipment is good.'

I frown at Cooper. I'm sure tattoos should be done in a place better than this.

Daisy gathers things and we follow her back towards the front door and into a lounge.

'Could you open the curtains?' Daisy asks, using her elbow to clear a space on a small table. A few books fall to the floor, but she doesn't seem to mind.

Cooper climbs over a stool to get to the window and he pulls open the curtains, letting in the afternoon light. Daisy picks up some clothes from the sofa and throws them on to an armchair. I know this place will be unsettling Cooper. It couldn't be more different from his immaculate bedroom at Keystone.

'Should be just enough space for you,' Daisy tells him. 'If you take off your top, I'll get ready.'

Cooper is definitely hesitating and I don't know where to look as he pulls up his T-shirt. He passes it to me and I'm trying to act like this is OK and normal, but his jeans are low on his hips and he's more toned than I'd imagined. I can't help glancing at where his flat stomach disappears beneath his belt. I pretend that his T-shirt in my hand is fascinating, but it smells of him and I think I might be more lost to this boy than I'd realised.

Daisy drags the table nearer to where Cooper lies on the sofa. He's rearranging a cushion under his head, but still doesn't look comfortable. Daisy grabs a stool for herself.

'Anywhere you want to sit is fine,' she tells me. The armchair is closest, so I move the clothes that Daisy threw on it. She looks at me. 'Cool hair by the way.'

'Thanks,' I reply. I keep my face expressionless, but she's no idea what her words do. She just gave me a topped-up cup of liquid sunshine to drink.

Daisy puts on some thin, plastic gloves, the type you see in horror movies.

'What's with all the writing on your arms?' she asks Cooper.

I've got so used to seeing words written there, that I'd forgotten what they might look like to a stranger.

'T.S. Eliot,' Cooper says.

Daisy lifts his arm to look at them, some smudged, some easier to read. 'Weird,' she says. 'But nice.'

Cooper's eyes usually shine when he talks about his poet, but Sancha and Orla have poured earth over his brightness.

'This,' he says, twisting his arm to show the underside of his elbow, 'is the best line ever written.'

Daisy peers closer. '*His soul stretched light—*'

'Tight,' Cooper corrects her. '*His soul stretched tight across the skies.*'

'What's that even mean?' Daisy asks.

There's a sinking disappointment in Cooper.

'Whatever you want it to mean,' I say. Because I don't know much about this Eliot guy he's obsessed with, but I do know that his poetry does something to the air.

'This one's good,' Daisy says. '*Until her teeth were only accidental stars.* It sounds like they've been punched out and left jagged.'

Cooper nods and stares at the words.

'So,' Daisy says, looking at the tattoo design in my sketchbook. 'Just the name and this trail of stars?'

'Yes,' Cooper says.

She bends her head over a piece of paper and begins to write Cira's name. It's strange, seeing someone copy something I've done. And even though it's about something so sad, it fills my stomach with wildflowers.

'Like this?' she holds it up to show Cooper.

'Yeah, that's good,' Cooper says. He looks at me and smiles and clenches his teeth.

'She hasn't even started yet,' I laugh.

'Getting prepared,' he says.

'Point exactly where you want it,' Daisy says and Cooper shows her.

Daisy leans over him, her bare arm against his bare skin and I know she's just doing what she's got to do, but it creates a shambles in me. Especially when she rubs some liquid soap on to his chest and begins to drag a razor over the bit where the tattoo will be. Cooper looks at me and I almost laugh because neither of us thought that this was part of it. Daisy lays the paper flat over the right place. She rubs over the top of it and begins to peel it off, showing Cira's name transferred to where it will always be.

'Try not to move,' Daisy says, picking up what looks like a pen with a weird swollen bit where she holds it. 'If it gets too much, tell me.'

'OK,' he says, closing his eyes.

I see the needle touch the skin over Cooper's heart.

'How long have you been doing tattoos?' I ask Daisy, partly because I'm interested, but partly to distract Cooper from the pain.

'I've done a few on friends,' she says. 'They pay me less than in a shop because I'm still learning.'

'You're not going to make a mistake?' I ask.

'I hope not,' Daisy says.

Cooper's eyes are still closed. A drip of sweat slides from his forehead and into his hair. I'm such a mix of emotions right now. I want to protect him, but lean over and kiss him all at the same time. I want her to stop hurting him, but more than anything I want to feel him beneath my palm.

'You still there, Dusty?' he asks, barely opening his mouth.

'Not going anywhere,' I tell him.

'Good,' he says.

Daisy concentrates and I watch as little jabs of colour cut through the drawn lines. It's red, so I can't tell if it's Cooper bleeding.

'So,' Daisy says. 'Why the name Cira?'

A heartbeat of pain crosses over Cooper.

'She's my twin,' he says.

'Does she know you're having this done?' Daisy asks.

'I hope so,' Cooper says.

I want to tell him that Cira does. That she's nestled next to his heart and can feel the vibrations of the needle, can see the inked stars filtering through his skin to catch in her hands.

'I've got a brother too,' Cooper tells her. 'I'll get his name when this one's healed.'

'People you love are the best tattoos,' Daisy says, focused intensely. 'So, what are you two doing in Newcastle? You don't sound local.'

'Travelling through,' I say, too quickly. I swear the truth

must burn like a beacon above our heads, but Daisy doesn't seem to notice.

'All around the UK?' Daisy asks.

'Until the money runs out,' Cooper says.

'Where are you staying?' she asks.

'We haven't figured out tonight yet,' I say.

Daisy's hand is steady. She doesn't look away from the tattoo she's creating.

'There's a party up at Jesmond Dene,' she says. 'If you want to come.'

'Where's that?' I ask.

'A park we go to, by a waterfall.'

Cooper opens his eyes and looks at me.

'Will your friends mind us being there?' I ask.

'Not at all,' Daisy says. 'It's not really like that round here. And you can show them my tattoo.' She laughs. 'So it'll be free advertising for me.'

'Sounds good,' I say, even though I can tell that Cooper is trying to communicate that he's not sure it is. And I'm trying to tell him, *I think we can trust her.* And at least we'll have somewhere to go, while we figure out seeing Poppy again.

'Are you going to get one done, Dusty?' Daisy asks, without looking up.

Before I came here, I definitely wasn't, but now I'm tempted. It's art, after all, but a permanent type.

'How much does it hurt, Cooper?' I ask him.

He opens his eyes again. 'A lot,' he admits. 'But less now than at the beginning.'

'Bearable?' I ask.

'Yes,' he says, though he's got sweat above his top lip.

'You two make the cutest couple,' Daisy says. 'You should get each other's initials.'

Neither of us tell her that we're not a couple.

Cooper looks at me again. 'I could have a D,' he says. 'And you could have a C.' As though of course this makes perfect sense. And the thing is, it does.

'DC,' Daisy laughs. 'When you hold them up together, you'll be Wonder Woman and who else?'

'Wolverine,' Cooper smiles. 'We've got to do it, Dusty.'

'Yeah,' Daisy says. 'You do.'

She blows across the tattoo she's inked and I've got to say it's not looking so great at the moment, bleeding a bit, with the skin all raised red. And I'm not sure it's something I want to happen to me.

Daisy sits straight and stretches her arms above her.

'I'll get a mirror,' she says. 'Bear in mind that it'll be back to front and not at its best yet.'

She stands up and goes from the room. Cooper sits and looks down at his chest.

'How does it look?' he asks.

'Sore,' I say. 'I think she's done a good job, though.'

Daisy comes back, carrying a mirror specked with toothpaste.

'There you go,' she says, holding it in front of Cooper.

'Will it take long to heal?' he asks.

'A few weeks, if you look after it properly.' Daisy gets what looks like cling film and lays it flat over the tattoo, smoothing over the top of it until there are no creases. 'Don't get it wet for two weeks. When it's time to take this off, you've got to wash it twice a day with soap and then moisturise it.'

Cooper looks over the mirror at me.

'I'll remind you,' I reassure him.

'Your turn?' Daisy asks me.

I get up and go and sit next to Cooper, wishing he'd put on his T-shirt again, so that it's easier to think straight.

'We're really doing this?' I ask him, my arm against his arm, fizzing sunshine to my stomach.

'Looks like it,' he says.

'Where are you going to have them?' Daisy asks.

There's no way I'm taking off my top and sitting here in my bra. And anyway, I want it somewhere I can see it.

'Inside our wrists?' I suggest.

'On your pulse point,' Daisy says. 'Cool.'

'You OK with pain?' Cooper asks me.

I look at him with a half-smile. 'What do you think?' I say.

He takes my hand in his, still hot with sweat from his own tattoo. I squeeze it tight, holding out my left wrist for Daisy.

'You know,' Daisy says. 'I think Accidental Stars would be a cool name for my business.' She rubs liquid soap on to my skin. 'What do you think?'

Cooper's smile makes him glow. 'Sounds good,' he says.

Daisy drags a razor over the inside of my wrist, even though there's no hair there. I don't look away as she puts the needle on my skin. I don't move at all with the sudden searing burn. I thought I'd pass out, but I like it. The ink transferring from the sharp tip, deep into me.

Cooper squeezes my hand again. 'OK?' he asks.

'Yeah,' I say. 'It's fine. It's actually good.'

I watch as Cooper's initial transforms a blank space of nothing into everything.

Chapter Thirty-Two

Amira: *Hi, Jen, it's Amira. How are you?*

Jen: *Amira? Is Poppy OK?'*

Amira: *Yes, yes, sorry I should have said straight away. Poppy's fine. She's lovely, actually. Obviously a bit nervous, but she's settling in. My cat has already taken to her.*

Jen: *Is she coping without Dusty?*

Amira: *She misses her a lot. It's why I'm phoning.*

Jen: *She knows we haven't found Dusty yet?*

Amira: *Yes, she does. I'm being honest with her about everything. But I'm concerned that the loss of Dusty is too much for her to cope with.*

Jen: *It was Dusty's choice to run away.*

Amira: *They were separated before that.*

Jen: *They're allowed to speak every day.*

Amira: *That's not enough. Poppy is lost without her sister.*

Jen: *It wasn't an easy decision. I know it's not ideal.*

Amira: *It couldn't be further from ideal.*

Jen: *Well, if there's one good thing to come out of all of this, it's that at least Poppy is with you. She deserves a bit of luck. They both do.*

Amira: *Poppy glows when she talks about Dusty.*

Jen: *Bless her.*

Amira: *Jen, I'm not going to keep Poppy without Dusty.*

Jen: *You're not keeping her? But we organised this as a more permanent placement.*

Amira: *It will be. But I'm going to make space for Dusty. I can clear out the study. I don't use it often.*

Jen: *What do you mean?*

Amira: *It's not a huge room, but it'll fit a single bed.*

Jen: *You're going to take both of them?*

Amira: *They can't be split up, Jen, we both know that. Jen? Are you still there?*

Jen: *Yes. Yes, I am. That's the best news.*

Amira: *I'm not going to tell Poppy yet. Not until you've found Dusty safe. Are you any closer to that?*

Jen: *We're working on it.*

Chapter Thirty-Three

Cooper and I sit on the railings of the bridge in the dark, our legs hanging over the edge. It's a very big drop to the water below, so I don't look down. Cooper already finished his burger in about three mouthfuls and is licking cheese sauce from his fingers, close to where my initial is seared into his skin. My own wrist throbs with a satisfying ache.

I didn't think it'd be possible to be happy without Poppy beside me and I wish I could tell Cooper, but I don't, because my life has taught me to keep my thoughts locked in. That anything I love, I lose. And so I sit and stare out over a city sparkling with a thousand lights and tell myself that this moment is enough.

'Do you know, I wish I could be in a band,' Cooper says.

Far below us, lights hit the water. Behind us, cars drive over the bridge.

'You can be in a band, Cooper,' I say.

'I saw a film once,' he says. 'And the guy in it was a guitarist in a school band and I wanted to be part of it so much it nearly made me sick.'

'One day you'll meet people who want to be in one with you,' I tell him.

'You think?' he asks.

'I know,' I say.

'I'd like to have had the same chance as others, that's all.'

'I know.'

I lick my fingers clean and look in my rucksack for a biro. Cooper doesn't ask what I'm doing, he just watches me, his legs swinging over the drop.

'I'm going to write our story,' I say. 'How we want it to go.'

Cooper's hyacinth girl words curl along my left arm, but the other has all the space to rework our future. The first thing I write is *rock star*.

Cooper grimaces. 'I don't want to be one of those,' he says. 'I just want to play music.'

I don't change the words. 'What else?'

'Just to stay out of jail,' he says.

'I'm only writing positive things,' I tell him.

'OK,' he says. 'I'd like to walk out of my house without someone having to follow me. Every day, be able to go where I want without being watched.'

I nod. I so get that. It was one of the worst things about being at Keystone.

I draw a pair of shoes, walking down the centre of a road.

'And I'd like to have kids,' Cooper says.

'How many?' I ask.

'Four.'

I draw them in a row. Four stick kids with the same hair as Cooper.

'Shit,' I say.

'What?' Cooper looks over his shoulder to the policeman I'm looking at, walking definitely towards us. Cooper stares back at me. 'What do we do?' He looks down at the river below us.

'Don't you dare jump, Cooper,' I say. 'Don't you dare fucking jump.'

The policeman must see the shift in Cooper, as he starts running. I don't move. It's like I can't. I've become a part of the bridge, welded to it.

The policeman's running towards us, one hand pumping the air, the other on his belt. He's running and I watch and he's in slow motion, but he's not, because he's fast and now he's right below us, breathing hard.

'That's not the best place to sit,' he shouts up. He's trying humour and it takes all my strength not to tell him to piss off and leave us alone.

'It's a bit cooler up here,' Cooper shouts down to him. 'There's a bit of a breeze.'

The policeman laughs. 'It's a hot evening,' he says,

‘but you can’t be sitting up there. We’ve had motorists phoning in about you.’

‘Sorry,’ I say. ‘We’ll come down now.’

He waits, watching us, arms folded across his chest in a way that only police officers are able to do. I start to move, but my legs are shaking.

‘You want me to go first?’ Cooper asks.

‘I’m fine,’ I say. Already I’ve one foot on a kind of rung and I look up at him. ‘You better follow me.’

My hands are slippery with sweat, but if I fall now, it’s only a short way to the pavement. I feel the policeman’s hand on my back and I jerk away. He holds up his hands.

‘It’s OK,’ he says. ‘I’m only helping you.’

I look up at Cooper, but he’s not starting moving, he’s only sitting there.

‘Come on,’ I shout up.

The policeman is looking at him too. Cooper begins to follow the route I took. I send him silent messages to stay calm, not to kick off, to do whatever the man says. And to run if there’s even a hint that he knows who we are.

But Cooper is all broad smiles and charm. ‘Sorry, officer,’ he says. ‘Probably a bit stupid of us.’

‘More than a bit,’ the policeman says. He’s looking at us as though he recognises us, but can’t figure out where from. ‘What made you think it was a good place to sit?’

‘We didn’t think,’ I say, grabbing Cooper by the hand and pulling him with me.

'We won't do it again,' Cooper says, bowing in a way that could irritate this man and send him from nice to nasty in a heartbeat.

I smile the sweetest smile I can manage and raise my eyebrows to the policeman. *This boy.* And turn and go and we walk slowly, Cooper squeezing my hand in a manic Morse code, which I understand completely.

We keep walking and I've no idea if the policeman is still watching us. We cross the road at the end of the bridge and follow the pavement round a corner. And then we run.

Chapter Thirty-Four

'Hey, DC,' Daisy says and I'm sure she's not pretending that she's pleased to see us, even though it's only been a few hours since we were first on her doorstep. 'How are the wrists?'

'They're good,' I tell her.

'Give me a minute.' Daisy leaves her front door wide open and I see her go into her kitchen.

'Is this a good idea?' Cooper asks me.

'Every idea is a good idea,' I say.

Standing beside Cooper fills me with all the best feelings. I barely want to breathe, in case I pop them.

Daisy comes back, a coat and blanket over one arm, a bag in the other.

'Right,' she says. 'I'm ready.' She closes the front door and walks through the middle of us to go down the steps. We follow her and I think Cooper will hold my hand, but he doesn't.

'Ryan is driving us,' Daisy says. 'My boyfriend.'

'We're going by car?' I want to grab Cooper to a stop. We're going with strangers, to a place we don't know, just like in Blackpool. Fear swells, sudden and suffocating, but I stay walking with them.

We stop by a car already filled with people. Daisy opens the passenger door and leans in.

'We've got two more,' she says.

I want to shrink and run away.

'There's no space,' the person driving says, who I think must be Ryan.

'It's all right,' Daisy tells him. 'One of them can go in the boot.'

'I'm fine with that,' Cooper says and he walks to the back of the car with her and even though he's only about a metre away from me, he might as well have stepped off the end of the earth.

I watch Daisy lift the boot and I don't know whether to put my hands in my pockets, or cross my arms, so I put them in my back pockets, but feel stupid standing like this.

The car door opens and a boy looks up at me.

'Getting in?' he asks.

I don't know you, I should say. *I'm not sure I want to.*

'Thanks,' I reply and sit in beside him, Daisy slamming the boot.

She gets in the front. 'Everyone, this is Dusty and Cooper.'

'Hi,' I say and I'm sitting here so close to this other boy, my whole leg pressed up against his. The person the other side of him reaches across, his hand outstretched for me to shake.

'I'm Haz,' he says and his eyes tell me I can trust him.

'Nice to meet you,' I say, keeping my voice steady, as though this is totally normal for me.

Ryan starts the car and I look over my shoulder to Cooper, but he's hidden under blankets. I don't even ask him if he's all right.

Daisy turns the music up so loud that I can't hear her conversation in the front. Ryan keeps looking over at her when he's driving and he's smiling wide. I tell myself to relax. That not every man is like that bastard with the wallet. That there were good people at the party in Blackpool. I tell myself that it feels good to be here. Adulthood is waiting with open arms and I'm ready to step right in.

The car park we stop in is empty.

'The moon is massive,' Haz says, getting out before any of us.

'Hunter's moon,' Daisy says.

'You know what they say about them.' Ryan laughs from his seat in the front, grabbing his keys from the ignition and his sunglasses, which is a bit weird as it's night-time.

Daisy is already helping Cooper out of the boot by the time I get to him.

'You been here before?' Haz asks me.

'No,' I say. 'First time.'

'Jesmond Dene virgins.' Ryan laughs again.

Cooper doesn't and he looks at me funny, like we shouldn't be here.

'Shall we explore on our own?' I ask him.

'You can't go wandering round here at night if you don't know it,' Daisy says, linking her arm through mine. 'You'll have a great time, I promise.'

I want to be holding Cooper's hand, but now I'm walking with Daisy and Ryan, and Cooper's behind me with the other two. Haz was right about the moon, it's massive and really low in the sky, shining on to the outside leaves of the trees ahead. We walk across an open space of grass, where there's another group of people a bit further away from us. I can't see them clearly, they're one shape, with bullet holes of sound.

'Have you got anything to swim in?' Daisy asks me.

'We're going swimming?'

'If you want,' she says, squeezing my arm. 'But you'll have to keep your tattoo out of the water.' She feels safe. I'm sure she's a good person. 'So, how did you and Cooper meet?'

'At school,' I say.

'Childhood sweethearts.' Her voice goes up a pitch. 'That's cute.'

'How did you and Ryan meet?' I ask, copying her question.

‘Work,’ Daisy says.

‘I’m her boss,’ Ryan tells me.

‘You’re so not my boss.’ Daisy swipes her leg towards him, but he dodges out the way and starts to walk backwards, looking at her. ‘I’m not going to warn you if you’re going to crash into anything,’ she says.

Ryan turns to walk normally and we head on to a path soaked in darkness.

‘Should we put on a phone light?’ Haz asks from behind us.

‘More fun like this,’ Daisy says.

In the quiet, there’s the sound of water. I can hear my own heart and my own breathing way too loud. The trees make patterns. Good patterns, I tell myself and I fill the gaps with colour that no one else can see.

Cooper is still behind us. I’m sure he is. There are footsteps and I try to separate them, to tell the three of them apart. We’re definitely walking alongside water now, louder all the time and further along there’s shouting. Happy shouting, I think.

‘Dusty and Cooper came up with a name for my business,’ Daisy tells Ryan. ‘Accidental Stars.’

I can just about make out the shrug on his face and the disappointment on Daisy’s.

‘You don’t like it?’ she asks, her confidence dropped.

‘It’s OK,’ he says.

‘He doesn’t have to,’ I tell her. ‘It’s your choice.’

‘What’s wrong with it?’ Daisy asks him, ignoring me.

'Nothing,' Ryan says. 'But there's not much right with it.'

'It's T.S. Eliot,' I say.

Ryan looks at me like I'm an idiot. 'Right.'

And I regret opening that door to mine and Cooper's world, to letting him have even a glimpse inside.

Light from the moon shows a stone bridge beyond the trees, torches scattered over rocks on the far side. Candles go right up to the edge of a waterfall that slides over the side and crashes foam into the pool below. It feels mad that it's here, right in the middle of a park.

There are more people than I expected, which makes me feel better, I think. I let go of Daisy's arm and wait for Cooper. I'm not going out of his sight this time and I'm definitely not going to drink anything other than the cans we brought. He's not far behind and is talking to the others and he's laughing and Haz laughs too. He looks at me and nods and smiles. *OK?* It's enough to lower my nerves.

We're together as we cross the bridge. There's a derelict building clear in the light, a massive wooden wheel on its side.

'What's that place?' Cooper asks.

'The mill,' Haz tells him. 'You can go in it.'

But we don't. We follow them left and on to the rocks, where people squeal at the sight of Daisy and jump up to hug her.

This is what my life was meant to be like. People are talking to us like we're just one of them. I haven't got a great, huge mark of *no hope* smeared across my forehead. I'm Dusty, with the cool hair and new tattoo.

I take another sip of beer. I've never had it where I want a day to go on and on. And even though it's technically night, this is the best moment of my life and if I could, I'd catch it in a jar and carry it with me always, proof that I was here with all these smiling people and their candles and guitars and the waterfall and the moon. With me and Cooper together in the centre of it all.

'Do you play?' Haz asks.

Opposite us, an older boy is singing with a guitar. His voice is kind of rubbish, but no one cares.

'A bit,' Cooper says.

'A lot,' I tell Haz. 'He's really good.'

Haz cups his hands around his mouth. 'Archie,' he shouts. 'Cooper needs to play.'

'No, I'm fine,' Cooper says. 'Honestly.'

'I need an excuse to get Archie off that thing,' Haz laughs.

Archie strums a last, dramatic note and gets up, holding the guitar above his head, steadies himself and walks across the flat rocks to pass it to Cooper.

'Do your worst, man,' he says.

They might not be able to notice, but I know that Cooper is terrified. The way his eyes glance to me, the fumbling of the guitar strap over his shoulder.

'What can you play?' Haz asks.

Cooper's fingers brush the strings. 'Um. A few things.'

'Bit of a Sheeran?'

Cooper grimaces. 'No.'

He strums something quietly, but it's a guitar, so it's never going to be that quiet and some people near us stop talking and watch. Cooper looks down and his hair falls across his face, protecting him from their eyes.

He starts to sing and more people stop talking, because Cooper's voice does that to you. And I look at him and think what a loss it is that every person in the world doesn't know he exists. This boy, whose soul is so bright that it's blinding.

Someone begins to join in with Cooper and others do too and it sounds like a proper song, with people singing different notes, high and low. I know the words and I want more than anything to join them, but I've never sung out loud in front of anyone, even in music in school.

There are tons of people singing now and Cooper gets more confident and he stretches out one leg and lets the song fly to the top of the sky. I thought that earlier was the best moment, but this is it. Maybe this is what it's all about, not just one good moment in forever, but lots of them. Grains of sand, building a castle.

Cooper loops the song and even Haz joins in, his voice low, the words wrong and it's perfect. Cooper finishes singing without a fuss, just does the final notes and lifts the guitar strap over his head and passes it to a girl who's reaching for it. And people go back to talking, like this is all just normal to them.

I link my arm through Cooper's and he puts his hand on my thigh and I'm so completely alive that I could die.

Cooper and I clamber with some of them down the rocks, closer to the water, in time to see Daisy in her underwear, jumping in the air, her fingers squeezing her nose, her other arm pointing to the sky. She crashes through the water and appears on the surface, screaming at the cold and Ryan is stripping off to his boxer shorts and does a weird, sideways roll into the water, roaring and shaking his wet hair.

'Coming in?' Haz asks me.

'Of course,' I say. Where there's water, I'll go.

I strip off my jeans, hesitate only when I realise I'm almost naked in front of a bunch of strangers.

'We're not meant to get our tattoos wet,' Cooper reminds me.

'We can be careful,' I tell him.

'It looks cold,' he says, still fully clothed.

'Have you ever swum in a waterfall?' I ask him.

'No,' Cooper says.

I reach for his hand and he holds mine. 'Then we must.'

I have to let go of him to strip off my T-shirt. Cooper looks at me and I can tell he's trying so hard to keep his eyes on my eyes and I turn from him and hope he's looking at all of me.

I sit on the rock and dangle my feet in the water and it's freezing, but I won't say, because I want Cooper to join me. Daisy swims over to us, her head above the surface, the light from the moon touching her legs. She holds up her hand to help me and I take it and let her lower me until I'm waist deep.

'Beautiful, isn't it,' she says.

I nod, the cold clasped round my lungs.

'Wolverine!' Daisy shouts up to Cooper. 'You can't leave Dusty in here on her own.'

'She's not on her own,' Cooper says, motioning to the others splashing about.

But he's taking off his shoes and I watch as he puts one of his socks in one and one in the other. He strips off his T-shirt and though I've seen his body before, I get the same jolt of electricity, as though I've touched a live wire and it's sparking through every part of me.

He unbuckles his belt and I should be stopping him, because he's got all the money we own in his pockets. But all I can think is that I've wanted to kiss many people in my life, but I've never wanted to have sex with any of them, until Cooper.

He runs the few steps and jumps.

'Your tattoos!' Daisy shouts, but Cooper lands deep in the water and it swirls over the transparent plaster that protects his sister's name.

He surfaces, spluttering, water over his skin and Ryan

splashes him before Cooper has even opened his eyes. Cooper wipes a hand over his face, laughing.

'We've got to keep these ones dry,' I tell him, holding hands with him to keep our wrist tattoos out of the water.

'You can't swim like that,' Ryan says.

'We don't need to swim,' Cooper replies.

I hold my other palm flat to the surface, feel the hum of the water.

'Careful where you step,' Daisy says. 'Loads of stuff gets thrown in here.'

'Thanks for telling us before,' I laugh.

Cooper looks at me.

'Waterfall?' he asks.

'We have to,' I say.

It gets louder as we approach it, water fizzing against our stomachs, bubbling over our free arms. I've got to remember it all, as I'm going to paint it later. The streaks of purple rock hidden beneath the dark green, the smooth of the water at the top, before the thrash of foam where it lands.

'Can we go behind it?' Cooper asks, his words disappearing beneath the sliding surface.

I pull him with me and it's a curtain we step behind. The sound changing instantly. There are no others, only the rush of water, and us.

'This would be a good place for you to tell me your name,' Cooper says.

In reply, I reach up to touch his face and he doesn't

move away. I trace my thumbs beneath his beautiful eyes, along the remnants of smudged black. I run my finger over the small scar on his forehead, feel his cheekbones beneath my palms.

Cooper steps closer to me and touches his hand to the back of my neck and my legs turn to dust. He bends his head to mine and my heart is going to break free from my ribs, my bones splinter. But I lean towards him and my lips are on his and I don't shatter. Cooper's lips are on mine and all the broken pieces of me find each other and my entire body throbs as it fixes back together.

His hands are in my hair and he pulls me closer. I press myself into him and I don't stop kissing him. I'll never stop kissing him. I feel his fingers on my back. Lower, until he's touching my underwear. I've never let a boy do this to me before and I want him to, but he's hesitating, so I guide his hand and now he knows what to do and nothing has ever felt so amazing as this. I become the rush of the waterfall, the bright of cold, turning to a heat that melts my skin. Cooper kisses me and touches me and I'm a star that explodes into all the darkness.

I can tell that he smiles, his lips on mine, the echo of his touch still in my veins. I want to do the same for him, but I don't know how. And if I fumble and mess up then I'll spoil it all. So instead, I kiss him and kiss him and hope that it's enough.

*

We go back through the water and I pull myself up on to the ledge of rock, my body filled with embers that want to be relit. I've a crazy need to help Cooper put his clothes over his wet body, so I can touch his skin again. He's smiling at me and it's different. It's him and it's me and it's *us*.

I pull my T-shirt over my head and it sticks as I pull it over my chest and down over my stomach. It's difficult to get my jeans on and it feels like we're doing the opposite of what we should be doing. We should be naked and touching.

I watch Cooper do up the button on his jeans and when he's done, he pulls me towards him and kisses me and I don't care who watches us, because all that matters is his body pressed so close to mine that there's no air between us.

'Get a room,' Daisy laughs, nudging into us.

We laugh with her and pull away from each other, Cooper giving me one more kiss and another.

'There's a fire pit in the mill,' Daisy says, wrapping a towel around her. She bends down to pick up a blanket and throws it at us. 'Follow me and I'll get you a spot close to it.'

I pick up my rucksack and Cooper wraps the blanket over my shoulders and we walk together over the flat rocks, down towards the derelict mill.

'You'll love this place,' Daisy tells us.

Flame light flickers through holes where windows would've been.

'I bet you wish you had your paints,' Cooper says to me.

And it's weird, because it's the first time I can remember

looking at something as amazing as the mill and I hadn't thought about copying it.

We walk with Daisy through a doorway with no door, into what must've once been a room, but now doesn't even have a roof. It has stairs, though, and we go past them, through another archway, to where loads of people are sat around a massive metal bowl with fire in it.

'Come and find somewhere to sit,' Daisy says and we go with her and people move up and actually make space for me and Cooper. Happiness swells within me to almost bursting.

The heat from the fire is instant, but still I put half the blanket over Cooper's shoulders, so we're snug together. Beneath the blanket, he holds my hand and I squeeze his, our Morse code. *We're here. This is happening to us.* I didn't think it was possible that an actual person could make you feel safe, but he's my iron bars against the world.

Daisy starts to dance really close to the fire and a girl with the guitar stops the soft song she's playing and starts a flamenco one. Daisy clicks her fingers above her head, her towel dropping, so she's dancing only in her underwear. One hand on one hip, her face laughing and serious all at once.

I open the rucksack and Cooper and I have one more beer left to share. I snap up the ring pull, bend to catch the fizz in my mouth and remember again that I don't even like the taste. But perhaps now I'll always love it, because whenever I drink it, it'll take me here.

I pass the can to Cooper, but he doesn't see me. He's looking at Daisy, who's taken off her bra and has twisted it above her elbow, an amulet that a goddess would wear. Her breasts are lit by the fire pit's flame and I have to nudge Cooper and it's like he wakes and takes the can and smiles only at me.

'Shall we live in Newcastle?' I ask him.

'Good idea.' His laughter is only cut short by his lips on the can.

Cooper's eyes widen and I look at what he's seeing, at Daisy pulling off her knickers, over one ankle and then the other. The girl with the guitar starts chanting Daisy's name and everyone joins in. Daisy weaves naked in a circle around the fire, the light sliding off her skin. She's Venus, stepped from that painting by Botticelli, but she's not standing in a shell, her bare feet are on the stone floor of the mill.

A boy opposite cups his hands over his mouth and howls to the moon and it spoils it. Someone throws an empty can at him and other people laugh, but the thing that was here between us all is broken and Daisy is putting on a T-shirt, pulling on baggy jeans that barely reach her hips. She wraps a thick woollen cardigan around her, the hood up, covering her hair.

'I mean it, Cooper,' I say, 'about living in Newcastle.'

'We are living here,' he says, looking at me again.

'No, I mean really live here,' I tell him. 'We could hide out and be close enough to see Poppy whenever we want.'

'My money isn't going to last for more than a couple of days,' Cooper points out.

'Then we'll get more,' I say. 'You can busk, Cooper. You'd be amazing at it. And I could do street art.'

'Street art?'

'I could sell paintings. We can do it, I know we can. It'll work.'

'You're serious, aren't you?'

'Totally,' I say. 'You've made money before from that farmer guy. And we've got this far without anyone finding us. Newcastle is massive, it'll be easy for us to hide.'

Cooper's smile lights up the darkness around us.

'Let's do it,' he says and he kisses me again.

There's the smallest space beside me, but it's here that Daisy chooses to sit.

'Having fun?' she asks.

'It's amazing,' I tell her.

Cooper drinks from the beer and passes it to me and I offer it to Daisy first.

'I'm good, thanks,' she says and so I drink some more myself. She leans towards me. 'What's your story then, DC?'

'What do you mean?' I say, my smile stuck.

'I think you're running away from something.' She looks me straight in the eyes. 'I'm right, aren't I?'

'Why do you think that?' I ask.

'Have you both left other partners? Left a trail of broken

hearts?' Daisy guesses. 'I'm not judging, or anything. If you've got to be with someone, you've got to be with them.'

'It's not that,' I say.

And there's something about her I know I can trust. I think that even if I hadn't been drinking, I'd still be tempted to tell her, because I'm thinking she could help us. Find us somewhere to live, help us get Cooper a guitar for his busking, lend us money for my paints.

'We're in care,' I tell her.

I feel Cooper tense beside me.

'Care?' Daisy says.

'Foster care,' I say. 'Well, at the moment we're in a children's home.'

'Children's?' Daisy sits back. 'How old are you?'

'Sixteen,' I say. She raises an eyebrow at me. 'Truthfully,' I tell her.

'And Cooper too?' She leans forward a bit, but she can't catch his eye.

'Yeah,' he says, taking a huge mouthful of beer.

'I thought you were older than that,' Daisy says. 'It was Ryan who thought you weren't. You won't tell anyone it was me who did your tattoos?'

'We haven't anyone to tell.' I smile, but she looks sad.

'Is the children's home in Newcastle?' she asks.

'It's complicated,' Cooper says.

'Why?' Daisy asks.

'It's not the nicest place to be,' I tell her.

Daisy finds my hand and holds tight to it. 'Then you can't go back.'

'We're not planning to,' I laugh.

'You've run away?' she asks.

'Kind of,' I say.

'So, they're looking for you?' she asks.

'We're good at hiding,' Cooper says.

I balance my sketchbook on my lap. It's a bit wonky, but I'm definitely not all-out drunk. The girl on my right passes me a box of chocolates. Everyone is passing them round and taking one and I don't even know whose they are. I look through them to find the one I like the best, but all the nut ones have gone, so I have a strawberry one and pass the box to Cooper.

He concentrates on choosing like a child would, all his world narrowing and becoming that pinpoint focus of bright wrappers. He sees me watching him and smiles.

'What?' He puts the whole chocolate in his mouth at once.

'Nothing,' I say. But there are so many words, in the centre of my bones, where storms can't reach, waiting for me to have the courage to say them.

'What are you going to draw?' he asks.

'Maybe the fire,' I say. 'But it'd be better if I had paints.'

I like the way that people's faces are broken up by the flames. How they crack and re-form, are mended.

'It'll still look good.' Cooper's words blur slightly. 'Maybe even better in black and white.'

Daisy is sat the other side of the circle now, her back to the fire. Smoke obscures her. The man she's talking to keeps moving his hand in front of his face, keeping the smoke away from his eyes. I start by drawing him first, the flames playing shadows across his cheeks and his eyes dark. It'll be good to do the detail, but first I concentrate on the form, his outline. It always gets me, how the paper is blank and then filled with someone's life. I draw him into existence, when he hadn't even known that he'd disappeared.

Cooper puts his hand on my back, beneath the blanket, his thumb stroking its own flame through my T-shirt. It makes it difficult to concentrate, but there's no way I'm going to tell him to stop.

I begin to draw the girl opposite, light from the fire showing the perfect lines of her braids, the tracks of skin between them. She's talking so intently with Daisy, but then they're both looking over at me and Cooper. Daisy points at us.

'Shit,' I whisper to Cooper.

'Gone wrong?' he asks, looking at my sketchbook.

'No,' I say. 'Don't look, but I think Daisy is telling people about us.'

Cooper blows through his lips. 'I thought it was too good to be true.' He looks across at Daisy, even though I told him not to. 'They're definitely talking about us.'

'Do we run?' I'm pretending I'm still drawing, but I'm only going over and over the same line, pressing the pencil harder than is good for it.

'It depends,' Cooper says. 'Do you think they'll call the police?'

'I don't know,' I say. 'If they do and we go now, they won't be able to catch us.'

'Fuck,' Cooper says and his eyes are more than sad. They're beaten down, defeated. 'I just want to carry on like this, you know?'

I reach for his hand. 'We will,' I say. 'But not with these people.'

My own disappointment falls from a height on to my chest.

'Do we leave the blanket?' I ask.

'Nah, we take it,' Cooper says, his jaw set hard. 'But let's go quietly. They won't think we're running.'

I put my sketchbook in my rucksack, but Daisy is coming over, her face glowing in the flames. She crouches in front of us, blocking our escape route.

'We've had an idea,' she says. 'It's wild, but hear me out.'

'You were telling people about us?' Cooper stares at her.

Daisy's face changes. 'Not in a bad way.' She touches Cooper's arm and I know his mind will be spinning as much as mine. 'Mel and Shak have been together like forever and we all know they're engaged.'

'Engaged?' I'm totally lost.

'Yeah, I know, they're young. But they're perfect together.'

'What's that got to do with us?' Cooper interrupts her.

I grip tight to the strap of my rucksack. It won't be too hard to dodge round the side of her.

'Mel's parents don't approve of Shak, even though he's the nicest guy on the planet.'

I look over to where Mel and Shak sit, their faces beaming at us through cracks of smoke.

'They've talked for ages about going to Gretna Green,' Daisy says, and I only realise now how drunk she is.

'Where's that?' I ask.

Cooper takes the blanket from our shoulders and folds it under his arm.

'Where people run away to get married,' Daisy says.

Her smile is expectant, but I've no idea what she wants me to say.

'It's your solution,' she carries on. 'If you two get married, then you won't have to go back to that place. You'll be free to do what you want. They won't be able to touch you.'

A flare of hope unfurls in me, even though I know it's mad.

'They'd know you were serious about each other,' Daisy carries on. 'They wouldn't be able to split you up.'

'We're sixteen,' Cooper reminds her.

'That's the point of Gretna Green,' Daisy says. 'It's known for it. That you can marry young there.'

Her words seem to suspend in the air, where I can't quite reach them. It doesn't help that the beers I've had are melting the broken mill around us.

'Come on, DC,' she slurs. 'This is the best idea ever.'

Cooper and I look at each other. I can't even begin to work out everything that's in his eyes right now.

'Shall we do it?' he asks me. And his smile is enough to turn my bones to ash.

'Get married?' I ask him.

'Yeah,' Cooper says. 'Stay together.'

'Forever?'

'Whatever forever looks like,' Cooper says.

'What if it looks like a long time?' I ask him.

Cooper kisses me. 'Then I want it with you.'

'And if our forever is a short time?'

'I still want it with you.'

And even though Daisy is sitting next to us, Cooper leans into me and kisses me properly and it's the best thing that could ever exist, kissing Cooper. The mill and the people and the flames disappear and it's just us, only me and him and his mouth on mine and his hands on my back and my hands in his hair and it's all I want, for however short or long our forever might be.

Daisy is clapping and nudging us and Cooper and I start laughing. Mel and Shak are walking over, hand in hand.

'Coming to Gretna?' Mel asks us.

I look up at them. 'You mean right now?'

'The best time for a double wedding,' she says.

Daisy stands and pulls Cooper and me to join her. 'You're so going to do this.'

'Do I need a dress, or anything?' I ask.

Daisy nearly falls over as she touches my arm. 'You're beautiful enough as you are, Dusty.'

'How do we get there?' Cooper asks.

'We're driving,' Mel says.

'Is it far?'

'Less than two hours,' Mel says, leaning into Shak and he stumbles a bit to keep her standing. 'We've had the route planned for months.'

'And now you've got an even better excuse to go.' Daisy hops from foot to foot, as though she's dancing on hot coals.

I'll be further away from Poppy, but only for a short time, and she won't know as she'll be asleep. We'll be back when she wakes up, with the best news.

I look at Cooper. 'Ready?'

He pulls me to him. 'Our life starts here,' he says and he kisses me on the lips, in front of them all.

Chapter Thirty-Five

We leave the darkness of the path between the trees, and the car park is in front of us, with only four cars in it. It feels quiet without the background rush of the waterfall, only our feet crunching across gravel. The moon is fierce in the sky and there's one bright star hanging almost below it.

Shak gets a key from his pocket, holds it towards the car and the lights flash as it unlocks.

'You're definitely sober?' Cooper asks him.

'As I'll ever be,' Shak laughs.

'He hasn't had much,' Mel assures us. 'And he can take it.'

Cooper looks at me funny, but there's no way I'm backing out now. I could tell if Shak was drunk and he's been walking in a straight line and talking normally. I open the back door and get in and Cooper follows me. He's still got the blanket and he puts it over both our legs, as though we're old people.

'What?' he asks, when I laugh.

'Nothing,' I say. 'It's brilliant.'

There's a seat belt in the middle, so we can sit close together. Shak reverses the car, faces the right way and begins to drive.

Cooper gets something from his pocket and I see that it's the sweet wrapper from when we were sitting around the fire. He rolls it into a straight line and twists it into a circle, his smile blazing as he takes my hand and puts the ring on my finger, tucking the ends under each other so that it stays in place.

'It's official now,' he says.

'I'll never take it off,' I tell him.

'I'll buy you a better one.'

'You don't need to,' I say. 'This is the best one.' And I kiss him again, his lips spinning havoc in my blood. 'Poppy will live with us. You OK with that?'

'Of course,' he says.

'Will they let us have her right away?' I ask.

'We'll be married,' Cooper says. 'They'll have to.'

A million butterfly wings cover me in beating colours of light.

'And Casper can come and visit,' I say. 'And live with us if he wants.'

'All of us together.'

'I'll have an art studio. And you'll have a room for your music.'

'We'll have to earn a lot,' Cooper says.

'We will,' I tell him.

We're out on the main road and even though it's the middle of the night, there are still cars driving around.

'You know, you'll have to tell me your real name now,' Cooper says.

'Is that in the marriage rules?' I laugh.

'It's the eleventh commandment,' Cooper says.

'Commandments aren't to do with getting married.' I laugh again and Cooper is laughing with me.

Shak looks at us from the mirror in the front and smiles. He's driving with one hand on the wheel and the other on Mel's lap and I remember that it's not just us, that they must be buzzing too. This car feels crammed full with the best feelings.

We're on a motorway, a long, straight road. Cars come the other way, their lights spreading long beams towards us. They manage to almost hypnotise me and make me realise I'm knackered, but I don't want to go to sleep and miss any of this.

Cooper's head is heavy on my shoulder, his hair against my neck, his breathing slower. I can't imagine now that there was a time before Cooper. BC. It makes me want to laugh and to wake him and tell him that I think he's the home I've always been searching for.

I touch the sweet wrapper on my finger, its crinkled gold lighting my bones. The cellophane plaster on my wrist, lifting round the edges from where it got wet. Beneath it, Cooper's initial, forever carved.

There's a sudden jolting of the car. Mel screams and I'm thrown forward against my seat belt, into a scraping sound of metal. I can see, so clearly, Shak spinning the steering wheel, his profile of terror. Cooper grabs my arm and outside the lights of other cars get left behind. Our car is lifting and it's turning, but it can't be because we should be driving. The sound of screaming and the sickening crunch of the roof buckling beneath us as we land.

I'm squashed and I can't move and I don't understand where the road is any more. A hissing noise and silence and my forehead is wet and I look towards Cooper and he's bent in on himself, the ceiling crushed against him. His eyes are closed.

'Cooper?' I scream. 'Cooper!'

Shak is in the front and he unbuckles his seat belt and has to stop himself from falling.

'Are you two OK?' he asks. 'Are you OK? Is he breathing?'

He's kicking open his door and pulling Mel with him.

'I don't know.' I'm crying and there's a strange face at the window, but it's the wrong way up.

Someone is pulling at the door, but it's all mangled out of shape. And they're reaching in from the front. It's a man and he's leaning across Cooper and pressing fingers to his neck and I want to ask, but I can't. There's no voice in me.

‘What’s your name?’ the man asks me.

But I can’t speak.

‘Where are you hurt?’ he asks, but he’s upside down to me and it makes me feel sick. So I close my eyes and wish myself back to the mill, back to the waterfall, back to when strangers were singing and Cooper was playing his guitar.

‘We should get them out,’ I hear someone say.

‘No.’ A woman’s voice. ‘We mustn’t move them. They could be injured.’

‘What if it explodes?’

There’s a long, long stretch of quiet.

I open my eyes. Cooper is still beside me. I reach out and put my hand on his chest, above where his sister’s name is written.

‘I know you want to see him,’ I whisper to her. ‘But please let him stay with me.’

Chapter Thirty-Six

A woman crouches close to me. She touches my arm, but I can't feel it. She tells me to keep awake, but I don't want to, I don't want to see. There's a smell of burning, but I don't think anything is on fire. A sinking smell of melting rubber.

'Cooper,' I say, but he doesn't reply. I won't look at him, he wouldn't want me to. But I want to see him. I'm torn, paper, metal. Ripped from one world to another.

Another siren. There's movement outside. The woman wears green and there's someone the other side, beyond the crumpled window by Cooper.

I'm listening to them speaking and I'm doing what they say. They put something tight around my neck. I don't like it. I can't breathe, but the woman looks me closely in the eyes and she's stroking my hand and she says that I'm fine.

I'm able to move and they help me.

‘Where’s Cooper?’ I ask.

‘He’s right here,’ the woman says. ‘We’re getting him out too.’

‘Is he awake?’ I ask.

‘Yes,’ a man says and I’m not sure I believe him, but he’s lifting me, somehow, between the front seats.

‘Cooper?’ I say, but he doesn’t speak.

They lie me flat on a stretcher, but I sit up and push them away. They don’t know. Where we were going, where we’re meant to be. I lash out at them and try to get up and a woman wants me to lie down, so I hit her and she steps back, but she’s not angry and she’s still talking.

‘We’ll get Cooper free quicker if you stay here,’ she tells me.

I stand and watch and wipe wet from my eyes, above us the lights from an ambulance swing into the sky.

There are so many people around the car with wheels the wrong way, helping Cooper.

I’m crying and the woman’s arms are around me.

‘We’ve got to get you safe in the ambulance,’ she says. ‘Get you checked over.’

Tears block my throat, fill me so deep that I’ll drown. I swim through them, find the only words I need, but never want to say.

‘Is Cooper going to die?’ I ask her.

I search her face for the truth. She’s making me lie down again, won’t look me in the eye.

'He's conscious,' she says, 'which is a good sign.'

'He lost his poems,' I tell her and they're lifting me and I wonder if his book had kept luck close and when it was stolen, there was nothing left to bind him to safety.

They're lifting me. Above me, there aren't any stars. They're taking me from where Cooper is trapped in the car and I feel the rope that ties me to him being stretched, pulling the muscles in my heart until I know they'll snap.

There's too much unnatural light. Sounds of cars the other side still driving, a river of them, a hum of water.

I grab a man's hand where he carries the stretcher and I tip, but don't fall.

'I need to see Poppy,' I tell him.

I'm higher from the ground, the stretcher guided into the ambulance and there are straps and noise and it's too bright. The woman holds my hand again.

'Was Poppy driving?' she asks.

It's the strangest question, spinning to a place in me that should drag laughter. Poppy, driving. I imagine her serious face looking out of the windscreen, hands gripped tight to the wheel.

'She's my sister,' I tell her.

'Do you know where she went?' the woman asks. 'Was she injured?'

I stare at her and shake my head. I'm too tired to say.

Cooper's eyes were closed, his body bent in on itself.

'Have they got Cooper?' I ask.

A man is fixing something above my head. He looks down at me and smiles.

'This isn't the way you were expecting to end your evening, I bet,' he says and he's trying to make me happy, but he doesn't know what I've just lost.

'Everything is going to be OK.' The woman strokes my hair from my face. It's so tender that it punches a hole through my bones. 'You're going to be fine.'

But they're closing the ambulance door and Cooper isn't here.

'No!' I shout and I hadn't meant it to be so loud, but I need them to listen. 'I'm not going without him.'

'We've got to leave them to help him,' the woman says.

There are straps across me, pinning me down.

'Please,' I sob. 'Please.'

But we're moving and the siren is screaming and I'm leaving Cooper. He's in that destroyed car, without me.

They take me through the doors of the hospital, the ceiling a line of light. It's the road we were on, before our car spun off. The memory of the sound makes me want to vomit. Cooper's closed eyes.

They stop and move me on to a bed.

'Where's Cooper?' I ask.

'He's in safe hands,' a doctor says. 'We just need to concentrate on you for a bit.' But she's not understanding, she doesn't get that I don't care about the cut she fusses over on my head. I use my elbows to jab away her arms and she looks at the nurse and I know exactly what she's saying in her silence.

'Tell me,' I yell.

The nurse tries to hold my hand. 'He's being well looked after,' she says. 'As soon as I know more, I promise I'll tell you.'

'Why isn't he here?'

'You can't be together right now as we need to check you both over. But he'll have people helping him, just like you have.'

The doctor lifts my other wrist, feeling my pulse, checking my skin, prodding my bones. They don't see where I'm really broken. They don't know that none of their plasters or medicines or machines can fix me.

'Cooper!' His name is a tornado smashing everything in its path. But he doesn't reply.

'Tell us your name, honey,' the nurse says. His eyes are golden and kind, but I blink him away. My fingers touch tight to the ring Cooper gave me. 'We need to contact someone for you,' I hear him say. 'Do you have a mum or a dad we can get in touch with?'

I shake my head.

'Whoever you live with will be worried,' the nurse says.

'I live with Cooper,' I say.

He nods and touches my arm, but he's hiding something from me, I can tell.

'What's happened to him?' I ask.

The nurse sits beside me on the bed. 'Cooper's head took quite a knock, which caused mild concussion.'

'Concussion?'

My blood turns to clay, hardening and cracking.

'Don't look so worried.' The nurse smiles at me. 'He's going to be fine.'

He's going to be fine. He's going to be fine.

'I need to be with him.' My pulse can't keep beating without Cooper beside me.

'He's awake. And asking for you.'

But he's somewhere in this hospital, without me.

The nurse starts writing something on his clipboard.

'Is he in pain?' I ask.

'He's had some medication to manage that. He might have a headache for a couple of days, but that should go.'

'We're getting married,' I say. 'At Gretna Green.'

I won't cry.

The nurse stands and hangs the clipboard from the bed.

'You don't look eighteen,' he says.

'You can marry younger there,' I tell him.

He pauses. 'I'm not sure they do that any more. I think they changed the minimum age.'

I close my eyes, but it doesn't stop the tears coming.

Even if Cooper and I had got there, we still wouldn't have made it.

'Honey.' The nurse reaches over to hold my hand. 'It can still happen.'

I have to find a way to believe it.

I'm useless, lying here, staring at the creases in the curtain that surround the bed. Beyond it, are the noises of the hospital. But no one I know. I can't hear Cooper.

I turn myself on to my side, push myself up so that I'm sitting. My head hurts, a dull, stretching ache. I stand up, leaning on to the bed, and I wait, expecting someone to come in, but no one does. I find the gap in the curtain and pull it back before I can change my mind.

There's an empty bed opposite, but others are screened off either side of it. Can I just go in and look and see if Cooper is there? I haven't really got much choice. Walking feels strange, as though I've stepped outside my body and someone else is moving my legs and someone else makes my hand open one of the curtains and I'm standing looking at strangers, a woman beside a girl.

There's a hand on my shoulder and I tense, ready to strike, or run, but it's the nurse with the kind eyes.

'How are you feeling?' he asks me.

'Where's Cooper?' I ask.

The nurse is still for a second and looks at me.

'They've moved him to the ward,' he says.

‘Why?’ My heart wrenches from its place. ‘What’s wrong?’

‘Nothing’s wrong.’ He smiles. ‘It’s a good sign. He’s there because we’re confident he’s OK.’

‘I need to see him,’ I say.

‘I thought you might, that’s why I was coming to get you. I’ll take you up there.’ The nurse links my arm through his and holds my hand. ‘OK?’ And his kindness causes a crack in the earth that I’m going to fall into.

My head feels filled with the fire pit’s smoke. Daisy was there, dancing. Cooper was kissing me. And now I’m here, in a hospital corridor, the floor too shiny and grey.

We walk past other people, but I won’t look at anyone. I don’t want to be reminded that I haven’t got a mum with me. And I haven’t got my sister with me and now I’m further away from her than ever. I made a promise to Poppy and I’ve failed her again. *I’m sorry, I’m sorry, I’m sorry*, I whisper.

The nurse leads me into another room and we walk the length of it and I try to count my steps to calm the wreckage in my mind. We stop and the nurse pulls back a curtain and I’m standing staring at a bed where Cooper lies. A white sheet is pulled up to his chest.

‘Why are his eyes closed?’ I ask.

He’s lying there so still.

‘He’s sleeping.’ The nurse puts his hand on my back, urging me forward. ‘He took quite a hit to the head. His body needs to rest to help it process the shock.’

'But he'll get better?' I feel so small, a child, asking for a miracle.

'I think he'll be fine. Do you want to sit with him for a while?'

I nod, frightened to speak again.

The nurse moves a chair next to the bed, helps me to sit next to this boy whose life has been in parallel with mine. Since the first time my stepdad hit me, since my mum first forgot I existed, since Poppy and I were moved from one foster carer to the next, my path has been waiting to cross with Cooper's.

'I'll leave you two together,' the nurse says. 'But I won't be far if you need me. If you're worried about anything, press this button here and we'll come straight away.'

I want to thank him, tell him that his kindness is a life raft, but he's gone, pulling the curtain closed behind him.

Cooper doesn't move. He has a bruise on his forehead that disappears into his hair, his skin deep purple, fading to black.

'Cooper?' I say, touching his arm through the sheet.

He opens his eyes. 'Dusty.' And in the middle of this nightmare, he's smiling at me. 'You're OK?'

I'm trying to smile too, because he's here and he's safe, but I want to be back hidden in the folds of the angel with him, I want us to be nestled together under the stars.

'Are you hurting?' I ask.

He shrugs. 'It's OK.'

There's a cut on his lip. I lean down and kiss him, so gently that we barely touch. But it's enough to remind my heart that he's here.

'You've cut your forehead,' he says.

'I'm fine,' I tell him.

Cooper reaches out his arm for me and I lie down next to him. He puts his palm to mine, our hands together.

Along his arms, his poet's words.

In this valley of dying stars.

'We didn't quite make it,' he says.

My chest collapses in on itself.

'We can still keep going,' I whisper.

I look into Cooper's eyes, see him nod and try to smile.

'Yeah,' he says. 'Let's do that.'

Chapter Thirty-Seven

A policeman comes in, the same one who tried to speak to us an hour ago.

'Ready to talk?' he asks. 'Shall we try again with your names?'

'I'm Wolverine,' Cooper says.

'I'm Wonder Woman,' I say, and it's madness, because we're laughing so much, but this is the worst thing that could be happening.

Cooper is wincing and holding his side and that makes me laugh even more.

'Although you're not, are you?' the policeman says, pouring cold water into my veins. 'We've got a Cooper and a Dusty, haven't we?'

'*The* Dusty,' Cooper says. 'Not just *a* Dusty.'

'Isn't there a singer?' the policeman asks.

I'm named after Dusty Baker, you dumbass, I want to reply.

All my laughter is shut so suddenly in a box I can't reach it.

'Would you like to fill me in on what you've been up to?' he asks.

'No,' Cooper says.

'How about who was driving, then?' the policeman asks.

'We don't know.' It's the same answer we gave him earlier, so I don't know why he's asking again.

'You just happened to get into a stranger's car and you don't know who they were, or where they were going?'

'We never said we didn't know where we were going,' Cooper says.

The look in his eyes rips me apart.

A different nurse walks in, ignoring the policeman.

'How's the head?' she asks Cooper.

'Hurting,' he says.

She puts her hand flat to his forehead and touches his cheek gently with her palm. 'It will for a while.' She turns to the policeman. 'To be honest, they've both gone through a big trauma, they need to rest now.'

'Right,' he says. 'I'll be outside.'

'Can we leave?' I ask the nurse.

We've got our rucksacks and if the policeman isn't expecting it, we could easily outrun him.

'Cooper's not well enough yet,' she says.

'I am.' He sits up.

'We need to monitor you for a few more hours,' she says. 'They'll be bringing round some lunch soon. Do you think you can eat?'

'Yes,' Cooper tells her, lying back down again, me in his arms.

'You two lovebirds.' She smiles and leaves us in a cage the size of the world.

Cooper and I both look to where the curtain at the end of the bed is pulled back. It takes me a second to understand that it's Jen standing there.

'Dusty.' My social worker looks genuinely pleased to see me.

'Is something wrong with Poppy?' I ask, sitting up.

'She's fine.' Jen smiles.

'I need to see her,' I say. 'She's expecting me and Cooper.'

'We'll let her know you're OK,' Jen says, 'but I'm not bringing her here. She's been through enough.'

'If you're wanting to make me feel guilty, it's working,' I say.

'The only thing I wanted was for you to be safe,' Jen says.

'We have been safe,' I tell her.

'We didn't know where you were, Dusty.' She steps towards us. I think she'll hug me and I want her to, but I don't want her to, and she must be able to tell because she keeps her distance.

‘You can’t have looked that hard,’ Cooper says.

Jen’s smile towards him isn’t so friendly. ‘You must be Cooper.’ And it’s there, a flint of anger in her eyes and I hate her for it.

‘It’s been the only time I’ve ever felt safe,’ I tell her truthfully.

Jen shakes her head. ‘You were never in danger at Keystone,’ she says.

I laugh. ‘You serious? You think that being pinned down was OK?’

I can tell she’s shocked, but only for a second. ‘I know what happened. They told me they had to put you in a hold.’

‘And you’re fine with that?’

I hate the anger that’s boiling in me now. But Cooper’s hand is on my back, grounding me.

Jen takes a big breath, as though she’s the one whose insides are scorching her.

‘You can’t keep accusing people at every place you live, Dusty. We’re on your side. We’re trying to help you.’

I jump up and get so close to her face that she’s forced to step back.

‘Are you saying you never believed me?’

The walls feel like they’re crawling closer. That I’m still in that car, with the roof caving in, but it’s not stopping and I know it won’t until it crushes me.

I feel Cooper grab my arm. I swear it’s the only thing that stops me hitting her. He pulls me towards him.

'It's not worth it,' he tells me and he makes me sit on the bed with him.

We lift our feet from the floor and sit facing each other. He holds my hands and I hold his and he draws circles with his thumb inside my palm. I want to kiss him, but instead, I move our hands so that we're grasping each other's wrists. Beneath his tattoo of my initial, I feel the beat of Cooper's pulse.

Chapter Thirty-Eight

Cooper and I sit in the back of Jen's car and she's driving me further away from Poppy. We're moving too fast and I want it to stop.

I feel every turn of the wheels below us, waiting for the car to leave the road and spin the wrong way round. But if it happens again, maybe we can rewind time. Cooper and I will be with Shak and Mel, heading towards a future where we can wake each day together, can watch the sun set and the moon rise, his poet's words on his lips as he kisses me. The loss of it all cuts a knife through my skin, deep into my core.

I rest my head on Cooper's shoulder, but he's a block of stone.

Keystone is as we left it. And even though it's the afternoon and the sun is bright, it feels like darkness hangs suspended above the house. We go up the path, staring at the ground, at our footsteps walking where we don't want them to go.

John is standing with the front door open and I don't want to look at him and his wiry beard. I only glance at him long enough to see him try to pat Cooper on the shoulder and Cooper pull away.

'Good to have you back,' John says.

'It's not good to be back,' Cooper replies.

Liv is at the bottom of the stairs, almost in the place where we last saw her.

'Hey,' she says, more to Cooper than to me. 'I'm glad you're OK.'

'We're not,' Cooper says and we walk up the stairs holding hands, along the corridor, all the way to the other stairs, up to Cooper's room. We don't knock on Jemal's door to say hi, which makes me feel guilty, but my head is too scrambled to think and I lie down on Cooper's bed before he even closes the door.

We're alone, curled together, and I stare at his words written all over the wall. It feels like all my bones have been plucked out and I've been left with a terrifying nothing filling me so full that it's hard to think.

Cooper has one arm around me. His other hand strokes my hair, his fingers gentle against the fragile china of my skull. Keeping all the memories of me and him safe, where no one can see them.

We ignore the knock on the door.

'Dusty?' Jen walks in, but I don't look at her. She walks into my line of sight, so I turn my head the other way. 'I need to talk to you about something.'

I don't answer her.

'Preferably alone,' Jen says.

She's mad in the head if she thinks I'm going to leave Cooper.

'Do you want me to go?' Cooper asks me.

'No,' I tell him. 'If she wants to speak to me, she can do it with you here.'

'That's fine,' Jen says. 'I've got some really good news for you, Dusty.'

I sit up, Cooper's arm falling from me.

'Is Poppy here?'

I see Jen shake her head, but she's smiling.

'No,' she says. 'But you are going to be with her. At Amira's.'

'I can visit?' I ask. 'When?'

'Better than visit,' Jen says. 'Amira has made space for you to stay there.'

'To stay?' Her words are slow to make sense. 'You mean I can live with Poppy again?'

'I absolutely mean that,' Jen laughs.

'So you won't separate us?'

'Not if you don't make us,' Jen says. 'Amira is a great foster carer. Poppy really likes her and I think you will too.'

I turn to where Cooper sits beside me.

'I'm going to be with Poppy.' I'm smiling so wide inside, but the relief of it makes me want to cry.

'That's great,' Cooper says and I reach out for his hand, but I can feel him shaking.

And it's this, the touch of his skin on mine, that makes me realise what this means.

I look back to where Jen stands. 'What about Cooper?' I ask her.

'I'm not his social worker, Dusty,' she says. 'My concern is you and Poppy.'

She might as well have just pressed my nuclear button.

'Well, I'm concerned about him.' It's only the Morse code of Cooper's hand that keeps me from hurling every ounce of anger at her face. 'Even if you can't be bothered.'

'It's not that I'm not bothered,' Jen says. 'But even if Amira had space, which she hasn't, it wouldn't be allowed.'

My lungs haven't got the air they need. 'Poppy can come here,' I say.

'No,' Jen says. 'She can't.'

I gulp in a breath, to stop myself from screaming.

'Do my feelings ever even come into this?' I manage to ask.

'You know they do,' Jen says.

I want to hack every word from her throat and choke her with them.

'You can't do this to me.' She can't give me the earth and take away the sun.

'I thought you'd be pleased.'

'Pleased to be leaving Cooper?'

'That's not what I meant. This is a good thing, Dusty. A really good thing. Do you know how hard it is to place siblings together? Especially ones your age.'

'You want me to be grateful?'

'I want you to see the bigger picture.'

There has to be a different way. A picture with me and Poppy and Cooper in it.

'What if I refuse to go there?'

'Refuse to be with Poppy?'

'You really just said that?' Fury falls on me, makes me unable to move. 'You know how much I love my sister.'

'But I don't know what you're asking now.'

'If I don't go to Amira's, then you'll have to find another place for us to be together.'

'There's no other option.'

'You're seriously making me choose between Poppy and Cooper?'

'No, Dusty,' Jen says. 'I'm not giving you the choice.'

Cooper sits up beside me.

'When does Dusty have to go?' he asks, his hand still tight in mine.

'Cooper, no,' I say.

'In two days,' Jen says, ignoring me.

'Can I talk to her on my own?' I hear Cooper ask.

'That's fine,' Jen says. 'I've got to drive back now in any

case. But you need to promise me, Dusty, that you won't try anything stupid again. If you do, I know for a fact that you'll lose your placement at Amira's. And then you'll have absolutely no chance of living with Poppy again. You've got to trust me that we know what we're doing.'

'We're not going anywhere,' Cooper says.

'Good,' Jen says. 'I'll phone you in the morning. OK?'

I glare at her. My heart feels like it's being smashed under tumbling rocks. 'Do you think any of this is OK?'

'What I know,' Jen says, 'is that I'm relieved you're safe. Because you both could've died.'

She looks like she's got no energy left, that she's given up. It's always like that. Every adult always gives up on us in the end.

'Well, we didn't,' I say.

'What would Poppy have done without you?' she asks me.

'That's a low blow,' Cooper tells her.

'Did you give her a thought when you ran away?' Jen says. 'The hurt that you caused her?'

She knows exactly what these words do to me.

'Close the door on your way out,' I tell her.

Jen goes without another word.

Cooper and I sit together in the silence of his room. I touch his arm, but already I can feel a gulf trying to stretch between us.

‘We could run away tonight,’ I whisper to him.

‘John will probably be camped out by the front door,’ he says.

‘He’ll have to fall asleep at some point. Then we can sneak past him. And if we put a towel over the kitchen window, we’ll be able to break it silently.’

Cooper shifts on the bed so that he can look at me.

‘You’ve got the chance of a good foster carer, Dusty,’ he says. ‘Remember how it felt being with Chris and Guy? You can have that again.’

‘But you won’t be there,’ I say.

Cooper brushes my hair from my face.

‘If Cira were waiting for me,’ he asks, ‘what would you tell me to do?’

I can’t bear how violent his agony must be, the impossibility of walking by her side again.

‘I’d tell you to go to her,’ I say.

Cooper nods. ‘I’m never going to be the reason you’re not with Poppy,’ he says. ‘I won’t take you from your sister.’

‘You don’t have to,’ I say. ‘I choose both of you.’

Cooper looks devastated. ‘We don’t get to choose, Dusty. Jen’s right, we never get to choose.’

I touch my fingers to his lips and hear the quick intake of his breath.

‘Don’t leave me, Cooper,’ I say.

‘They won’t let me stay here, Dusty, not after this.’

'You really think they'll move you?'

'I'm only here until they sort something else, then I'll be gone.'

'From me?'

'Never from you.' Cooper holds my face in the palms of his hands. 'I'll be in your life as long as you want me to be.'

'That's forever, then,' I say.

'Then forever it is.' Cooper smiles the saddest smile and I hold him so close that there's nothing between us, the heat in my veins fusing his heart to mine.

Chapter Thirty-Nine

We're walking down the corridor, Cooper's hand in mine, when we see Jemal. I feel so happy and sad to see him all at once.

He stops on the top stair. 'You're back,' he says.

'I'm sorry we went without saying goodbye,' Cooper says.

Jemal shrugs and I know there's not much we can do to put it right, so we follow him without talking, into the kitchen.

Alfie looks up wide-eyed from the table. I'd forgotten how young he seems. He looks happy to see us, but just for a moment.

'You left.' He accuses Cooper more than me.

'Only for a bit,' Cooper tells him.

There are little sparks of hatred in Alfie's eyes. I don't blame him. Cooper and I now belong in the long, long line of people who've let him down. Guilt grinds deeper, but it's mixing with my own anger, because I'm back here and it's the last place in the world I want to be.

'I'm glad you're both safe,' Kelly says and she reaches to touch my arm, but I won't let her.

The meal is weirdly quiet. John talks mainly to Kelly about the football and every word he says is winding me up. It literally feels like he's got a key in my back and he's turning it and turning it and he'll keep going until I detonate.

John draws an invisible diagram on the table, to emphasise his point.

'It's people kicking a fucking ball around,' Cooper says. He shoves in another mouthful, ramming down the rest of his words.

Casey starts to clear the plates, before John has even finished eating. It's the smallest rebellion on her part. A silent *fuck you* and she's no idea how much it means to me.

I don't want to stay down here for dessert, but Casey made it, so I do and Cooper does too. John's pretending to be all casual, but I feel his eyes on us, even when he's not watching. Liv is having a go at Jemal and I want to tell her to stop, but I don't have the energy. I'm only embers. I'll either scorch to a flame, or disappear.

I sit cross-legged on Cooper's bed, my sketchbook open on my lap. Outside the window, the dark sky is broken by the brightest moon. I'm drawing Cooper, sitting on the chair opposite me, looking down at his guitar. His hair is falling over his eyes, tucked behind his ear on one side. I won't draw the bruises on his skin. In this picture, we're still free.

I want my pencil to capture the brilliance of him. I draw the outline of his shoulders and the way his arms hold his guitar as if it might break. His poet's words cover the wall behind him and I find the ones I want to write on the page.

'There is always another one walking beside you,' I read.

Cooper looks up and his smile lights me and destroys me. How can the universe have given me the best soul it could find, but now it's taking him from me?

Through my tears I see him put down his guitar and come to me. He circles his arms around me, and he kisses me and it should take us to the best place, but the hurt is ripping each and every one of my ribs from my chest.

'I don't know if I can hold on to hope any more, Cooper.'

He clasps my face in his gentle, ink-smudged hands.

'You can,' he tells me.

'I'm not strong enough.'

'Don't you ever say that,' he says. 'You hold up my world, Dusty. On your own.'

I pull him down to lie with me, his body against the length of mine. And his kisses are enough to blaze through the chaos of my world, branding his name on to my skin.

The door opens and John is standing there looking at us together on top of Cooper's bed. He's taking up the space, the silence. *This is our time*, I want to scream at him.

‘Separate rooms,’ he says. But this is my only safe place right now, in a sea filled with sharks. ‘I mean it, you two.’

We ignore him. Cooper’s arm stays around me, his muscles rumbling with fire.

‘You either go to your room now, Dusty,’ John continues, ‘or we’ll help you get there.’

Cooper tenses. ‘You’re going to have to.’ He looks at me and in his eyes I see the colour of a soul that no one else bothered to find. It’s luminous and it’s pure and it’s mine.

I don’t kiss him, not in front of John, because if John tears me from him, I swear to God I’ll kill him. I just stand up, when every part of me is yelling at me to stay. I let go of Cooper’s hand, when all I want to do is hold it closer.

John stands to the side and it takes a strength I didn’t know I had to keep on walking.

Chapter Forty

I'm woken by the loudest noise. A dragging, banging and it's Cooper's voice, yelling.

I grab my trackies, stumbling, trying to walk before I've even got them on. I yank open my door, to see John and Rina either side of Cooper, barely enough space for them on the stairs coming down from his room. His face is spiralled out of control with anger, but when I look in his eyes, it's total terror I see.

'Get your hands off him,' I scream and I know I'm going to make everything so much worse, but I'm scratching at Rina's arms and John is trying to put his body between us, still gripping tight to Cooper.

'Calm down, Dusty,' John says.

Kelly runs up the main stairs and I step away from her. She's breathless, palms flat towards me, slowing as she gets closer, as if I'm a wild animal. Well, she's right, I am. Caged and ready to fight.

'What's he done wrong?' I ask.

But they don't answer, only keep dragging Cooper past me.

'Scott's outside,' Kelly says. 'Shall I get him?'

'Who the hell is Scott?' I shout.

Cooper is grabbing on to the banister, but it's only with one hand and John is too strong and pulls him from it.

Something is very wrong. They'd normally be pinning him down where he is.

John looks over his shoulder. 'Look after Dusty,' he tells Kelly.

She steps towards me, but knows she stands no chance. I'm a fuse attached to dynamite.

'Swear to fuck, if you touch me,' I warn her.

'Let's wait in your room,' she says. 'It'll be easier for you.'

Alfie opens his door, squinting from sleep. 'What's happened?' he asks.

It gives me the seconds I need to push past Kelly and run down the stairs to where a policeman stands in the hallway.

'You can do this the easy way, or the hard way,' he says to Cooper.

'You're arresting him?' I say. 'He hasn't done anything wrong.'

'No one is arresting him. Scott's only here to help us,' John says, struggling to hold Cooper.

Cooper turns to look at me. It's like all the storms in

the world have hurtled into him. Hurricanes trying to uproot him.

'They're getting rid of me.' His words erupt into the space between us.

'They can't,' I say.

'They can,' he says.

'I'm coming with you,' I tell him.

'Dusty,' John says, readjusting his grip on Cooper. 'Don't make this harder for him.'

Anger explodes from Cooper's lips. 'You think she's the one making it hard for me?'

'OK, son,' the policeman says. 'Keep it down.'

'I'm not your fucking son.'

I've never seen fury in Cooper like this, his shoulders ready to rip through his skin, his face twisted with hatred.

The policeman just stares at him and it's this that throws bolts of lightning to my blood. He's not seeing Cooper. He's only seeing through him, as though Cooper doesn't even exist. That Cooper is *nothing*.

I lunge towards him, but his hand is fire-quick to stop me from punching him in the face. Kelly grabs me.

'This isn't helping Cooper,' she tells me.

I lash out at her and the beads on her wrist break all over the floor. I'm trying to get free of her, of them all, so that Cooper and I can run and keep running. But I feel like I'm drowning in my anger, and it's too difficult to breathe.

'Dusty.' It's Cooper's voice, dragging me back to the surface. 'It's OK.'

'Don't lie to me,' I cry.

'I'm not,' Cooper says. He's suddenly standing so still. 'We always survive.'

His words fill the air with the oxygen I need. I stop struggling and turn to Kelly.

'Let me go to him,' I beg her. 'Please.'

She looks to John, but he shakes his head.

Cooper glares at him. 'You're a bigger piece of scum than I thought.'

'Right,' the policeman says. 'Time to go.'

'Your car, or ours?' John asks him.

And I hate him more than I've ever hated anyone. Speaking about Cooper as though he's just a *thing* to shove into their car.

'Mine'll be safer,' the policeman says.

They start to pull Cooper outside. They're taking him away and the panic slices right through me, a blade dipped in boiling oil, dragged across my chest. I want to scream, to kick, to break the walls of this place apart, but I can't move.

'Wait,' Cooper shouts, trying to free his arms. He manages to turn enough to look at me. 'Dusty. Tell me your real name.'

I look into his eyes and I'm reaching for him, but they won't let me touch him.

'Alice,' I tell him.

'Alice?' Cooper laughs. 'You serious?' They're dragging him from me, but he's smiling. 'Alice Cooper,' he says. 'Look it up. We were always meant to be.'

They pull Cooper down the path and push him into the car. Through the window, I see him raise his arm. He peels the transparent plaster from his wrist, kisses his tattoo and holds it towards me. I rip the plaster from mine, his initial inked into my skin. I kiss it and hold it up for him to see, but already the car is moving. Cooper keeps his eyes locked on mine and I think he's going to open the door and escape. But he doesn't and the car turns down a different street. And he's gone.

Chapter Forty-One

I stand in Cooper's room, my hand to the wall, touching his poet's words. Now I know the true meaning of hollow. My body empty of everything. Hope, light, stars, all gone. Only the shadow of my veins are here, with the echo of Cooper's hurricane whistling through them.

This is the dead land. I trace the outline of the letters on his wall. His beautiful, messy handwriting.

After the sunsets.

Cooper.

You pieced me together. You made me complete.

I lie in his bed, in the silence of his room.

Kelly stands in the doorway, but she doesn't come in.

'You've got to eat, Dusty,' she says. 'And then maybe you can phone your sister.'

I stare at her, my skin goosebumps before a storm. 'Where've they taken Cooper?'

'You know I can't tell you that,' she says.

'You have to,' I say.

Kelly steps closer, but stops.

'He's safe,' she says. 'In a place that's better suited for him. And that's surely a good thing, right?'

There's a deep pain in my head. I close my eyes, but it spreads into the darkness.

'Get out,' I say.

'You'll meet other friends, Dusty.'

I bite down into Cooper's duvet, in this bed surrounded by the smell of him. An avalanche of rage falls so fast that it fills my lungs, suffocating me so I can no longer move.

Jemal doesn't knock, he comes in holding a plate with a sandwich on it and puts it on the floor next to the bed.

'We're watching a film if you want to join us,' he says.

I want to thank him, but I just shake my head.

Outside the window, the sky turns from blue, to grey, to black.

I only go downstairs, as far as my room, for the one thing I want to get. Cooper's sweatshirt is on my pile of clothes on the floor and I pull it on, surrounding myself with him. If I close my eyes, I can almost imagine he's here beside me.

But he's not.

And Poppy's not with me.

In a house full of people, I'm totally alone.

I need air and try to open the window, but it goes only as far as the safety latch. Of course it fucking does. I'm trapped, the word sticky in my brain, peeling away to leave bullet-sized holes for me to fall into.

I need the air that somewhere Cooper breathes. That somewhere surrounds my sister. I need it to surround me. To breathe it deep enough. I pick up a chair, because the only way to get it is to smash the window.

My phone rings.

I stand, holding the chair and the phone is ringing. I grab it and hold it to my ear.

'Dusty?' It's my sister's voice, an anchor to hold me.

'Prim?' I drop the chair and sink to the floor.

'Yes,' she says. 'It's me.'

'It's late. You should be in bed.'

'Amira said I could stay up for a bit, because we're celebrating.'

Celebrating?

My world has been torn inside out, but Poppy stops me spinning off into the darkness.

'What are you celebrating?' I ask her, even though I know what her answer will be.

'That we're going to be together,' Poppy says.

I'm going to be with my sister. And it's this that drags me back from the edge.

Four Weeks Later

Poppy is sitting opposite me at the kitchen table. Amira's home isn't like any we've been in. It's got pictures all over the place and there's love clear enough to touch.

I hold the phone tight in my hand.

'You've got to do it,' Poppy tells me. 'You promised Cooper.'

I think she might love him as much as I do.

'And after this, you can phone Terence,' she says. 'The gallery man you told me about.'

I barely mentioned it to her, this dream of a future. How it felt when I stood with Terence in front of the paintings. The terrifying and brilliant freedom he gave me to speak my thoughts. Yet here my sister is, holding the card for his gallery in her wise hands.

I key the number into the phone. It rings and then rings again and I'm about to hang up when a woman answers.

'Northern School of Art,' she says. 'How can I help you?'

I look over to Poppy, her smile still shining.

'I'm phoning about studying at your college,' I say. 'Am I too late to start in September?'

'Never too late,' the woman says.

I laugh, relief rushing in like the tide.

'Have you had a look around the campus?' the woman asks me.

'Not yet,' I say. There's a beat of silence. 'But my carer says she'll come with me.' I'm surprised how proud I am to say it. That my foster carer, Amira, will be by my side.

'That sounds good,' the woman says. 'There are lots of options here for you.' And she's saying more, her words a whirl of everything I hoped they'd be.

I nod, even though she can't see me and I say all the right things and Poppy holds out her arm to show me the words she's written on her wrist. *You did it.*

'And what's your name?' the woman asks me.

'Dusty,' I tell her.

'Dusty,' the woman says. 'That's one to remember.'

Amira is a miracle worker. I'm not allowed to know where Cooper is, but she persuaded Jen to let me write to him. When I first sent him a letter, he wrote back straight away. And then I sent him a book of T. S. Eliot's poetry, which Amira helped me to find. Poppy laughs, says it's too romantic and I guess it would be, if missing him didn't peel a layer from my skin.

'The days will go before you know it,' Amira tells me. 'When you're eighteen, you can see Cooper all the time, as much of him as you want.'

Poppy giggles.

'Not like that,' Amira says.

And I think, *yes, like that*, and I count off another day from the calendar Amira let me paint on my wall.

Until then, I'll keep Cooper's letters in a pile beside my bed, pages filled with the words of this boy I know I love, my favourite on the top.

Hyacinth girl, in his handwriting that shines all the best colours to my bones. *You have existed.*

Author Note

Dusty, Cooper and Poppy are inspired by the many brilliant children in care who I've had the privilege of working with. However, the darker parts of this book are not a figment of my imagination. Of the approximately 85,000 'looked after' children in our care system, around 20,000 have been taken from their brothers and sisters, just like Dusty and Poppy are, and separated from those they love most in the world. Half of them are living away from the area they call home. And many of them are pulled out of school with no warning, even in the middle of their GCSEs, to be moved miles from everyone and everything they know.

There are many brilliant people who work in the care system, however there are also those who see it as a way to make big money. Most children's homes are businesses, with a focus on profit. And behind too many of their doors (and the doors of some schools) traumatised children, like Cooper and Alfie in *This Boy I Hardly Know*, are being restrained on a daily basis, by the very adults they thought would keep them safe. Young people who've experienced it talk of the terror they felt, the agony of the 'hold'. I know of a child who vomited out of fear during a restraint.

These children are not numbers on a form. They're resilient, gutsy, important members of our communities, who've survived complex, challenging early years. They have hopes and dreams of their own that need to be heard. My hope is that this book makes them feel seen. That they'll know how valuable they are. That they have every right for their light to shine.

Acknowledgements

To my beautiful mum, who taught me about bravery and how to recognise it in others.

To my husband Miles and our boys Albert, Frank and Arthur. You all rewrite the meaning of happiness.

Thank you to my siblings Anna, Emma, Lara and Philip. Life's journey would have been far trickier without you all holding my hand.

To my Uncle Martin and Aunty Jacqui, thank you for your love. And to Abby and Kitty, for bringing extra sunshine into our home.

To Ruthy, Lucy and Mari – the very best of friends.

To my fantastic agent, Kate Shaw – thank you for loving Dusty instantly and fighting her corner from the moment you met her.

Thank you to my wonderful editor, Eloise Wilson – you have held this story with such care every step of the way and been so patient with all my last-minute tweaking of tiny points! Thank you to Rob Farrimond and Jade McGrath for your determination to spread the word about my book far and wide. And to Kate Grove, thank you for working tirelessly to create a truly perfect cover. Thank you also to Susila Baybars – how lucky I've been to have you as my copyeditor again!

Thank you to all the fabulous librarians who do so

much to help spread a love of reading – in particular to Caroline Wheelhouse, Debbie McCullough and Susan Morgan-Jones – your support has meant so much to me. To all booksellers, for all the hard work you do to put stories in people's hands, especially Ness and Jules at The Book Nook.

To Wren Furneaux – thank you for reading the very first draft, for taking the time to chat and for your brilliant thoughts. Thank you Abie Longstaff, for also reading at such an early stage, for loving Dusty and reminding me about hope.

Thank you to Louisa Reid – it's not every day that one of my favourite authors gives me my first line! To Nikki, for all your bookish wisdom and for always being there. Sandi for my notebook! And the rest of my fantastic writing group – Deb, Allie, Lucy and Suzanna.

To Chloe Davis – you were as determined as I was to get Dusty's story published! And Lily Colburn, for showing me courage on another level.

A massive thank you to The Royal Literary Fund – your invaluable grant enabled me to keep writing. I am forever indebted to you.

Thank you to my writing spirit, for staying close.

And all the children I've met in the care system – you've added immeasurably to my life. To you and all those I haven't met yet, I hope this book makes a difference.